One Click Love

T. GEPHART

Published by T Gephart
Copyright 2020 T Gephart
ISBN: 978-0-6487943-0-1

Discover other titles by T Gephart at the retailer of your choice or on Facebook (https://www.facebook.com/pages/T-Gephart/412456528830732), Twitter (https://twitter.com/tinagephart), Goodreads, or tgephart.com

Cover by Hang Le
Editing by Insight Editing Services
Formatting by Elaine York, Allusion Graphics LLC
www.allusiongraphics.com

One Click Love

To Gayle,

Oprah has hers and now I have mine. Never underestimate
what a generous, strong, and thoughtful friend you are.
I'm blessed to have you in my corner and can't thank you
enough for your kindness and support.

Want a man who is not only hot but knows how to handle a blaze?

Well ladies, it's your lucky day.

John "Mack" McPherson is 6'3" of fine with a six-pack that makes men half his age question their gym regimen. Teddy-bear brown eyes with brown hair, his graying temples let you flirt with just enough silver fox so you know you've got yourself a real man. But don't let the body and face fool you, he's incredibly smart, with medals for days and won't think twice about putting his own life on the line to save someone else. Brave, dependable, and needing someone equally awesome, Mack is ready to be snapped up by a feisty female who isn't scared to play with fire.

John,

Not sure how feisty I am now, but I'm fighting my way back. Little scares me though, and I'm not someone who breaks easily. Not interested in playing mind games, so if your idea of a good time is heading to a club where we pretend to be into the scene, then it's probably for the best we don't meet. I expect honesty and a half-way decent orgasm I don't have to give myself. Other than that, open to negotiation.

Let me know if you're game,

Hayden.

Chapter 1

Mack

"**N**ORTH. MY OFFICE. NOW!"

You'd think with a wife and a kid on the way, North had better things to do than fuck with my day, but clearly I'd overestimated his ability to multi-task.

His head snapped up from the radio he was testing, sly-ass grin he always wore beaming on his face. And any doubts he was behind my latest headache were firmly put to bed.

"Something you need, Chief?" My problem child had the nerve to smile wider.

Should have known it was too much to ask to celebrate my forty-fifth birthday without dealing with his shenanigans. Seriously, what the hell was I even thinking?

"I need," I tried to keep a lid on it, "for you to get in my office." I pointed to the doorway I was currently standing inside and hoped he wasn't going to make me ask again. I was already in a mood and repeating myself only made things worse.

"No problem. Be right there." North tossed me a wink, chuckling under his breath as he ambled slowly—couldn't have moved slower if he fucking tried—to my office.

I swear some days I honestly wonder where I went wrong with him.

Riley North had come into my life just over ten years ago.

With two shitty parents who both succumbed to injuries following a horrific drunk-driving accident, the eighteen-year-old kid found himself orphaned overnight. I'd not only been the first on the scene, but the person who'd had to knock on his door and tell him. And there was no way I could walk away from him after I saw the shithole he'd been living in, knowing he would probably end up in a body bag like his folks a few years down the line. Didn't even think twice about it either. Just told the kid to pack whatever he wanted to keep and get into my truck. And the rest we kinda worked out as we went.

Of course, he really tested my patience, and still did. But there was no prouder moment in my life than watching him graduate from the academy and having him serve alongside me in the FDNY. But that didn't mean he still didn't like to press my buttons from time to time. Case in point, the current state of affairs.

"You just couldn't help yourself?" I shook my head, closing the door behind us. "Couldn't let me have just this one day in peace."

"C'mon, Chief. It's your birthday! And at your age you need to celebrate every single one; never know when they're going to run out." His smug grin widened.

I scrubbed my face with my hand wondering whether he was right and I really was 'getting old'. "I swear, North, one of these days—"

"Happy birthday to you, happy birthday to you, happy birthday dear Chiiieeeeef, happy birthday to you!" Leighton burst through the door before I could even finish yelling at Riley. And if the off-key singing wasn't enough, in his hands was a cake straight out of my mother's 1980's *Wilton's* Buttercream collection, and wouldn't have been out of place in a retirement home celebrating someone named Mable's century. With enough candles on there for Mable too—it was a wonder the smoke alarms hadn't already gone off—those assholes either couldn't count or had a hard-on for melted wax.

He wasn't alone either, the whole company was piled either beside or behind him, every single one of them wearing equally annoying grins. It seemed my request for a quiet, uneventful birthday had been totally disregarded, and there wasn't a goddamn thing I could do about it.

Leighton lowered the cake on top of the paperwork covering my desk, increasing the chances of igniting something other than my temper. The scent of vanilla and powdered sugar competed with deodorant and chrome polish, something not entirely unpleasing except for the audience that accompanied it. Men crammed into my office, looking at me with expectation as Riley leaned in and stage-whispered, "This is the part where you make a wish and blow them out. I hear the mind is the first to go, but don't worry, Chief, we've got your back."

I rolled my eyes, flipping him off before blowing out the stupid candles. I still wasn't done yelling at him, but it was hard to be angry when I knew his heart was in the right place.

"I hate all of you," I laughed, not really sure why I hadn't just taken the day off. "But since you're so insistent on celebrating my big day, I expect a coffee to go with this cake."

"Coming right up, Chief!" Tibbs saluted, shuffling his way back to my doorway. "And happy birthday."

Each of the men took turns in giving me their best wishes with their own personal brand of amusement. From giving me shit for being a dinosaur and asking me if I'd filled in the forms for my senior discount, to inviting me out on the town when we all got off shift. I couldn't help but smile as I shook their hands and kicked them out of my office. They might've been a huge pain in my ass, but I still loved the bastards.

"Okay, so are we done with the fun and games now? Good, now go ahead and delete that fucking profile and bring me back a piece of cake."

Riley chuckled, leaning back against his chair as he raised an eyebrow. "What profile?"

"Seriously? You're too smart to act stupid, North. Just pull it down and let's move the hell on."

He blinked, his smile dropping for the first time that morning as he looked at me seriously. "Chief, honestly. I don't know what you're talking about. Aren't you yelling at me about the box of *Depends* I left in the break room?"

"No, you moron. I'm annoyed at that stupid profile on the dating website. Look, I know it's been a while since I divorced Melinda and—" I wasn't able to finish, his eyes clouded in confusion as it became apparent he wasn't that good an actor. "Shit. Where the hell is your wife?"

Quinn North was not only the love of his life, but an equal thorn in my side. I swear the two of them treated it like sport. And while I loved her and was grateful she'd joined our little family, if there was a gold medal for interfering, she'd have a neck full of the suckers.

Riley's face contorted, laughing his ass off as he pulled out his phone and dialed the woman in question. Judging by his reaction, it had been a solo mission on her part. "Wow, she totally outdid me. Don't know if I'm annoyed or proud." He only had to wait a minute, the mother of his soon-to-be-born child answering it almost instantly. "Quinn, something you want to tell me?"

My single status had been a recent hot topic.

Riley had been trying to get me to date before the ink was even dry on my divorce papers, and Quinn. . . well, let's just say pregnancy hormones had only increased her need to be in my business.

My morning had started so uneventful.

Got to the stationhouse around seven forty-five and sat at my desk. Ignored the pinging from my phone because it was my birthday and assumed it was just well wishes. There'd be at least a couple from my parents who had relocated to Florida and probably my younger brother, sister-in-law and my two nephews. Nothing strange about a few extra messages when you were celebrating. But when the notifications kept buzzing, I knew something *else* was going on.

Never in a million years was I expecting an inbox with so many unread messages I was beginning to think some asshole had targeted me for a cyber-attack.

Should have known better.

Instead, what I found was notification after notification alerting me to "matches" for datemyfriend.com. Because clearly there weren't enough dating apps on the market, a new one had been launched a few months ago with datemyfriend.com allowing "friends" to help their single buddies out by putting up a profile. Then, the *victim*—because there was no better word for it—had forty-eight hours to claim the profile before it and all evidence—and the account—dissolved into internet lore. Guess it was supposed to deter shitheads from setting up accounts as practical jokes. All good, right? Yeah, perfect, except until those forty-eight hours expired my only options were to sit tight and wait for the timer to run out or to claim the account and return the messages. I couldn't delete the profile. Only the person who set it up could, unless I flagged it as harassment.

It was tempting.

He pulled the phone away from his ear. "She says she's doing it for your own good and that you should at least try it. Honestly, it's probably easier than arguing with her. When Quinn gets an idea . . ."

There was no need to finish that sentence. I'd have better luck pissing on a forest fire than getting Quinn to change course.

"Well, tell her in two days it ain't going to matter." I rolled my eyes, annoyed I was going to have to endure two more days of a flooded inbox.

Riley laughed, passing on my sentiments before asking how she was doing, ignoring me and my mood.

Jesus.

More notifications, I frowned at the screen, tempted to check it out.

What the hell had she written?

Quinn was creative for sure, and had skills with Photoshop, but surely even then there couldn't be more than ten to fifteen women interested in an over-forty fire chief who hated nightclubs and overpriced microbrews.

My eyes floated to Riley, his interest still on his wife rather than me as I clicked the link which took me to the landing page. It wouldn't hurt just to look, and unless I accepted the Ts and Cs and activated it, there'd be no harm done.

Wow.

Where the hell did she get those photos?

In what I assumed would be standard, there was an array of pics Quinn had uploaded. What was unexpected, every single one of them I'd never seen before. There were a couple of photos of me in uniform, even one in my turnouts when I was running drills with the men. And some that were more candid, me in civilian clothes. But I hadn't posed for any of them. She'd obviously been around and taken them when I wasn't paying attention. Always knew she was a talented photographer, but it was kind of weird looking at myself through someone else's lens.

"Chief, you good for tomorrow night?" Riley raised an eyebrow, clear it hadn't been the first time asking.

Zoning out had made me miss whatever he'd said the first time, shoving the phone into my drawer as I tried to refocus. "Tomorrow night for what?"

"Dinner. You know, for a *proper* celebration. You are not spending it throwing cards at Cap's house." The phone still pressed against his ear.

Great.

Because dealing with his BS on my *actual* birthday wasn't enough, we had to have an encore.

I leaned back in my chair, folding my arms across my chest. "You know what, kid. No. I know you mean well, but I think I'm going to spend my time off exactly how I want it. Besides, you might want to take some of your own advice and take Quinn out and celebrate. After the baby comes, who knows how many opportunities you're going to get."

It probably would have been easier if I'd just agreed. Gone to dinner and smiled, with the probability of it being a good time fairly high. But as much as I hated disappointing people, I'd wanted zero fuss and that had yet to transpire. In fact, it had been the exact opposite. Which meant when our shift was over, I was going to do whatever the hell I wanted. And if that meant playing cards with a buddy or sitting in my condo watching cable, then so be it.

Riley swallowed, looking surprised I'd turned him down. "Mack, it doesn't have to be a big deal. We can keep it small."

"Kid, I love you." I shook my head, shooting him a grin. "And I appreciate it, trust me. But let me have this one." While I knew my earlier anger about the whole dating thing had dissipated—especially since I knew he wasn't the mastermind behind it—I wasn't willing to concede. All of his—often misguided—intentions in the world weren't going to convince me otherwise, the chances of "a quiet dinner" turning into a sideshow still very real given the two of them.

He nodded, knowing my chances of backing down were probably low. "Hey beautiful, let me call you back." His call ended a second or two later, his attention solely on me. "Look, if you change your mind—"

"Not gonna happen. Now get out of here and call her back before she freaks out." I smirked, gesturing to his phone. "And how long does it take to get me a coffee and a piece of cake? What the hell was the point of blowing out the fucking candles if I don't get a taste."

"On it, Chief." Riley grinned, moving to the door.

It was only after he'd left that I let my hand go back to my drawer and pulled out my phone. There was my smiling mug, reproduced more than was necessary. And assuming ladies liked what they saw—I liked to lead by example and kept myself in shape—they could scroll down and get my particulars.

Oh, for fuck's sake.

Want a man who is not only hot but knows how to handle a blaze?

Seriously? Could it be ANY more cliché? I had to wonder if Quinn was deliberately trying to make it sound like a bad porno, or women genuinely responded to that shit. Not like I was an authority.

Well ladies, it's your lucky day.

John "Mack" McPherson is 6'3" of fine with a six-pack that makes men half his age question their gym regimen. *Was that supposed to be a compliment? It sounded like it should be and yet . . .* **Teddy-bear brown eyes with brown hair, his graying temples let you flirt with just enough silver fox so you know you've got yourself a real man.** *Oh for fuck's sake, Quinn. Teddy bear, silver fox—it was like I was an asshole with an identity crisis. I thought it was supposed to be a profile, not a fantasy novel.* **But don't let the body and face fool you, he's incredibly smart, with medals for days and won't think twice about putting his own life on the line to save someone else.** *Finally,* mention of my service and something I was actually proud of. **Brave,**

dependable, and needing someone equally awesome, Mack is ready to be snapped up by a feisty female who isn't scared to play with fire. Wait, that was it? Twenty years in the FDNY reduced to a sentence? She talked more about my abs than what I did for a living, surely that wasn't right?

I wasn't sure whether to be appreciative—if not slightly embarrassed—by her favorable analysis or be mad she was making me sound like a fucking pin-up for *Playgirl* magazine. Not to mention she hadn't written anything about what I actually liked to do. Knowing my luck most of my "matches" would be women I had nothing in common with. Wasn't even going to touch her call out for a *feisty female who isn't scared to play with fire* bullshit.

Laughing to myself, I shook my head wondering why the hell I even cared what she wrote. Not like I was going to do anything about it. She could call me fucking Santa Claus and it wouldn't make a difference, because there wasn't a chance in hell I was meeting the woman of my dreams on a dating website.

Ignoring my resolve, my phone lit up again with more incoming messages vying for my attention. And much to my amusement, I wasn't as pissed as I initially was. If I didn't know myself better, I'd think I was mildly entertaining the thought of checking out some of those messages. Not because I thought I'd end up with anyone, but because the curiosity was getting the better of me.

"Here you go." Riley burst in, balancing both a cup of coffee and a cake-filled plate in one hand. "I know you're trying to watch your waistline, so we cut you a smaller piece. Wouldn't want you to get fat as well as old." His face morphed into a horrified grimace before settling into a smirk.

I didn't bother shoving the phone away, folding my hands across my chest as he lowered the coffee and cake onto my desk. "I'm not fucking *old*."

"No? Must be the surly attitude then that's got me confused." His eyes dropped to my screen, the dating website still open on my internet browser.

I waited, expecting some wiseass comment because that kind of material would have been too hard for him to resist. He knew I'd been looking, and whether it was for curiosity or any other reason wouldn't have meant shit, but surprisingly his eyes snapped back up to mine and his mouth stayed shut.

"Something you wanna say, North?" I asked, because I was slightly unnerved by the lack of comment. It wasn't like him to bite his tongue and I liked it better when I could see the trouble coming.

"Well, I better get back in the bay. Tibbs needs help checking hoses." He tipped his chin to my desk. "Enjoy."

And without so much as another fucking word, he turned on his heel and he left.

His hasty exit was so out of character it had me uneasy. And what the hell did he mean, *enjoy*? Was he eluding to the coffee and cake or the freaking website?

"Jesus." I grabbed the phone, and against my better judgment claimed the goddamn profile. "I already know I'm going to regret this."

Chapter 2

Hayden

THE LAST TIME I'd been asked out by a man I'd worn Levi 501s, Doc Marten boots and a see-through lace T-shirt. My padded push-up bra had turned my sweet little B cups into majestic Cs, while my dark brown matte lipstick hadn't budged despite the bottles of Zima I'd been swallowing all night. Surrounded by a cloud of cigarette smoke and CK One, I'd locked eyes with a guy across a crowded dancefloor while Pearl Jam blasted out of the speakers. My heartbeat quickened as he threaded himself through the gyrating bodies, not dropping his gaze as he made his way over to me. His lip ring caught the light, twinkling against his beautiful lips as he leaned in closer and offered to buy me another drink. I hadn't even thought twice, abandoning my Zima on the bar—and my common sense—and running my hands up and down his arms. They were toned, not overly muscular but athletic, and covered in tattoos. And instead of buying me a drink, we made out in a dark corner.

He was magnetic, and dangerous, and made my toes curl with just his kiss. So obviously when our lips finally separated and he asked me out, I readily agreed. Little did I know that ten years after that first kiss in that crowded nightclub, I'd end up Cooper's wife.

Of course, when we took the walk down the aisle, the lip ring had been removed and his tattoos were usually covered by starched white shirts, and that wasn't the only thing that had changed. Much to my mom and dad's delight, he decided to go back to college, me having to work two retail jobs just to keep our rent paid while he gave up on the rebellion and became a cog in the machine we both used to despise. I got it, I did. We were no longer in our twenties and at some point we needed to grow up. But while Cooper was praying at the altar of corporate America, he forgot about me.

And I'm a little ashamed to admit I forgot about me too. My dreams were put on hold while I did whatever it was that made him happy. I stopped worrying about taking care of myself and gained thirty pounds, dying my hair blonde with drugstore bleach instead of maintaining my natural light brown at the salon because it was cheaper and easier to hide the grays. And sex . . . well I couldn't even remember the last time I'd been touched. It had to have been years. YEARS since he'd made me feel like anything other than his fat, boring wife who hadn't even bothered to finish community college.

When the hell did I give up? I couldn't even remember how it happened, and other than looking in the mirror and being horrified at what was looking back at me, there wasn't a lot I'd gotten from the divorce. And no, it wasn't the extra weight I was carrying or the mediocre home-dye job that made me cringe. It was the lack of myself that I saw in the reflection. I was a ghost. A faint echo of who I used to be, and I vowed never to let anyone— let alone a man—ever make me feel like that again.

I dried my eyes for the last time, promising I was done feeling sorry for myself.

It had been a year since I'd gotten the courage to move out and file for divorce, the finalized paperwork having arrived earlier that morning.

And I was free.

"Well, at least you didn't have kids with him." My sister-in-law, Gayle, joined me on my bed, handing me a glass of champagne. "That would've made it worse."

"Yeah, probably the only smart thing I did. Although, people usually have to have sex for that, and let's just say it wasn't high on either of our lists of priorities." Although, as much as it had been my decision to keep my womb unoccupied, I knew my chances of becoming a mother had become remote. It wasn't so much a regret as a slight ache in my heart. Still, the impending menopause my mother warned me was looming at my door wasn't helping either.

"So, what are you going to do to celebrate?" Gayle lifted her flute to her lips, savoring the champagne. "You want to go out? Have a nice dinner? See a movie?"

As adequate as all those options sounded, I'd just spent the better part of twenty years with one hand on the snooze button and I didn't want to continue the trend.

"I want a one-night stand."

Gayle coughed, the champagne getting caught in her throat. "Sister, you've got to warn a girl before you come out with something like that."

Maybe she had a point, but I'd gone from my middle-finger-in-the-air twenties, to my apologetic-conforming-self-conscious thirties. And at forty-two, I think I was done being polite. Besides, we'd already established I hadn't had a male-provided orgasm in God knows how long. And if that was how I wanted to ring in my renaissance, then I was allowed. Hell, Cooper hadn't waited as long. And while I had no proof he'd been unfaithful during our marriage, he'd seemed to quickly replace me after I'd left. She was the typical Stepford-wife clone, perfectly coiffured hair but probably sucked dick like a Dyson. And she was welcome to him.

But unlike him, I didn't want a replacement.

In fact, a relationship was the last thing I wanted. Please. I wanted to play the field a little, enjoy myself, and after being condemned to one average penis for so long, I was looking forward to spending a little time at the buffet.

"I'm serious, Gayle. I want sex. No strings. Just someone who is going to make me feel good for a night. I don't even care if they lie to me, it's not like we'll ever see each other again. So give me some ideas. *Tinder*? *Bumble*? Where should I start looking? Because even I know going to a bar and finding a guy is no longer a thing."

She nodded, commiserating that internet dating was very much my reality. "Yep, it's all about swiping and finding matches these days. Guess we need to find you a site and set up a profile."

That's what I loved about my sister-in-law, there was no judgment. My brother, Matthew, had gotten lucky when he'd found her, she was the best. Cooper had won custody of most of our friends after the divorce—I was the whore who left my husband. And those I'd had before marriage had been lost during my boring, need-to-please stage. Which meant I came up kind of empty on my contact list, Gayle rapidly becoming my best friend. So I guess I'd gotten really lucky too.

Setting my glass on the dresser, I pulled out my laptop and typed *online dating* into the search bar. I was positive I was going to be inundated with a million options, but despite what millennials thought, people my age *did* know how to use the Internet, and we still wanted to have sex.

"Oh! What about *Date My Friend*?" She pointed to one of the sponsored ads. "I've heard really good things about it. They run background checks on everyone on the site. Your profile can be active while they run the search but anyone found with outstanding warrants, avoiding credit collection agencies or felony charges gets booted and/or handed over to the police. Also, while you need to put in a real name and Social Security number, it's kept private. No need to exchange personal information, everything goes through an app. So if he ends up being a jerk, you don't need to file a restraining order."

Had to admit, keeping as much of myself private did seem pretty appealing. While my divorce settlement hadn't been huge, the sale of our house had given me enough for a down payment on a small, one-bedroom condo in Inwood. Hard to believe I'd been able to afford to stay in Manhattan, but property prices were favorable, and I'd scored an adorable little place in a gorgeous neighborhood. I'd spent the first part of my marriage supporting my husband and the rest of it more than contributing my share to the mortgage. I was done paying someone else's bills.

"Yep, the less they know, the better." I'd already clicked on the website and was reading the fine print.

It was exactly how Gayle had explained. Real information had to be provided and you were free to use the service while they ran you through their "checks." Then you could be handed over to the appropriate authorities if you were anything other than the model citizen you claimed to be. But there was only one catch, a friend had to sign you up.

Hmmm. Well that was interesting.

"I guess you're going to have to do this." I swiveled the laptop toward Gayle. "Apparently a *friend* needs to create the profile."

Gayle smiled, cracking her knuckles. "Probably because friends are better at seeing all the good qualities."

I rolled my eyes, not needing to hear yet another pep talk. "Just don't lie. No need to give my poor prospective fling a heart attack when he's expecting a tall, thin runway model and I show up."

She elbowed me, her fingers already busy typing. "Just shut up and let me write."

Even though it killed me, I didn't edit the profile once I'd claimed it. While Gayle was incredibly generous in her description of me and my virtues, I would probably be the first to admit I wasn't exactly objective when it came to my selling points.

Those thirty extra pounds didn't do wonders for my five-foot-five frame, and while my self-dyed blonde hair didn't look out of place with my gray eyes and pale skin, it was a far cry from the luscious, glorious locks I'd seen on Fifth Avenue.

And yes, I knew I wasn't ugly. But I just wasn't feeling great about my body—like almost every woman in America—and was just being honest about it. Still, curvy women with ordinary features got laid all the time, so clearly I just hadn't found my target market.

Shifting through prospective "dates" later that evening wasn't as much fun as it sounded. What I hoped would be like flicking through an IKEA catalog, felt more like looking at mug shots. Firstly, I didn't believe half those profile pictures were accurate. Maybe like twenty years ago when the photo had been taken, but there was literally no way a forty-five-year-old man looked like that. Not unless he'd had some major surgery done. And I was totally cool with that—hey, I wouldn't mind getting a little nip and tuck if I had some spare cash—but I highly suspected *Rob from Staten Island* hadn't gone down that road.

And if the whole photo bait-and-switch wasn't enough to turn me off, there was the bullshit their friends had written about them. *Likes long walks on the beach, looking for my other half, enjoys the theater and ballet*—please, most of these guys were just looking for a quick lay and they—or their friends—were regurgitating what they thought women my age wanted to hear. Newsflash, not every woman over the age of thirty is interested in a man "to grow old" with. We weren't a Ming vase that needed to be put on a shelf and adored.

Some of us liked to be *fucked*. Properly and thoroughly fucked, so that we didn't have to fake an orgasm. Sure, slow and passionate love was nice too, but it didn't mean that was all we wanted. And why the hell did anyone think we wanted long walks on the beach? We weren't border collies. And screw the theater and the ballet, that would be hours of my life I'd never get back. I'd rather a decent meal in a non-crowded restaurant or better still, pizza on the couch.

Wasn't there a man who was decent looking, knew how to have a good time, and maybe—if I wasn't asking for too much—up for starting a little trouble? Someone who—

HOLY SHIT.

My throat tried to swallow but I was having a hard time of it while my eyes widened.

He was . . . well, there was no other word to describe it but breathtaking. John McPherson was a forty-five-year-old firefighter—it didn't explicitly say but if the uniform shots were anything to go by—who gave new meaning to hot. He had a warm smile and kind eyes, but left *nice* on the side of the road and became something else. He was toned and muscular, his body obviously conditioned either for work or for pleasure. *Please God, let it be pleasure.* And his profile—absolutely nothing about walking or soul mates.

My finger hovered over the MATCH button, wondering if a man like that wasn't looking for some twenty-something supermodel to take to the Fireman's Ball. Not that I knew if fireman's balls were still a thing, but if they were I bet he would look amazing in his dress blues. As for the rest of his uniforms, he was rocking the fuck out of those turnouts.

There had to be at least seven or eight photos, each of them more amazing than the last, and every single one of them showcasing his *assets*. They didn't have the same vibe as the other guys, the resolution of the photos definitely from the current decade as well as showing him from all angles. Not like the kind of photo spread that was conducive to hiding physical flaws, he was either exceptionally good looking or the photos were of someone else. But those eyes. Man, something about them was just so trustworthy I couldn't believe it was anyone other than the firefighter he'd been described as. If someone was catfishing, they'd gone to some serious effort. Of course hot didn't disqualify you from being a rude asshole with shitty conversational skills, luckily I was interested in a different kind of oral.

Pushing away old insecurities, I clicked on his name with a steady resolution to stop giving a fuck. The worst thing he could do is reject me and I'd been numbed to that kind of hurt after years of indifference, so who cared what a stranger thought. And, if by some miracle he was looking to play with someone closer to his own age, then I'd have missed out simply by not taking the chance. I was soooooo done with missing out.

Deciding I was too old to play games, and with no patience to learn what was acceptable dating ritual in the current decade, I accompanied my marked interest with a note.

John,

Not sure how feisty I am now, but I'm fighting my way back. Little scares me though, and I'm not someone who breaks easily. Not interested in playing mind games, so if your idea of a good time is heading to a club where we pretend to be into the scene, then it's probably for the best we don't meet. I expect honesty and a half-way decent orgasm I don't have to give myself.

Other than that, open to negotiation.
Let me know if you're game,

Hayden

Then deciding to not wait for a response either way, I closed my laptop and went to retrieve that half bottle of champagne Gayle had left in my refrigerator. Dating was less complicated and more fun the first time around, although I was able to appreciate being in my pajamas and not having to wear Spanx as I sipped on my drink.

See, there was always a positive. I just had to find it.

Chapter 3

Mack

SIMULTANEOUSLY LOVED and hated the end of a shift.

Those twenty-four hours either dragged ass or flew at lightning speed, and both scenarios left you fucking tired. I rarely got any sleep at the stationhouse, too busy making sure shit was running at its optimum level and keeping my men in check. No shit, some of them were like fucking toddlers and you'd think they didn't have enough to do. But there wasn't a one I'd trade. Nope, when that bell rung and they piled into the engines, they left their bullshit at the door and became some of the finest men I'd ever seen. That they were mine—well, that just made me a little prouder.

Part of me hated not going out on the calls. As an officer and senior staff, I spent a lot of my time pushing papers around and dealing with administration. It was a necessary evil, and a team is only as good as their leader. Plus, I'd hoped the change would've kept my marriage together, but that was a losing battle that probably went on longer than it should.

"Want to go grab some breakfast, Chief? I have an hour before I have to be home to get Quinn to our appointment." Riley stood at my door, already in civilian clothes, keys dangling from his fingers.

My head lifted, meeting his eyes as I shook my head. "And risk you being late? Your wife will have your balls and then come after mine. Go be a daddy and tell the little sucker hi from me. And make sure you call me so I know everything's kosher. It could be any day now. That last month is a crap shoot."

Riley laughed, rubbing the back of his neck nervously. "You're telling me. Had the bag packed for over a month and make Quinn run drills just to be sure. Never thought I'd be this anal, I swear I'm turning into you."

"There's worse things you could be."

"Yeah. There is." He swallowed hard, shifting on his feet. "Look, Chief, about that dating thing."

"North, if this is the part where you tell me to go get laid, save it. We're both tired." Besides, last thing I wanted to do was admit I was considering it. Fuck, then I'd never hear the end of it. Nope, he could go on believing I was still annoyed while I worked out whether I wanted to look through a million messages.

"Okay, Mack. Well, whatever you do today, try and have some fun or something. I don't know, maybe crack a smile just to see if you still can." The smart ass grinned. "And I know you already turned me down, but the dinner invitation tonight still stands. You can wow us with tales of the good old days, tell us what it was like before running water and electricity."

"Get out of here, North." I chuckled, leaning back in my chair as Riley shot me a quick wave and headed out the door. Lord, that kid of his was going to be a handful and I couldn't have wished it on a more deserving man.

I was still wearing my grin as my phone rung, the name on the screen enough to make me lose whatever jovial mood I'd had.

Melinda.

Guess I should be grateful she didn't call yesterday, counting my luck from not hearing from her a little premature as I lifted the phone to my ear, already regretting answering it.

"John," she purred, doing her best to sound like a phone sex operator. "I'm so sorry I forgot your birthday. Will you forgive me, sweetheart?"

Part of me wished—and I'm ashamed to even admit it—that she had some kind of psychological disorder. That her behavior was due to an imbalance or—I don't know—a fucking trauma. Not because I was a hateful bastard and wanted her to suffer, but so it made some kind of fucking sense. However, no, she was okay in the head department, and for some reason evil bitch was stuck as her default.

"Why are you calling me, Melinda? I know it's not to wish me a happy birthday so why don't you just cut to the chase." My fingers squeezed the bridge of my nose, wondering how the hell we'd stayed married so long. North had never liked her, warning me before I slipped a ring on her finger and thankfully saving the I-told-you-so after.

She gasped, having the nerve to try and sound shocked. "I don't know why you think I can't just call to wish you well. You know, there was a time when you loved me and—"

"And that was a long time ago. But screwing around and then taking the house and the car will correct that. So tell me, what is it that you want?"

"Well," she took a breath, pausing for maximum effect. "Todd and I were trying to have a baby and well, we're having some difficulties in the *swimmer* department. All those procedures cost so much money and aren't covered by insurance. You were always so amazing with Riley, and I know how good a man you are—"

"Whatever you were going to ask, don't." My hand squeezed the phone, bewildered she'd taken fucking psycho to a new level.

"Because I'm trying to be respectful here and I can guarantee if you ask it, I'll lose the ability."

"C'mon John, don't pretend like it would be so difficult for you to just fuck me while I lay there and look bored. You did it for years and never complained. Who knows, you might even enjoy it."

Never raised a finger to a woman.

Not even as a joke.

But the one on the other end of the line would test even a saint's resolve.

"I'd rather stick my dick in a blender, Melinda, and turn the fucking thing on. And do us both a favor, lose my number." I ended the call, tossing the phone on my desk while I tried to wrap my head around her request. And in what alternate universe she'd thought I'd agree.

I'd wanted kids—a son, a daughter, didn't care as long as they were healthy. After seeing Riley grow into a man and having a hand in it, I wanted more. But she'd always thrown my job in my face, telling me I'd leave her to raise them on her own. And when I traded turnouts for a desk, I was fucking over the moon when she told me she'd reconsidered. Months we tried, the shit eating me up while I'd tempered my disappointment so I didn't hurt her feelings. That was until I found the birth control pills she was secretly taking. Can't say it didn't chafe me that she'd lied, had me believing we were planning our future when really she was just biding her time. But now she wanted to have a kid with whoever the fuck *Todd* was and looking to me for stud services.

Jesus Christ.

Had she always been that bad? No wonder I didn't fucking date. If my judge of character was so off the mark, I couldn't trust myself not to end up with a serial killer.

Maybe Riley and Quinn were right.

Maybe I just needed to go get laid and stop worrying about trying to be everything to everyone, and what was it North said . . . *go have some fun?*

Wow.

Melinda had either thrown me more off kilter than usual, or I was way more tired than I thought.

And without debating which of those two was responsible for my reasoning, I picked up my phone, scrolled to the newly downloaded app and opened the inbox of doom. It was going to take a while, probably better if I did it at home after a few hours' sleep.

Most of the messages were different versions of the same.

I got sick of the hose/pole jokes real quick, likewise with the puns on fire/flaming/heat etc.

And sure, some of the more *colorful* messages made me hard in all the right places, but not one of them were original in any way worth remembering.

Except for one.

Hayden.

The honesty and lack of BS was both refreshing and fucking attractive. Not to mention she hated crowded nightclubs, which was a woman after my own heart. I couldn't stand the places, would happily never step foot into another one again unless it was to fill out an arson report.

I hadn't even bothered to look at her picture, immediately hitting the reply so I didn't lose the message in the sea of not interested.

Hayden,
Not interested in nightclubs or any other place I

can't hear a woman when she talks. Mind games and lies are also on my list of disinterests.
As are half-way decent orgasms.
Sounds to me like you've been settling, and if a man can't see to it that you're properly satisfied, then he's not worth your time.
Since our interests seem to be aligned, I say we grab a coffee and see what else we have in common.

Mack

Not sure what I was intending to write but I sent it before I had a chance to reconsider. It was probably more direct than I would have liked but something told me she would appreciate that. And if she didn't and thought I was an asshole then I guess her lack of a response would speak loud and clear. No harm, no foul.

It was only after my message was floating through the intersphere that I clicked on her profile and checked her out.

Wow.

She was beautiful.

None of her photos looked photoshopped, uploaded without bunny or cat ear filters and about as honest as her message. Large slate gray eyes that smacked you right upside the head, her blond hair twisted in different directions and rested just above her shoulders. She had curves, the sexy kind like the old-school pinup girls I saw in my grandpa's garage. Wish she hadn't covered up with so many clothes, the full body shots only teasing me with the visual.

But what I saw I definitely liked, with nothing about her being ordinary. And I bet that theme went far beyond just her looks.

Well, maybe my judgment wasn't so bad after all.

Not that any of it mattered, she still hadn't said yes to anything, and there was a very real possibility she'd tell me to take my TEDtalk and shove it up my ass.

I was still gawking at her photos when my phone pinged, the alert letting me know there was a message from none other than Hayden herself.

John/Mack,

You're either extremely confident or extremely cocky. Not sure it matters as long as you can back it up. Assuming we follow your logic—about men being unable to satisfy me not being worth my time—your invitation and by extension the use of *my time*, must mean you can. Coffee sounds great. I get off work around 7 p.m. and hoping it's not too presumptuous to assume you have no plans for a Tuesday night. Probably being a little more eager than I should, but talk of decent orgasms will do that every time. Are you on the Island or somewhere in the outer boroughs? There's a great place in Hudson Heights—Caffeine and Me—that's open until late, but up for suggestions.

Hayden

I laughed, interested beyond measure if she was as forward face to face. After all, it was easy to talk a good game when you were behind the safety of a screen. But take that away and people could be different. And I really, *really* hoped she wasn't.

With a grin on my face, I typed back my reply.

Hayden,

It's just Mack, and I like to think I'm a little of both—confident and cocky—but you can absolutely bank on me being able to back it up. As you guessed, my Tuesday night is free, just got off rotation actually so the timing works great. But if we're throwing out suggestions without worrying about presumptions, let's do dinner instead. I'm in Midtown, and there are lots of places to eat. Can I pick you up from work? Happy to provide references from the city to prove I'm not a deviant and willing to take my chances you aren't either.

Mack

I wasn't even sure who I was anymore. Flirting with some woman on a dating app I'd never met, spoken to, and knew very little about. Not that the insanity of it all made me rethink my offer. Nope, it just made things more interesting. Truth be told, I was kind of enjoying it, liking the back and forth and seeing where it ended up.

And lucky me, I didn't have to wait too long.

Mack,

Yes to dinner, but no to picking me up from work. As compelling as your references are, I'd prefer to meet you there. And since we're doing dinner, let's meet at 8 so I can go home and change. There's this cute little Italian place in Midtown called Gino's we could try. I've heard it's a little loud and crowded, but the pizza is really good and service is quick. I can call and

get a reservation if this works?
Let me know.

Hayden

Was she shitting me? *Gino's*? The pizza place right around the corner from our firehouse? We'd had more Gino's than was probably legal, most of the station being on a first-name basis with all of the staff. Not to mention it was like a ten-minute walk from my condo. If there was some Higher Power trying to throw me a sign, I'd say it was well and truly received.

Hayden,
Meet you at Gino's at 8. I'll take care of the reservations.

Mack

Short and sweet, which was my only option unless I wanted to embarrass myself. Flirting was fine, but talking about coincidences and heavenly signs was too far over the line. So instead, I picked up the phone and called Gino's, the number having been dialed so many times before, I knew it by heart.

"Gino's."

There was only one female who could answer the phone so clipped and impatient and get away with it, probably on account the restaurant shared its name with her dad and her grandpa before him.

"Vera, it's Mack. How are you doing?"

"Mack! Hey, I'm doing okay, well as good as I can be when my brother is busy flirting with customers, leaving me to do all the work. How are you? You need a delivery?" Her disposition improved knowing it was me.

"No delivery this time around, but I will take a table for two around 8 p.m. if you have one. I'll even set your brother straight while I'm there, let your dad know he can send him around to polish the engines anytime he starts slacking off."

She laughed, something she usually reserved for North, Tibbs or Leighton. Well basically *anyone* else in my crew under the age of thirty. "Just as long as I get to come and watch. And a table for two at 8 is no problem, I'll put you at a table along the back wall away from the kitchen."

"Thanks, Vera, appreciate it."

"My pleasure, Mack. See you then."

Guess she would be. Who knew when I turned down Riley and Quinn's invitation I'd have actual plans? Not that I planned on broadcasting it, the shit I'd no doubt catch enough to have me shutting my mouth and saying nothing. And as long as no one walked into Gino's and saw us, they'd be none the wiser.

Best it stayed that way, at least for now.

Chapter 4

Hayden

SO MUCH FOR me and my bright ideas.

When I'd suggested coffee with John, sorry, *Mack*, it was no big deal. I wasn't playing the hard-to-get game, and dragging it out for a week before we finally met served no purpose. Honestly, I was too tired and worked too many hours to bother with the pretense. We either clicked or we didn't, and if his fancy words ended up being nothing but talk then I would have preferred not to waste a whole week wondering.

But dinner had not been part of the equation.

Not that dinner in itself was a problem, we all had to eat, and usually by the time I finished my shift at Target, I was starving.

So I'd agreed, willing to kill two birds with one stone and glad cooking and dishes were going to be someone else's responsibility at least for one night. And I'd heard the food at *Gino's* was good.

The problem *was* my wardrobe.

Or more to the point, the lack of options in *it* suitable for a date.

There wasn't a chance I'd be able to squeeze into my old Levi's and lace T-shirt even if it wouldn't make me look ridiculous. Which left me with yoga pants, work clothes, and a printed floral dress I'd worn to my cousin's wedding last spring. It was also February in New York, so unless I wanted to suffer hypothermia there was a greater chance of me turning up in my work khakis and red polo than slipping into the dress.

Lucky for me, the realization had occurred *before* I'd left the store, running to the ladies' department and putting my employee discount to good use. And as tempting as it was to pour myself into one of those beautiful knitted sweater dresses and pair it up with equally stunning knee-high boots, the allure of not wearing control undergarments won out. So I settled for a pair of skinny—ironic since I was not—jeans, knitted sweater and woolen blazer to both keep me warm and stop me obsessing about how my butt looked in my new jeans. I also picked up some new panties and a bra, just in case.

Then I raced home, furiously pulling off labels before throwing myself into the shower and redressing. It was the quickest turnaround in history, my makeup being applied with one hand while I tried to tame my errant hair with a hairdryer.

It was a losing battle, the kinks and waves kicking out disobediently despite a healthy amount of hair product and a generous amount of heat.

Oh well, with any luck he'd be too interested in my boobs to even worry about my hair. I smoothed down the front of my new sweater, my old B cups having swelled to Cs without the aid of a push-up bra.

I was nervous.

There was no way around it.

As much as I wanted to not care what he thought, Mack was, *hopefully*, going to be the first man—other than my disinterested ex-husband—I'd been naked in front of for twenty years.

Which was why I had to get it over with as soon as possible.

Tossing insecurity out the window, and throwing myself at someone I wasn't in love with was the plan. So if—and that was a HUGE *if*—I did find someone I cared about later down the road, I wouldn't be hauling extra luggage he didn't deserve.

Ha! Look at me being delusional in thinking I'd ever fall in love again. Yeah, because being in a long-term relationship had worked out so stellar for me the last time. And considering I didn't have another twenty years to waste, I'd say it was better if I just tucked that idea back into the far recesses of my mind where it belonged. I allowed myself one more look at the mirror, fussing with lint that wasn't there before grabbing my keys and heading to Midtown.

It would have probably been smarter to leave my old Ford sedan at home and taken the subway. But I was tired, it was already so dark, and I wanted the option to get the hell out of there in a hurry if I needed to. So driving—however impractical—was the better option.

Not sure if it was better or worse having time to contemplate. The time spent from getting from my humble little condo at the top of Manhattan to the bustling center giving me time to mull over every good and bad thought. I had purposely not asked Mack about himself, wanting to keep things casual and distant. It would be easier that way.

The plan was we have dinner, and if things were going well, I'd *casually* invite myself to his place, and then sleep with him. Sure, there was the possibility he'd turn me down, which is why I was giving myself the whole dinner before broaching the subject. And if I read the situation wrong, asked and was turned down, well I'd just wave him goodbye, get back in my car and find some other guy who was willing. No sweat. But as I got closer, I was starting to have some doubts whether or not I was going to be able to go through with it.

My sedan eased into a parking space not far from *Gino's*, a few deep breaths needed before I got out of the car and made my way to the entrance. I ignored my sweaty palms, wiping them down the front of my new jeans as I edged my lips into a smile and walked to the hostess desk.

"Hi, I'm meeting a friend. Is there a reservation for Joh—I mean—Mack?" My manufactured confidence doing its job so my voice wasn't shaking.

The hostess looked me over, her dark brown eyes surveying me with more interest than I would have liked. "Suuuuuure, right this way."

Her voice was artificially sweet, as was her smile, glancing at me over her shoulder multiple times as she led me through the dining area to a table where a man was already seated.

The man was huge.

His big body was folded into the chair while his wide shoulders protruded from the backrest. Muscular and obviously tall as well, his head was down, studying his phone intensely as we neared. And I was almost going to tell my overly friendly escort she had to be mistaken when he turned and looked up.

Oh.

Holy.

Hell.

Those kind brown eyes I'd seen in his photos weren't half as sweet as they'd seemed. Heat licked at his irises, simmering warm as he smiled, and making what I'd thought was a handsome face turn into waaaaaaaay out of my league.

He was gorgeous.

A sharp jaw that looked to be freshly shaved, his short brown hair military neat, and lips so inviting I couldn't stop staring.

The chair scraped against the floor, his body coming to full height as he stood, and I had to take a minute to appreciate what all those photos had failed to capture.

Gorgeous had been inaccurate.

Sexy as hell was closer.

Breathtaking even more correct.

"Mack?" I stupidly asked, ignoring the fact I'd been led there and I knew it was him. I guess part of me was still grappling with disbelief, and more to the point, wondering what a man like him was doing still single. And why the *hell* he'd agreed to meet me.

"Hayden." He nodded, holding out his hand politely before turning to the hostess who still hadn't left my side. "Thanks Vera, I've got it from here."

Vera?

Her smile indicated they'd been more familiar than Mack just knowing her name.

Great.

Trust me to pick the one place in the whole of Manhattan that employed one of his ex-girlfriends. Although a man like that probably had a few, so it was bound to happen sooner or later.

"Hi." I accepted his handshake, delving back into that manufactured confidence I'd been rocking earlier and smiled. "I hope you haven't been waiting long."

Vera tipped her head to Mack, eyes glancing down at our clasped hands before her grin edged wider. "Enjoy your dinner. Your waiter will be here shortly." And then thankfully left before making it more awkward.

"Friendly staff." My palm heated, the touch of his skin making me feel warm all over. "Hopefully that's a good sign."

The contact between us broke, his hand sliding away as he moved closer. "I should have probably told you before." *Oh-uh here we go.* "But this place is right near my stationhouse, and we come here a lot."

Well that was comforting, hopefully meaning he'd only traded orders with Vera instead of bodily fluids. Not that it was any of my business, I just preferred to eat dinner without worrying about a jealous ex spitting in my fettucine.

"That's great," I lied. "Obviously the food is decent or you wouldn't keep coming back."

A waft of his cologne spiced the air between us, his hungry eyes simmering. "The food *is* decent."

With the heat of the restaurant and my overactive hormones making me feel too warm, I shucked my coat and hung it over the back of the chair. Mack took a step like he was going to pull it out for me but stopped when I shook my head and sat down before there was a discussion. Chivalry was fine except that wasn't why I was there, and I was already doubting we were going to make it to the naked stage, so it was probably best we got the show on the road.

"So Hayden, that's a pretty name." He retook his seat, smiling as his eyes did a subtle sweep of the hot mess in front of him.

"Thanks." I picked up the menu, trying to read the words while simultaneously convincing myself I had a shot. He'd seen my photos, right? Surely he hadn't been expecting a Victoria's Secret model and got me by mistake.

"How was work?"

His question pulled me from my conflicting thoughts, wondering if I should just outright ask if he'd matched me by accident. "I'm sorry?"

"*Work*, you said in your message you were working until seven," he repeated, not seeming to be annoyed by my apparent lack of attention.

I waved my hand, not having anything positive to say about how I earned a paycheck. "Oh, it was fine. Retail. You know, any day *Karen* doesn't want to talk to my manager, or no one is murdered in the dogfood aisle, it's a success."

He eased back into his chair, completely ignoring his menu while he looked at me. "Sounds interesting. You have many murders in the dogfood aisle?"

"Not as many as I would like." I huffed out a laugh, hoping to God he knew it was a joke and I wasn't harboring dark murderous thoughts. That sure as hell wouldn't help my cause to get laid. "So how was your day?" I attempted small talk, having decided on some kind of pasta.

"Slept, ate, did laundry. Typical day off," he offered. "And of course, messaged you."

Ah yes.

Of course.

I couldn't help but wonder how many other messages he'd sent. If I was the first—maybe not, he'd had hours he could've filled—woman of many or if he would work through them one at a time. He'd been very attentive, not glancing down at his menu or his phone since we'd sat down, and paying me enough interest that I believed I was his sole focus.

"You guys ready to order?" A pretty waitress placed two water-filled plastic tumblers down on our table. "I can give you the specials if you want? Oh hey, Mack!" Her attention turned to my date. "Aren't you sick of this place on your days off? Looking pretty fine." She winked before turning to me. "You and your friend need more time?"

She hadn't called me his date. Probably assuming a man as good looking as him would have someone suitably gorgeous on his arm. But while my insecurities weren't going to be disappearing anytime soon, I wasn't going to let some pretty, young nobody make me feel less than. I got enough of that at work. So I wasn't enduring it at dinner, especially when I wasn't getting paid.

"Actually, we're on a date." My lips spread into a grin. "So maybe you could suggest a nice red?"

"Oh?" She looked honestly surprised before shooting her eyes back to Mack. "A date? Really? Wow, okay. Ummm. Maybe the pinot?" She was either not sure about her wine selection or still reeling from the shock of Mack being on a date with me.

"Hmm." I tapped my finger on my chin, pretending to consider it. "I think I'll go with a glass of the merlot instead. And the ricotta and spinach cannelloni, thank you."

"Merlot sounds great." Mack grinned, handing his menu back to our waitress. "And I'll take the lasagna, thanks, Brooke."

She collected our menus, not bothering to write down our order before scurrying off. No doubt to confer with *Vera* where they'd share collected information. Next time I went out with a guy, I was asking a lot more questions before we settled on a venue. Or just flat out asked to meet in a hotel room.

Then.

Silence.

He didn't talk, ignoring both Brooke's hasty departure and the fact he was staring. My hands knotted in my lap, trying to find some of that bravery I'd had earlier. While I knew I was far from a beauty queen, I'd made more of an effort than I usually did. My clothes were new and well fitted, I'd worn makeup, done my hair—nothing that screamed celibate divorcée.

I cleared my throat reaching for the tumbler of water and taking a drink. His eyes hadn't left my face or my body for more than a few seconds since I'd walked in. And while initially I'd assumed he'd been attentive, I was beginning to second guess.

"Not what you're used to?" I tipped my head to the side, not willing to sit in the silent scrutiny any longer. "If you want, we can just get the food to go and then go our separate ways." I angled for my purse, ready to cover my half of the check.

He reached across, grabbing my arm. "No. No, you're not what I'm used to, and no, I don't want to get the food to go."

My brow arched, wondering what was going on in that big beautiful head of his. "So, if I'm not your usual type, what are we doing here? I already told you I'm not interested in mind games, but what I should have said is I'm not interested in *any* games, period."

"No games, Hayden." His arm had yet to move. "And we're here because I wanted to have dinner with you. Still do. Thought that's what you wanted too. But if that's changed I'm not going to hold you against your will."

Well that was a relief! Because honestly apart from the whole bigger/stronger vibe he had going on, I was positive Vera and Brooke would spring into action like a pair of trained ninjas and stop me from leaving.

"I don't know if I want to stay," I answered honestly. I was fairly sure I wasn't getting close to getting an orgasm—half-way decent or not. And to be honest, having dinner while people he knew watched us was a little more than I'd bargained for.

"Is it me or the place?" He asked so honestly, I almost laughed. Like there was a universe where a woman wouldn't want to have dinner with him. Certainly not the one we were in.

"Hayden, is it me? Have I done something that makes you want to leave?" He leaned forward, his warm brown eyes turning serious as he kept his voice low. "Because if I have, I'd really like to know. And apologize."

"Here you go." Brooke interrupted our moment, two wineglasses being laid on the table in front of us. "Your food should be out shortly. Oh, and Uncle Gino said dessert is on him."

Mack turned to Brooke, lifting out of his seat and reaching for his wallet. "Tell Gino thanks, but I've got this one." He pulled out some bills and placed them on the table. "We'll also take the tiramisu, and if you can wrap it with the rest of our order to go, that would be great."

"You're leaving?" Brooke echoed my thoughts.

Not sure why I was surprised, I'd offered to do exactly that not long ago. And even if he'd said no initially, he was allowed to change his mind.

"Yep." He held out his hand, waiting for me to take it. "We've had a change of plans."

Huh?

He was taking me with him?

Both confused and curious, I accepted his extended hand and stood.

After all, it was a weeknight and I'd gone to the trouble of dressing up, the least I could do is see what he had in mind.

Just as long as we ate.

Because whether I was his type or not, I was starving.

Chapter 5

Mack

HAYDEN WAS BEAUTIFUL.

Not pretty.

Not cute.

But beautiful.

Like a classic Chevy with rounded fenders, or a movie star from a black and white movie, there was something about her that was undeniably compelling. And fuck, was I glad I'd taken a chance and suggested dinner because coffee sure as shit wouldn't have been long enough.

Unable to stop looking, I knew I was probably making her uncomfortable. No woman wanted to be gawked at like a piece of meat, and yet there I was, keeping my mouth shut so my tongue didn't polish the floor.

She was curvy, her jeans and top doing a fine job clinging to her body, a sample of what was underneath. And her huge gray eyes were so expressive, it was like they were having their own conversation.

We ditched the table, the wine, and the pretense, moving to the counter by the door. Our order had been changed to go, and I was planning on still having dinner with Hayden even if we were changing the location.

"You ready?" I asked, grabbing our food Brooke had so helpfully boxed up and taking Hayden's hand. "We should probably get going before dinner gets cold."

It was a gamble.

A total roll of the dice whether or not I ended up with her handprint across my face. But I liked playing the odds as much as the next guy so figured it was worth the risk.

"Where are *we* going?" She buttoned up her coat, her breath coming out in a smoky huff in the cold air.

"My place, it's not far and there's no audience. Figured it will be less noisy, too."

I waited.

Anticipating either a few choice words or a right hook, but hoping for neither.

She dropped her hand from mine, taking a step closer and tilting her chin back so she could get a good look at me. "You *really* want to take me back to your place?"

"Yeah, I do," I laughed, willing to bet she was as surprised as I was at the invitation. Well, it wasn't much of an invitation considering I hadn't asked. "Hayden, I'd like to have dinner with you, what do you say?"

Her eyes glanced down the busy street, people coming and going despite the cold. "How far? I'm parked around the corner."

"I'm two blocks on 10th, why don't I walk you to your car and we can park it closer," I offered, not loving the idea of walking back later when it was darker and colder. And there wasn't a chance in hell I would let her do that trek alone. "Better be quick though, I can already feel the pasta cooling down."

Her head bobbed, giving me a nod in the affirmative as she directed me across the street. Parked not too far was an older model Ford Taurus, the lights blinking as we got closer and she hit the keyless entry.

Not waiting for an invitation, I walked to the passenger side, hopping in beside her as she started the ignition. Other than when I was in an engine, I liked to be behind the wheel. But given the circumstances and the company, I really didn't give a shit, grateful we were going to hopefully pick up where we left off.

"Make a right and get on 10th, I'll let you know where to park." I pointed up ahead, the car easing away from the curb as she entered the flow of traffic.

The stereo was on, tuned to some popular rock station and playing songs I barely recognized. I remembered when my old man said that about the stuff I used to listen to, and there I was, spewing the same thing.

"What?" She turned, catching me in a smile. "And if it's to complain about my driving, I'll happily pull over so you can walk."

I laughed, having learned a long time ago never to complain about a woman's driving. "My sister-in-law drives like a maniac and I made the mistake of telling her only *once*. She left my ass on the 95 and I had to walk three miles in the Florida heat. Now I either shut my mouth and accept the ride gracefully or drive myself. So no, it wasn't about your driving."

"So . . ." She waited for me to continue.

I tapped the speaker in the door. "The music. I never thought I'd see the day when I didn't recognize what was playing on popular stations but here we are. Everything is auto-tuned, over manufactured—there's no telling who the hell it is anymore. Was just thinking about how much my complaining sounds like my old man."

A smile edged on her lips as she nodded. "Oh, I'm with you there. I remember being in a moshpit for Soundgarden, people smuggling in weed and beer. Don't miss the flannel though, I look hideous in plaid."

"Ha, I find that hard to believe. I can't imagine there is anything you don't look good in."

Her eyes darted to me before going quiet again, the smile slipping from her face. And either she thought I was feeding her a line, or she wasn't very good at taking compliments. Neither sat well with me.

"Just up here, if you pull around the back, the garage has a couple of extra spaces for visitors. Fingers crossed we get lucky tonight."

Fuck.

Not what I'd meant to say.

"I mean, hopefully there's a vacant space," I added, probably making it worse.

She followed my directions, doing me a favor and ignoring what I said as she pulled to the front of the roller door. "Do we need to press something." She glanced at the metal box to the side, my ass already out of the seat as I went to input the numbers.

The door rose slowly, giving me time to get back into the car before she could drive through. "Take anything that's free on the far left. I think there's a gap between the Wrangler and BMW."

"Wow, this must be a really nice place." Her eyes widening at the rows of imports, shiny hood ornaments lining most of the garage.

Even a shithole with minimal square footage and no windows cost a fortune in my part of town, but my dad had bought into the co-up years before the neighbors had fancy cars. And when the folks made the move to Florida, he'd sold it to me. Lucked out considering it was right around the time of the divorce.

"Yeah, it used to be. Most of the old families have moved out so don't really know who my neighbors are anymore. They seem to have expensive tastes though."

She eased the Taurus into the space, cutting the ignition before we both exited the car. Even under the bright yellow security lighting she looked beautiful, taking a minute to appreciate the view as I grabbed the food and we walked to the elevator.

"I'm on four." I pressed the corresponding button, leaning back against the wall as we started to climb.

We didn't speak, taking the ride in silence until we got to my floor and the elevator door opened.

"You always lived here?" she asked, following me down the hall to my condo.

My fingers twisted the key in the lock, my front door popping open. "When I was younger, then back again in the last few years. It's really close to work too." I hit the hall lights, gesturing for her to go through.

"Ahhh yes, the fire station." She walked in front of me, looking over her shoulder as I followed. "We didn't even get to talk about your exciting job."

"Well, you can ask me about anything you want while we eat." I stopped at a doorway. "Kitchen or couch? I know it's probably easier at a table but I thought I'd give you the choice. I'll be honest, most nights I park myself in front of the tube and just eat there."

Her eyes lit up, clueing me in that she liked the suggestion. "Oh, I love eating on the couch. It's the only time I get to watch any T.V."

With the debate settled, I lowered the food onto the coffee table and flicked on the lamp. "Make yourself at home, I'll grab some plates from the kitchen."

I didn't leave her long, grabbing a few plates, forks, and a couple of beers before heading back to the living room.

"No merlot unfortunately." I held up the bottles, feeling a little apologetic. "Not much of a wine drinker."

She didn't hesitate, twisting the cap off the beer and taking a swallow. "So why didn't you order a beer at Gino's?"

"Because I was trying to impress you," I laughed. "Not saying I don't drink it, I just prefer this." I raised the icy long neck.

It was her turn to laugh, shaking her head as I opened up the plastic containers and dished out the pasta. "Mack, surely you don't have problems impressing people. Seriously, I'm still wondering what the hell you're doing with me."

"Why would you say that?" The notion made heat crawl up my neck. "I didn't say so at the restaurant because I couldn't trust the words to come out right, but you're beautiful, Hayden. Why the hell wouldn't I want to be with you?"

"Wow, you are *really* trying. I guess I should be thankful, but you don't need to pretend," she grimaced, shaking her head.

"What's that supposed to mean? I'm not pretending anything." I was confused, wondering what I'd said to make her question my motives.

She huffed out a breath. "Look, you seem like a nice guy. Probably too nice for what I need right now so I'm going to cut you some slack. But I haven't done this," she gestured between us, "in a *really* long time. I haven't had compliments and flirty conversation, and I can't even remember what it feels like for a man to want me like that. I know you probably were looking for a nice night without the drama and unfortunately you got stuck with me."

Didn't need to be told she had baggage, managed to work that out all on my own. But hearing her say I was too *nice* for her made me irrationally angry.

"Since you've been honest with me, I'm going to pay you the same courtesy." I looked her in the eyes, making it clear I was serious. "But I'm not *stuck* here with you. I invited you, and I'm not in the habit of doing things I don't want. Now, I can't change what's going on in your head, or what kind of things happened to put those ideas there in the first place. But if you can leave them at the door for a few hours and just enjoy dinner, I promise you won't regret it. Either way, I think you should eat before you leave. Pretend it's for my ego if that makes you feel better. But sending you out in the cold after working a long day when we have a perfectly good meal in front of us doesn't sit well with me. You think you can give me that?"

North had always accused me of being too intense, warning me to dial it back. And I wasn't sure if it was that or something else that had shocked her into silence. Last thing I wanted to do was scare her, but I didn't know another way to get my point across. Not in a way where I thought she'd believe.

"Sound good?" I asked, handing her a fork before taking one for myself. "Mmm, this lasagna smells delicious and I'm starving."

Deciding to sideline the conversation for a bit, I forked some of the noodles and started to eat. It was probably better I didn't say anything else, worried my little outburst had scared her and she'd be tempted to stab me in the neck with a nail file or something. Still while my delivery wasn't great, I didn't regret it.

And thankfully after a few minutes watching me eat, she decided to get in on the action too. Taking small bites of her cannelloni, she made a start on her meal. Still wasn't sure the minute she was done she wouldn't head to the door. But as long as there was still food to be consumed, I had time to convince her to stay. Not even sure what I was hoping to achieve. Maybe get her to see she deserved to be treated well, and that those compliments I'd paid her weren't even close to what she was due.

"It is *really* good." She was the first one to speak, her lips wrapping around the fork and savoring the mouthful. "How's yours?"

An opening.

And I sure as hell was gonna take it.

"Amazing, you want to try?" I angled my plate, encouraging her to take some. "Gino's red sauce is legendary. I know the place isn't going to win any gourmet food awards, but I would eat there every day of the week and not complain."

Her forked pierced my lasagna, a small—but encouraging—smile on her face. "Sounds like you already do if the staff's reaction is anything to go by."

I rolled my eyes. "Yeah, not everyone is as good a cook as I'd like. The rookies are brutal. Unless it's something you can toss into the oven and reheat, they're clueless."

"And you? How good a cook are you?" she asked, taking a little more of my lasagna before going back to her pasta.

"Well, considering it's been a really long time since I've been a rookie, my skills have vastly improved. I also like to eat—nothing like a good motivator." I smirked, picking up my beer and taking a swig.

I was underselling my skills in the kitchen by a long shot. Able to cook most men under the table. But since she was having trouble accepting I wasn't too good to be true, I figured it was the better option.

She also grabbed her beer and took a mouthful, pointing the bottle at me. "So what exactly do you do at the fire station? You drive the truck? Handle the hose? Do both?"

"I'm the Battalion Chief, but I did my time on the front line."

Her eyes widened, her hand slowly lowering the beer. "Does that mean you're the boss?"

I chuckled, probably liking it a bit too much that she was impressed. "One of . . . I have subordinates, but I answer to people above me too. Lots of paperwork, but highly rewarding. What about you?"

There was some hesitation, her guard still up. "I work at Target. I'm a sales associate. But I also do some medical transcription from home; I get to put my fast typing skills to good use." She gave me a tight smile.

"Sounds to me like you work harder than I do. Bet that discount is pretty sweet." My shoulder nudged hers, shooting her a wink.

Her body seemed to relax as her grin brightened. "Sure is. Hey, can I ask you a question?"

"Shoot." I waved my hand, not having anything to hide. "What is it you want to know?"

"Why the dating site? I would think a good-looking guy with a great job wouldn't need the help."

"You think I'm good looking?" My lips twisted into a grin, unable to focus on the rest of her question.

"Come on, you must know it." She gave me a playful shove. "Surely you've looked in a mirror. I'm surprised people aren't pulling fire alarms just hoping you turn up."

I laughed, not so secretly pleased she liked what she saw. "Yeah, that doesn't happen. Maybe for some of the younger guys, but it's been a while for this," I reproduced her earlier gesture between us, "for me too. Apparently, too long. I was gifted the profile as a birthday present."

"Oh really?" She leaned forward, interested. "Who set yours up?"

"My . . . urm . . . Quinn."

Yeah, hadn't really thought that one through, had I?

"*Your* Quinn?" Her question one hundred percent anticipated. Figuring it was easier to just tell her the whole story, I settled back into my seat. Besides, maybe if I volunteered a little more information, she'd do the same.

"Quinn is . . . well complicated would be an understatement. She's my daughter-in-law. I took in a kid when he was eighteen. He didn't have a family, so I made him part of mine. No formalities or anything on account he was already of age, but trust me, that kid needed a lot of work. We don't share the same last name, and most of the gray hair on my head is because of him, but I couldn't have loved him anymore if he was mine. Riley. Quinn is his wife."

She swallowed slowly, an emotion I couldn't read clouding her eyes. "He was eighteen?"

"Yeah, he's almost twenty-nine now, works at the station with me. Has a kid on the way. A lot has changed since we first met," I chuckled, the time having disappeared quicker than I'd ever imagined.

"Wow, you *really* are a nice guy."

There was that word again.

Nice.

Didn't usually have a problem with it except its current usage was bugging me.

And another thing, if she kept looking at me like she was, I was probably going to have to kiss her.

"You should finish your pasta, we've still got dessert." I coughed into my hand, turning my attention back to my plate.

Yeah, kissing her was so on the agenda.

Chapter 6

Hayden

HEARING MACK HAD taken in Riley over ten years ago was startling. Sure, being a parent in your thirties wasn't strange, but it hadn't occurred to me someone would help raise what essentially was an adult. He didn't elaborate on the details but I could read between the lines, assuming Riley's circumstances had been less than ideal.

Wow.

Because being a heroic firefighter wasn't enough, he had to add adopting troubled youths as well. It was both heartwarming and overwhelming. Somehow, instead of securing a hot and insignificant one-night stand, I'd stumbled headfirst into an afterschool special. It was hard to relax, knowing I was making a big mistake. I should have gone with that guy from Staten Island. Sure, probably an asshole with a middle-age paunch, but at least I wouldn't be blinded with the shine of his freaking halo.

What would Mack think of me? Only charitable thing I ever did was throw in some loose change in the Salvation Army's red Christmas bucket.

Not on the same level.

Not even close.

God, I was disappointed.

Wishing he'd been a little less . . . magnificent. He was already too good looking, too sexy and too charming for anyone's good, and he'd also been incredibly sweet. It was either throw myself at him and disregard my conscience or walk away and let him be with a woman he deserved. And given my track record for not being overly charitable, I'd say my chances of doing the right thing weren't great.

And yes, I knew I was being hard on myself. Knew that if Gayle, or anyone else who cared about me heard those internal thoughts, they'd probably kick my ass. But valid or not, those shadows of self-doubt crept in all the same.

I didn't ask any more questions. Honestly, I was a little worried about what else he might say. He'd already called me beautiful and said so many amazing things, I wasn't sure I'd be able to recover. It was hard enough being beside him, feeling my skin tingle just by the way he looked at me. God, not sure what would happen if he did anything more.

Worried about the silence that had crept up between us, I did my best to make small talk. Nothing too personal, keeping things light and non-intrusive. We made it all the way through dinner and halfway through dessert before it all fell apart. Asking me what I'd asked him, why was I on a dating site.

Shit.

"My divorce was finalized," I volunteered, hoping it would be enough. "Figured it was time to get back on the horse."

I hoped he took it for the literal meaning I'd intended, and not think I was screening prospective candidates for a replacement.

Sadly, my meager explanation invited more questions.

"How long were you married?" Mack took another spoonful of the tiramisu, licking remnant mascarpone off his lips like it was no big deal.

Yum.

And the dessert wasn't bad either.

I tried to concentrate, thinking about how much I hated Cooper in the hope it would stop me from getting aroused. "Ten years, but we were together for twenty. Probably would have gotten less for murder," I joked, realizing too late it was the second *murder* wisecrack I'd made through the night. Because it wasn't enough I didn't have angel wings like he probably deserved, I had to cast doubts on whether he'd end up with a toe tag by the end of the night. My dating game needed some serious work. "I mean, it probably went on longer than it should have. The marriage was dead." *Shit, could I just stop?* "I mean, *over* a long time before we split up."

Great, because sounding pathetic was only slightly better than sounding psychotic. "How about you?" I asked, again realizing too late that I didn't want to know. It would just make things harder. Personal information shared wasn't conducive to a one-night stand and was none of my business.

"Been divorced for two years. We were separated for another two before we finally got around to the paperwork, and we'd been married for six. Had been too preoccupied with my career before then to settle down. It's not exactly easy keeping a relationship when you're a first responder."

Was he kidding? No relationship was easy, and it was hard to imagine what kind of woman would toss a man like Mack aside. Between Cooper getting his MBA—which I paid for—me working two jobs, and *him* then finding a job, we'd barely seen each other. And had he given me just a shred of appreciation—or even affection—I'd have stayed. Because it takes work, and that passionate spark of first love doesn't last forever.

Yet, Mack was—if I had to list his virtues again I was probably going to dry heave—amazing, and his ex just what? Just walked away? He didn't seem like the kind of man to screw around—I didn't have to know the guy to see how honorable he was—and I doubted he'd be the kind to beat a woman. And he'd been so friendly and attentive with me, and I was a relative stranger. I could only imagine what he was like when he was in love.

Lord.

I bet he was intense.

Old Testament kind of intense, where he laid down and volunteered to carve out his own heart to prove he was worthy.

"Uh-hmm." I cleared my throat, my efforts to keep my thoughts and my underwear clean struggled with the visual.

Mack turned, his face full of concern—because he was soooo fucking nice—as his fingers reached out and gently caressed my arm. "Are you okay?"

"Yeah, fine," I lied, my skin flushing warmer because of the attention and the contact. "Just fine."

"Yeah, you are." He grinned, his hand moving from my arm and pushing my hair out of the way. "And I know that was a cheesy one-liner, but I couldn't help myself."

Hell.

I didn't even try to argue, accepting his compliment while thoughts raced through my mind. Either I do what I'd set out to do or walk out the door. And my feet, like the rest of me, hadn't moved an inch. Guess that was decided then, my need to take it further greater than any of my other hesitations. "What else do you say when you can't help yourself?" I asked, both excited and terrified of finding out. Still, I wasn't backing down, finding bravery in that I'd probably never see him again so I could just say what I wanted.

"Why don't I just show you instead." He moved his mouth closer, his lips barely making contact.

Oh.

His lips demanded more, the brief whisper of a kiss deepening as his hand cradled my jaw. Without even thinking, I opened my mouth, allowing his tongue to slide in. My lips started to move, an action I was positive I'd forgotten, returning like it had been automatic. Me, an active participant, kissing him back.

"Mack," I moaned shamelessly, running my fingers through his closely cropped hair and arching into him.

Like something inside of me had awakened, I bloomed for him, kissing him, touching him, and letting him do both to me.

My brain kicked out of gear for a second, those pesky extra pounds and the feelings that came with them crept back in, my eyes opening wide when his hand slid up my belly.

He was looking right at me, his eyes filled with heat and desire and who knew what else as he continued to touch me, slipping under my knitted top and touching my skin.

For whatever reason he wanted me.

Wanted this.

Pushing the thoughts back, I gave into his touch, arching as his hand traveled up my body, his fingers cupping my breast.

"Hayden," he growled against my lips, no longer sweet and gentle as he pulled me closer.

"Please touch me," I begged, feeling like a million pin pricks were assaulting my skin. "Touch me."

I'd been starved.

So emaciated of affection that I needed his hands everywhere.

"I should stop." His hands hesitated, his mouth continuing to kiss me.

I shook my head, sucking in a breath and demanding, "Please. I need this. Don't stop. Don't you dare."

"Fuck me." His voice was raw, pulling down the cup of my bra, his fingers touching my soft skin. My nipples hardened on contact, stiffening under his palm as he kneaded my breast.

I wasn't sure if it was a curse or an invitation, my body writhing as my hands clawed at his muscular back. I loved the way it felt but wanted more, pulling the shirt from his pants and splaying my fingers across his firm abs.

Oh.

Oh.

Oh.

My breath came out in short, sharp bursts as he continued to kiss me. His hand had moved to my other breast, giving it equal attention while his mouth made me lose what was left of my mind.

"Take it off," he hissed, yanking at my top. And had I assumed he had wanted my help, I was mistaken, managing to whip the knitwear over my head. "My shirt, Hayden. Take it off."

Oooooooohhhhhhhhh.

Following his directions—because I very much wanted to as well—I fumbled with his buttons blindly, furiously working each of those frustrating things through the buttonholes until I could part it down the middle. My reward was a wall of toned, taut flesh that rippled under my fingertips.

While I'd been distracted, he also unclasped my bra, the pretty lace falling to my lap as I sat in front of him topless. I didn't even have time to be self-conscious, his mouth dropping to my neck and then lower, sweeping his tongue against each nipple.

"Mack, please." I wasn't even sure what I was asking for, needing more but not wanting him to stop what he was doing.

"I love the way you say my name." His words vibrated against my throat, my body tipping backward as he leaned me back. I was no longer vertical, the cushions of his sofa cradling me as I waited for what was coming next.

His hand swept down my stomach again, playing with the top button of my jeans while his eyes asked for permission. He hesitated, waiting until I nodded my consent before undoing them and then sliding down the zipper.

I had no idea what he thought about what he saw, if he was comparing me to other women he'd slept with or if he wasn't expecting me to be so soft and rounded. But I didn't have time to contemplate, his mouth coming back to mine as his hands roughly shoved down my jeans.

"If I touch you, are you going to be wet?" His words were rough against my mouth while his fingers edged at the seams of my underwear.

I nodded, feeling so hot between my legs I was positive I was dripping. "Yes. Very."

"Good." A smile slid across his face. "Because I'm going to make you come, Hayden."

Oh.

God.

Before I could ask how, his weight shifted, moving that amazing torso and sculpted abs out of my grasp as he shuffled the rest of my jeans down, taking my underwear with them.

I was bare.

That Brazilian wax I swore I'd never get again finally paying dividends as every single sweep of his hand was amplified. Everything was sensitive, more intense, his fingers not even close to my clit yet I was ready to burst.

"Open for me." His strong hands parted my legs, baring myself even more as he kissed each of my thighs.

Shit.

I hadn't had a man go down on me in at least seven years, my eyes opening so wide I was surprised it didn't scare him off. "Are you?"

"Yes." He flattened his tongue against my core, cognitive thought leaving completely as my body shook. My eyes slammed shut, my back arching as he did it again, his breath hot on my center as he lapped me slowly.

"Oh. Fuck," I cursed out, overwhelmed by sensations and too turned on to be embarrassed. I didn't care what he thought about my body. How many women he'd done it to before or what was going through his mind. I was selfish, desperate for release, the feeling building in my gut as I lost all sense.

Either it had been too long to compare, or oral sex had never been this good, his mouth doing crazy things as I was rendered speechless, unable to do anything but lie back and enjoy it.

I'd tried to reach out, touch his cock, his chest, his head—something so it felt like I was participating, but stalled out. My body so tightly coiled that basic movements felt impossible as I had no choice but to lay there.

Even though he was severely being short changed, he didn't seem to mind. His tongue and lips alternated kissing and sucking, the sensation almost unbearable.

"Mack, I—"

Not sure what I was going to say but I didn't get the chance, my body splintering as I came undone, my limbs shaking as waves of pleasure washed through me. I hadn't orgasmed so quickly in years, usually needing a decent amount of lube and the help of my trusty vibrator.

Mack's mouth stayed on me, teasing out the last echo until I was boneless, a puddle unable to move. His head lifted, a radiating smile twitching at his lips as he hovered above me. "Hadn't been my plan, but I can't say I'm disappointed."

"I'm not sure I can even think right now." I threw an arm over my eyes. "That was so far away from half-decent, I'm not even sure that was just one."

It was crazy, my body still tingling as I laid naked on his couch.

God.

I was naked.

Without an impending orgasm overriding my brain, awareness snuck in. Usually when I was naked I felt vulnerable, exposed. Even with Cooper, I'd unconsciously lower my hands and cover myself. Or on the rare occasion we'd have sex, I'd leave on a T-shirt. Funnily enough he never asked why or tell me to take it off.

And yet with Mack, I didn't hide.

But not because I didn't want to.

I was desperate to pick something up off the floor and use it as cover, glad the only light in the room was that of a single lamp. But I refused to give into that voice, forcing myself to be brave.

It doesn't matter what he, or any man, thinks, I reminded myself.

I'm brave, and strong, and—

"Hey, beautiful," his finger trailed up my stomach, not seeming to notice the silvery squiggles I tried to ignore whenever I got dressed. "Where did you go?"

My hand reached up to his jaw, caressing him as gently as he was me. "I was just thinking that I'm not ready to leave yet."

"Oh yeah?" His brow rose. "And what did you have in mind?"

Be brave, Hayden.

I reached over, pressing my palm against the fly of his pants and found him hard. Even doing what he had been, I was still a little surprised. A surge of excitement took over me as I slowly moved my hand. "It wouldn't be polite of me to leave you with this, would it?" I leaned closer, brushing my lips against his neck. I didn't kiss, just hinted at the contact, letting my breath heat his skin.

His chest expanded, taking a gulp of air as my fingers tightened against the fabric. "You sure you want to do that?"

"Yes, very sure." My lips moved to his pecs, swirling my tongue around his nipples like he had done to me. "Your body is amazing. Do you live in the gym?"

He chuckled, his fingers tracing the length of my spine as I worked my way down his impressive abs. "Glad you like it."

Inch by inch my lips traversed his torso, my hands exploring further south as they landed on the waistband of his pants. I didn't hesitate, popping open the button and easing down the zipper, his impressive length straining against the cotton of his boxer briefs.

"Jesus," he cursed, my hand disappearing underneath the fabric and wrapping around his length. I gripped him tight, feeling him throb within my fingers as I lowered my mouth and sucked.

His hands went to his pants, pushing them down low on his hips to give me better access. I had planned to take them off before I started but didn't want to waste the time, lollipopping him with my mouth while my fist continued to glide up and down.

It had been a while but I remembered the basics, finding my rhythm fairly quickly as my tongue swirled around the head and pushing his shaft deeper into my mouth.

"Hayden," he growled, gripping my hair as his body tensed. "You keep doing that and this is going to be over real quick."

My head lifted, my hand still pumping him slowly as I leaned forward and kissed his mouth. We both moaned, the taste of me still on his mouth as I jerked him off, feeling him get even harder.

His kiss demanded more, pulling me closer as his hands touched me. My breasts, my shoulders, my back—his fingers completely restless as he took my mouth.

"I'm not blowing my load into your hand, Hayden. That just isn't happening." He groaned against my lips. "Give me a second to get my clothes off and let's see if I can't find a better alternative."

"Fuck me," I moaned, not willing to leave it to chance that he had another option. "I want you to fuck me."

A noise that didn't sound human tore at his throat followed by a sharp hiss. "Fuck this shit." He kicked off his shoes, pulling his lips away from mine so he could yank off the rest of his clothes. Pants, socks, underwear all got dropped to the floor in a rush while I was treated to one hell of a show as muscles flexed and twisted, showing me exactly how *in shape* he was.

His body was incredible, hard lines and perfect curves that seemed to defy logic. Even when I was in my twenties, having sex with bad boys who liked to work out, I'd never seen anything as impressive. And I wasn't just talking about his body.

"Wow." I took a moment just to appreciate, whispering silent thank yous as I stared.

"Again, glad you like it," he smirked, the cocky grin from earlier making a reappearance. "Now let's take it to my bed, Hayden, where I can do this properly."

An outstretched hand waited for me, and I wasn't going to say no.

Chapter 7

Mack

IF I SAID I hadn't wanted to fuck Hayden, I'd have been lying.

But when I invited her to my condo to finish our dinner, that hadn't been part of the plan.

Not to say I didn't have a casual hook-up every once in a while, but Hayden had been different. I'd wanted to get to know her, too bad my dick had other ideas.

"You sure you want this?" I asked her one last time, laying her flat on my bed so I could get a better look at her.

I turned on the bedside lamp, the light it threw off letting me see her nod. "Yes, do you?"

Jesus.

"This isn't enough of an indicator?" I stroked my hard dick, wanting to be inside of her more than anything. "Okay, Hayden, enough talking."

Deciding to put my mouth to better use, I kissed her again. I loved her mouth, those sweet lips—hungry, opening for me on command as I moved on top of her. She was so receptive, pressing her tits against my naked chest, her pussy grinding against my shaft as my hands were on her everywhere.

I couldn't stop touching her, her body so amazing my hands didn't know what they preferred. I wanted it all—her hips, her ass, her tits, her thighs—my mind taking a mental Polaroid I was sure I'd jerk off to later.

Beautiful.

And so fucking sexy I wasn't sure how I'd gotten so lucky.

Her hips rocked, the friction between us making me crazy and I was done playing.

"I need a condom, sweetheart." I pulled my mouth from hers, her swollen lips parted as she panted. "Let me get one."

She looked confused, her eyes dipping to where my bare dick and her pussy had been grinding. "Oh. Of course. I just forgot."

"Don't worry, I've got it covered," I winked, pulling out a silver packet from the drawer of my nightstand. My fingers got busy, tearing the sucker open and rolling it down my shaft.

Her eyes stayed on me, following my actions as I pumped once and then twice, so hard it was almost painful. Last thing I needed was for it to be over before I'd even started. But if she kept looking at me like that, I wasn't going to have much say in the matter.

I leaned forward, my mouth moving from her neck to those pretty little nipples. Her tits were perfect, not so big I couldn't get my hand around and tips that got hard the minute my tongue hit them. Nothing more a man could ask for, my hands cupping them as I settled between her legs.

"Mack." It was halfway between a moan and a sigh, the way she said my name so fucking sexy I hoped she never called me John. I wanted to hear it again, to make her sound like that over and over, my name on her lips while I was buried inside of her.

She reached down, fingers gripping my cock and using it to rub up against her. It was hot how much she wanted it, desperate whimpers spilling from her lips as I teased her some more.

"You ready for me, Hayden?" My mouth moved to her jaw,

kissing her as I lined up against her opening. She was so wet, her hips bucking in anticipation, and if I had any resolve left, it was gone. "Yeah, you are."

I sank into her slow, letting her adjust as I gave her a little more, her eyes slamming shut as she tilted her pelvis. She felt amazing, gripping me tight as I got deeper, only getting halfway before I couldn't hold back.

"Fuck," I cursed, sliding in to the hilt, my hands on either side of her on the mattress so I wouldn't crush her under my weight. "You feel so good."

Those beautiful eyes popped open, giving me their attention as I took a moment to just enjoy it. "Yes," she breathed, arching her back off the bed. "More."

She wasn't going to have to ask again.

I slid out only to slide back in harder than the first time, shuffling to my knees so I could hold her legs. *Yeah, much better*, my hips rocking against hers as I got in deeper, her thrusts matching mine as we both lost control.

If I'd wanted to be slow and gentle, I'd seriously fallen short of the mark, pistoning inside of her as she reached down and played with my balls.

God, that felt good.

Fucking amazing, but it wasn't just about me. I wanted to see her come again, this time on my cock.

One of my hands reached between us, finding her clit. It was swollen and ready, my fingers circling it as I continued to drive into her.

"Yes, yes," she panted. "I'm so close."

I picked up the pace, faster and harder while I continued to tease, her mouth opening and her eyes peeling back wide as the first wave hit her.

"Mack," she screamed, my name bouncing off the walls as her whole body shook, her pussy tightening around me as pulses squeezed me like a fist.

"That's it, sweetheart. That's it." My need to come so nuclear I wasn't sure I could hold off. "That feels so good."

She shivered, her hands reaching up to her tits, playing with them as she continued to unravel, the visual enough to finish me off.

"Hayden." My hips jerked, my body detonating as I felt it straight from my balls. I couldn't stop, bucking against her while I emptied my load into the condom.

It was only when I slid my eyes back open that I'd realized they'd been closed, the view underneath me enough to make me hard again.

Her eyes were open too—glassy and bright—a satisfied smile plastered across her mouth while her hair covered my pillow like a mess of golden cotton candy.

"You okay?" I asked, still buried inside her as my fingers moved up her body. She shivered, breathing deeply as my hand made its way to her face.

She nodded, her smile getting bigger as she reached up to kiss me. "That was amazing. Seriously, a-mazing."

"It was pretty amazing for me too." I kissed her back. "Let me go get cleaned up."

Last thing I wanted was to get out of the bed, but I had the condom to take care of. "Bathroom is through there if you need it." I pointed to the adjoining room. "I'll use the other one down the hall."

Kissing her one last time, I pulled out and walked to the door. She'd sat up, looking at me leaving, shooting her a smile before I disappeared out the door.

I headed into the bathroom, took care of the condom, using the facilities before washing my hands and drying off. I hit the lights and strolled back to my room.

My bed was empty, the covers kicked back, but I could hear the water running. Giving her space, I slid back into bed hoping once she was done, she would join me. Considering the date hadn't gone as I'd assumed—dinner, and *not* sleeping with her—I wasn't sure where she'd land on sticking around. It wasn't like we knew each other. Hell, I hadn't even asked her last name or her phone number. All I had were the details she'd put on her profile, and a memory I wouldn't be in a hurry to forget.

The water stopped, rustling coming from the bathroom before the door slid open. She was wrapped in a towel, her hands clutching at the top to keep it together. "Hi," she grinned, sitting on the edge of the bed. "I should probably go get my clothes from the other room."

"Yeah, you could do that." I moved closer toward her. "*Or* you could get back in between these sheets with me."

It was greedy of me wanting her to stay. After all, she probably had work the next day and it was already late. But I wasn't ready for her to leave either. At least not until I had a guarantee I was going to see her again.

She hesitated, eyes cutting to the doorway like she was weighing her options. Hoping I'd sway her decision in my favor, I folded down the covers. Her eyes got wider seeing I was still naked and already half hard. "What do you say, Hayden? You want to get back in this bed?"

"Yes," she nodded, the appreciation she gave me inflating my ego. "I want to get in the bed."

"Then take off the towel, sweetheart." I tugged at the edge, encouraging her to let go. "Your body is too beautiful to be hidden away behind this, and I really like looking at it."

Her lips tightened, her mouth slamming shut like she wanted to say something but was holding back. Maybe that hadn't been the right thing to say, making her think all I was interested in was the sex.

I was just about to apologize, tell her that I was rusty at romance when she lifted her ass off the mattress. I watched with interest, thinking I'd probably blown my chance when she stopped, looking me in the eyes as she let the towel drop.

"Fuck," I cursed out, my intentions of being a gentleman forgotten as I leapt from the bed. "You're so beautiful." And before I could say anything else, I kissed her, her lips opening for me instantly as my arms circled her.

She was perfect, every single part of her amazing, and I needed her back in my bed.

So much for my apology.

The lamp beside me was still on when I opened my eyes, having fallen asleep around midnight. I'd intended to do more talking and less touching, but after seeing her naked standing in front of me like a goddess, my brain kind of stalled out. I'd taken her back to my bed and made her come three more times before I wrapped her in my sweat-soaked sheets. My arms kept her close against me, loving her cheek pressed against my chest. It was only after she'd closed her eyes that I did the same, not wanting to waste a second of it on sleep.

But as I became more aware, I noticed the place she'd occupied on my chest was empty, a quick glance of my bed showing me she wasn't there either.

Not good.

Hoping she was in the bathroom, I threw back the covers and slid open the door. The room was still dark, a couple of damp towels in the hamper in the corner but nothing else.

I didn't even have to check the living room to know her clothes—along with her—were gone too.

She'd left.

I couldn't have been asleep for more than a half hour, my sleep patterns erratic from rotating shifts. But in those precious minutes she'd slipped out of my bed, gotten dressed and left my condo without so much as a goodbye.

A quick survey of each room confirmed what I already knew. She was gone—no note—and other than the empty takeout containers still on my coffee table and the used condoms, no sign she'd even been there in the first place.

My phone was sitting in my pants on the living room floor, pulling it from the pocket as I sat on the couch. The screen lit up, showing a missed called from Riley and a couple of texts. Short of asking one of my friends in the NYPD to search a database— something I'd never do—the only way I had to get ahold of her was that app and those messages. I flicked across to our message thread and hesitated as I figured out what I wanted to say.

She was already skittish, so asking why she left without so much as a goodbye wasn't a good way to go. Not like I was owed anything. And as much as I wanted to see her again, I didn't want her to think all I was interested in was the sex. Considering we hadn't done much else, it would be a fair—if inaccurate— assumption on her part. But I couldn't just let it go either.

When it came to one-night stands, I wasn't exactly great at it. Not to say I couldn't do casual, but the few women I'd slept with since splitting up with Melinda had been more of a *friends with benefits* kind of arrangement. Sometimes that didn't work out, with the few casual hook-ups I'd attempted not lasting more than a week. The job, my attitude, my less-than-enthusiastic desire to hand another woman my balls again—take your pick as to why I was mostly riding solo. But Hayden was different. She was intriguing, interesting and fuck knows I wanted more than just one night. She wasn't like those other girls, and while I didn't know why, I wanted the chance to at least find out.

Hayden,
There's a 90's night at Club Retro in Brooklyn
on Friday. It will probably be too loud, filled

with obnoxious twenty-year-olds wearing faded band T-shirts of artists they've never heard of. But if you want to join me and revisit when music was still good and complain about the current state of affairs, I'd like the company. No plaid wearing necessary.
Mack

It didn't say half of what I wanted, but kept it casual enough so hopefully she'd say yes. Other than both being divorced and liking 90's grunge, there wasn't a lot I had to work with. And begging her for another date—despite wanting to—wasn't the way to go either.

And the irony that I was inviting her to a *club* wasn't lost on me. It wasn't even an accident, a million other venues preferable. But I was hoping, if nothing else, it would prompt her to call me out. At the very least, open a dialog. And if I had to pick—gun to my head, make a decision—a club I'd want to spend time in, one with a decent playlist would be my first choice.

I stared at what I'd written, hitting send before I had a chance to change it. The circle beside her name was red, signaling she was offline. She might've been in the car driving home and would probably go right to bed. But hopefully in the next few days she'd flick open the app and see my message, and if not, well then I guess I'd be trolling Targets and looking like a creep.

Either way, I had to see her again.

And I was going to do everything in my power to make that happen.

Chapter 8

Hayden

EVERY PART OF my body buzzed.

My hair was still damp, too tired to blow it dry after my shower, so I'd laid a towel over my pillow before climbing into bed. But it would be hours before I got any sleep. And I didn't need the digital display of my phone clicking over minute by minute to know it was a fruitless exercise.

Mack was . . . amazing.

I think I'd used the word a million times since meeting him but hadn't found a better substitution. I pictured his gorgeous smiling face beside the definition of it in the dictionary.

And yet . . . so unexpected.

When he looked at me it was like he saw something else, a different version of myself I didn't know or hadn't met. And he *really* liked that woman whoever she was.

Even when Cooper and I first met and we were screwing like rabbits, it hadn't been as good. And anyone who came before— well, who even remembered. All I knew was he'd given me more orgasms in one night than I'd had in an entire decade. And wow, they had been better too.

He didn't fumble around, trying to stick it in before I was ready. No, he took his time, touching me, kissing me, teasing me so when he eventually got to my clit all he'd have to do was blow and I'd unravel.

His ex-wife had to be an idiot.

Hell, if sex with Cooper had been halfway near that level, we'd probably still be married. And not just because he'd given me mind-blowing orgasms either, it was because he made me feel *beautiful*.

It was utterly absurd how many times he'd said it, that at first, I thought he was playing some kind of angle. A line, a ploy, a strategy—a way to get me naked and horizontal. Which I'm not even ashamed to admit, he probably didn't need to bother.

I'd wanted a one-night stand.

Wanted random sex with a stranger without the tangle of feelings.

I wasn't even fussy, willing to sleep with someone who wasn't all that good-looking, that probably wouldn't even remember my name after.

But . . .WOW, he was none of those things.

He was gorgeous, with a body that was insane and took a kid who didn't have a family into his home. And then, if all of that wasn't enough? He worshiped my body like it was the most precious thing he'd ever seen.

I didn't even care if it was a lie.

Completely okay to play along with the *act*, and willing to pretend to be the dumb idiot who fell for it. My lapse in intelligence would have totally been worth it, and my ego, well it was still reeling.

Mack would be the man I would forever use as a measuring stick, and it sucked that I highly doubted anyone else would even come close.

Damn it.

Why couldn't I have met him later? Like after two or three meaningless hook-ups which were physically satisfying but didn't keep me up at night. Why did *he*—of all the men on that dating site—have to be my one-night stand? Such a waste, and just another example of how much I sucked at dating. I was overthinking which is exactly the opposite of what I'd assumed decent sex would do. Fucked into mindlessness was clearly a myth, and oh, I think I pulled a muscle where my abs used to be.

So since sleep was impossible and my body was still sore, I got out of bed and switched on my computer. I had medical reports waiting for me to transcribe and figured the time would be better spent earning money than daydreaming about a man I wasn't sure hadn't been a fantasy.

With my headphones covering my ears, I lost myself to words, procedures and treatments I didn't understand. My fingers automatically typing as I listened, my heart still beating too fast considering the subject matter.

It was only after I'd finished and emailed the reports that I'd noticed there was an alert sitting in my inbox, encouraging me to check my app for a message from Mack.

And I thought my heart was beating fast before.

My fingers twitched, hesitating for only a second before I grabbed my phone and logged into my account. And there, flashing like my overactive hormones, was Mack's name, the unread note sent only ten minutes after I'd slipped out.

Was he glad I'd left, relieved I'd spared us the awkwardness when we woke up together? Or angry I'd snuck out without saying goodbye? Maybe he was busy cataloguing his belongings, checking to see I hadn't taken something on my way out.

Gah, I needed to put myself out of my misery and just look. Because I was fooling no one pretending I wasn't desperate to see what he'd said.

What?

An invitation?

He didn't mention our date, the sex, or me leaving—nothing to even connect us to the night we'd had. It was like it hadn't existed, asking me to go to a music night in a club in Brooklyn.

What the hell?

Did he want to sleep with me again? Or was he trying to be my friend? It was confusing, mostly because I had no idea what it even meant.

It was weird, mostly because I couldn't work out if I was glad or disappointed that he hadn't asked why I'd gone. And also, because as much as I knew it wasn't a good idea to see Mack again, I was actually considering it.

Not smart, Hayden.

It would make more sense to find some other guy, go out and maybe try and get lucky again. I'd more than deserved a few fun nights without any attachments, past caring if anyone thought that made me a whore.

I couldn't decide, torn between the curiosity of untangling the mystery—and wanting to see him again—and saving myself the possible humiliation. What if I'd read the situation all wrong? What if he *hadn't* worshiped me, *hadn't* thought I was beautiful, and it had been so long that I didn't know the difference. Then that memory and the fantasy would be gone forever.

It was such a risk.

And one I wasn't sure I was willing to take.

"I'm sorry but that bag of potato chips was a dollar, not two ninety-nine." She tapped her foot impatiently, watching every item I scanned with laser-like focus.

"Ma'am, someone must have left them on the table with the discounted candy. As you can see there are no other potato chips on there." I tried to smile. Smile and pretend I didn't want to shove that bag of potato chips down her throat.

Oh, I knew it wasn't very *customer service* of me, wishing they'd just see the reason instead of arguing over a buck and some change. But just like the chances of me picking the winning combination for Powerball, it wasn't happening.

"*Ma'am,*" she glared at me, hands planted on her hips to go with the foot tap. "I don't think I like your tone. And if the ticket says they're a dollar, then that's what I'm paying."

One.

Two.

Three.

"I'm sorry if my tone offended you." I laced it with as much sweetness as I could stand. "But the *ticket* is advertising candy, so you'll have to pay the scanned price."

If there was a way for a person's head to explode, we'd be mopping brain matter off the floor.

She glanced down at my name badge, her lips disappearing into a thin line. "*Hayden*, I'd like to speak with your manager."

"Of course, ma'am." I couldn't help myself, tossing that little dig over my shoulder as I picked up the microphone for the intercom. "I'll just get her. Penny, please report to register five."

She glared at me. Not Penny, my manager who had yet to arrive, but one-dollar-chip lady who was mentally leaving a bad review.

Bad attitude with a tone I didn't like. Wouldn't give me my shit at a discount just because I was an argumentative bitch. One star. I was shaking in my tan khakis just at the thought.

It had already been a long day; my lack of sleep had already made me cranky as did the tightness in my muscles. I wasn't twenty-five anymore, and marathon sex was probably best followed with Advil and a few physical therapy visits. I was also contemplating putting a bag of peas on my crotch, my poor neglected vagina reminding me I should get more limber before attempting to sleep with someone like Mack again.

I bet he wasn't even sore.

Rolled out of bed like he'd taken a leisurely stroll around the neighborhood, wondering why his sheets had been so sweaty.

Ignoring the scene that was happening to the side of my register, I continued checking people out for the last thirty minutes of my shift. It was only when I got to my locker that Penny caught up to me.

I really hoped she didn't want to talk to me in her office. She was new to the store so I didn't know her well, and while she was friendly and we got along great, it was always hard being reprimanded by someone who was ten years younger.

"Hey, Hayden, you have a minute?" Her blonde—salon dyed and glossy, unlike mine—hair bounced. "My office, please."

Here we go.

There was no point prolonging it. If Penny, or anyone else, needed to yell at me to make their life easier, then I was going to just let it happen. I was too tired to fight it.

I grabbed my bag, slinging it over my shoulder, as I followed her into the small back room. Penny waited at the door, closing it behind us as she directed me to take a seat.

She took a seat opposite me, nodding her head like she wanted an explanation.

"Look, there's no way those chips were a dollar. I wouldn't be surprised if she'd put them there herself. But if you want to write me up or give me some kind of warning, then it's fine."

It was the best I could do, hoping we could move it along so I could go home and soak my fatigued body in some Epsom salts and essential oils. I didn't even care how pathetic that made me sound.

Penny opened her mouth and laughed, smacking her hand on the desk, making me jump. "Are you kidding me? That bitch was batshit crazy. Hell, if it wouldn't get me a phone call from corporate I'd have told her how psycho she was being."

"I'm sorry?" I leaned forward, wondering where the polished professional who managed the store was, and when she was getting to my "disappointing" behavior.

"Hayden, I'd never say it on the floor, but some of these people yell at us just to make themselves feel better. They have their small lives and sad existences, just looking for anyone to tear down. Easier to yell at someone about three-dollar potato chips than tell their mother to stay out of her marriage. Or tell their wives if they have to spend another long weekend with that couple they met on the cruise they're going to set fire to the garden shed. They're terrible, the evilness eating them alive while they smile for trying to make you feel bad. So no, that tight-ass bitch did not get a discount, and if she calls corporate to complain then that shit will rain down on me. Sometimes you got to say fuck it."

"Not really used to saying *fuck it* in the workplace if I'm being honest," I laughed, slightly worried one of those Alexa Dots was recording the conversation to later be played back to HR.

"Oh, it's totally not acceptable. Out there." She pointed to the door. "In here, let it fly. You've been with the company for ages; I'm surprised you're not the one sitting in this chair."

She had a point, and it was honestly something I'd considered. But retail was always supposed to be something temporary, a job not a career. Of course I could never decide what I wanted to do and with only half my college credits completed and no degree, I didn't have a lot of choices.

"Yeah, not sure I want the responsibility." I grimaced, the memory of why I'd been summoned to her office still fresh in my mind. "I think I'll leave the headaches to you and I'll just come in, do the job and leave without the drama."

Penny nodded, either agreeing with me or willing to let it go. "Sure, I can see that. But if you change your mind, let me know. It would be good to have some decent people who actually have a brain in management."

"Well, if having *a brain* is the only criteria, I might have to reconsider. And thanks for the vote of confidence," I chuckled, taking the compliment and not overanalyzing it.

It was new. Accepting praise and not looking for some ulterior motive. Previously if someone said anything complimentary, I'd immediately assume they were being sarcastic or disingenuous. Out of all my habits, it was probably the hardest to break. Not to say I was comfortable with it. Lord, I wanted nothing more than to tell her exactly why I wasn't very smart, but I didn't, shutting my mouth and letting her live in her fantasy that I was.

Just like I'd done with Mack.

Mack.

"Well, if that smile is anything to go by, I'd say you've got some plans you want to get to," Penny chuckled. "Go. Go have fun. I'll see you tomorrow."

"No plans actually." I pushed away all thoughts of the hot fireman and his cryptic message. "Not unless you count curling up in front of the T.V. and binge watching some new diet docuseries on Netflix. I think I've watched about six. Paleo, vegan, more fat, less fat, more meat, plant-based—I think I've effectively ruled out food entirely." Just like accepting the praise, being honest was something new. Before the divorce I'd have smiled, not bothering to correct her. But if I was trying new things, then it seemed like a good place to start.

Penny gasped, screwing her face up in horror, "Oh, you need to stop that right now. Nothing good ever came of those T.V. shows. You need to hang out with me and my friends, we'll set you right."

She had to be kidding.

While I'd never outright asked her age—because who even does that—she couldn't be more than thirty. *Maybe* thirty-one with an amazing skincare regimen. Why Penny and her friends would want to hang out with me was a mystery.

So, unless they had a quota—a vacant spot in their crew for a charity case—I wasn't exactly sure where she was going with it. "You want me to *hang out*?" I asked, wondering if I'd heard her correctly.

"Sure, why not?" She responded like it was the most natural thing in the world.

Words of how crazy it was were ready in my throat. Everything about how much older I was, to her being my boss—all valid excuses. But I didn't.

"Thanks, I'd like that." I nodded, standing up from my seat. "Well, I should go. Thanks for the chat."

"Don't mention it. Have a good night, Hayden." She waved as I left her office.

I was still tired, still perplexed about what to do about Mack, but somehow felt lighter. Amazing how something so small could make me feel so good. And I fully intended to go, promising to push myself out of my comfort zone and make new friends. Let's face it, my old ones had made it very clear they'd sided with Cooper. So a clean slate was definitely the way to go.

The wind blew as I stepped outside the store, the chill in the air getting colder even though winter would soon be over. I was lucky it wasn't still snowing, thankful there was no white covering the streets. I'd needed new snow tires and had put them off longer than was probably safe. But as I got to my car and hopped in, the cold, my lack of funds for new tires, and everything else kind of faded away.

Nope, my mind was somewhere else. Or more to the point, on *someone* else and the message I'd reread while sitting in my car waiting for the heater to kick in.

I hadn't responded. Wanting nothing more than to see him again but worried about everything that went with it. And as I eased out of the parking lot, his words churned in my head over and over again, I knew I wasn't going to be able to let him go.

Maybe it could be a two-night stand? That could be a thing, right?

Whether I turned up to that club on Saturday night or not, I was going to have to speak to him at least one more time.

Chapter 9

Mack

NO RESPONSE.

I'd toyed with the idea of writing something else, being a little less casual in case I hadn't made myself clear. But something in my gut was telling me to leave it, and it had nothing to do with looking desperate.

So I let it go, the ball in her court as I went about my day, my thoughts never straying too far.

She'd read the message. The notation underneath the bubble said she'd seen it, and that little dot near her name had gone green at least once while I was online.

But I hadn't heard a peep.

Not from her anyway.

The messages in my inbox were still accumulating. More women than seemed reasonable had pressed on the match button beside my name, and if I'd had any other way of contacting Hayden, I'd have deleted the stupid app altogether.

I should've gotten her number.

Complete stupidity on my behalf, thinking I'd have time in the morning before she left. Hadn't counted on her leaving so soon though, or not bothering to say goodbye. I wasn't even mad, knowing she must've had a reason. And if not for the lack of means to call and tell her I wanted to see her again, I wouldn't be half as annoyed. It was right there and then I decided that if I was given a second chance, I wouldn't be wasting it.

"Heard you were at Gino's last night. With a woman." Riley was doing his best to look shocked, his stupid grin letting him down as he swung keys around his finger. "Are the rumors true? And before you answer, know Tibbs is already trying to get the security footage."

I shook my head, wondering how long it was going to take before one of them found out. Vera liked to talk, and despite him being married, she still had a thing for North. "You heard of knocking?"

"Why would I knock? I have a key." He scrunched his brow like he was genuinely confused.

"The key is for emergencies, or if I lock myself out. Not for you to come and go as you please." I clipped him over the ears as he took a seat beside me on the couch.

He chuckled, shoving the keys into his pocket. "It was a wellness check. Heard about the date, so I needed to be sure you were okay. What if you'd had some kind of senior episode and were wandering around in your tighty-whities babbling about communists?"

"Could have called, my phone still works."

"And missed out on all this fun? Not a chance." He stretched his arms, anchoring his hands behind his neck. "So, you gonna tell me? Or are we going to have to call Vera in for a debrief."

I was surprised it was just North, and the whole battalion hadn't joined him to get the skinny. The stationhouse was a family—a big, loud, meddling family—and personal business didn't stay private for long.

"Did you not tell me to go out and get laid? I believe it was your wife who set up that stupid profile in the first place." I rolled my eyes, the conversation not original since it was his usual go-to.

North's head snapped up, his hands raised in surprise. "Firstly, when have you ever listened to me? And secondly, you got *laid*? Wow, this is even better than I thought. Wait a second, I'm going to need a minute to recover from the shock and then you can proceed."

Me and my big mouth.

It wasn't like me to kiss and tell, but with North it was tough not to overshare.

"Be respectful," I warned, not in the mood for Hayden to be stationhouse fodder. "And I'm not telling you shit other than we went out and had dinner."

"I'll be respectful, but you're delusional if you think I believe all that happened was dinner. It's written all over your face, Chief, and you're forgetting I know what you look like when you're trying to bluff."

I needed to change my locks.

And get a better poker face.

"Why are you here, North? Other than to bug the hell out of me." I pinched the bridge of my nose, feeling a headache coming on. Trying to change the subject was probably a lost cause, but I figured I'd give it a shot anyway.

He sighed, chest rising up and down as he took a deep breath, letting the smile drop. "Quinn threw me out. And before you start, I didn't do anything. Well, maybe I left a wet towel on the floor, but we both know that isn't what it's about. She's uncomfortable and can't sleep, and if yelling at me helps her through it, then I'll do whatever she needs. She's carrying my baby, Chief. Nothing I wouldn't do for either of them. I was giving her some time to cool down, figured I'd pick up some ice cream on the way home."

"Jesus, North. You've come a long way, kid. And I don't say it enough, but I'm proud of you." I clapped my hand around his neck, getting a little emotional at how much he'd grown. He was a good man, and for whatever part I'd played in that, I was fucking pleased.

"Yeah, yeah, I'm amazing. Old news, Mack." He smirked, cocky grin spreading across his lips lacking the humility he'd shown less than a few seconds ago. "Tell me something I don't know, like who's your lady friend and what's she like."

It was tempting to shut my mouth.

To tell him to go buy Quinn some flowers or cake and go back home.

But the two of us had been through some tough times together, and there was probably no one in the world I trusted more. Plus, whether I wanted to inflate his ego by saying it out loud or not, he was really fucking perceptive. And if ever I could use some input, it was my current predicament.

"I hope I don't regret this." I shook my head, scrubbing my face with my hands. "Something about her has me so interested, it defies logic. Yes, she's beautiful, but other than basics, I know nothing about her. But I get the feeling she's got some baggage, has no idea how gorgeous she is, and probably has some self-esteem issues. She's skittish too, left this morning without saying goodbye."

I waited.

Waited for North to make some crack about her spending the night, or that I'd slept with someone I clearly didn't know well. But he didn't, shutting his mouth like he was actually giving it some thought.

"Have you sent her a text or tried to call?" It was a logical question, and I couldn't even be mad at him for asking.

"She didn't give me her number, or her last name, or an address except for a general area. I know she works at Target, but no idea which one. And yes, I realize what this sounds like. I sent her a message this morning on that stupid app, but she hasn't responded."

"Maybe she hasn't—"

"She saw it. Been online. Look, honestly if she'd rather not see me again, I can live with it. Not saying I'd like it, but I'm not going to camp at her door like a fucking rejected frat boy who's worried about his reputation. But when I got her alone, and she let down her walls a little, we connected. At least I thought I did. Thought it was worth pursuing."

Hearing it out loud wasn't doing me any favors. I sounded less like a grown-ass man, and more like a clueless teenager with no hair on his balls. But it didn't change the facts, nor did it quell the uneasy feeling I had on the way things were left. Sure, I knew what we'd done was consensual, and she'd been just as into it as I had. But the radio silence didn't speak volumes for me being the decent guy I was trying to be.

"Chief, all jokes aside, considering this is the first woman we've even discussed since the Wicked Witch of the West, I'd say it's worth pursuing. And yeah, I know there have been other women, we've already established you can't bluff for shit. But not even one has rated a mention." He slung his arm around my shoulder, pulling me in for an awkward sideways hug.

He always did have such a colorful way of referring to Melinda, not that I wanted to think about her or her latest request, let alone tell Riley about it. My parameters for sharing had a limit, and that surpassed it by a long shot.

"So? Got any ideas? Or did I just give you extra material to roast me for the next twelve months?" I hoped for both our sakes he could throw some extra enlightenment on it, or at the very least, forget everything I'd said.

Riley tipped his chin, meeting my eyes. "Nah, Chief, I don't need any extra material. I've got plenty to last me a lifetime. But I do think this is above both our pay grades, and we need some extra help."

"If you so much as breathe a word of this to anyone at the station, kid, I'll have you scrubbing bathrooms for an entire month." I narrowed my stare, my threat not an idle one.

"Relax, Chief. I'm not telling them shit," he laughed. "But I do think we should speak to Quinn. She will absolutely know what to do. Plus, if you come back with me, she's less likely to throw me out again."

It was my turn to laugh. "Using me for your personal gain is wrong, kid. I thought I taught you better than that."

"Hey, we're both getting something out of it. I see no victims here, old man."

It was tempting, but talking about Hayden behind her back didn't feel right. It was bad enough I was having the conversation with Riley, involving Quinn was too much over the line.

"North, as much as I would like to make your life easier, I'm going to take a pass. Go buy her the ice cream or whatever it is she wants and go be with your family, kid. And thanks for stopping by."

"Okay, Chief. And now that I know there's a chance you might be *entertaining*, I'll be sure to knock the next time." He shot me a wink as he stood. "And for what it's worth, anyone who spends more than five minutes with you knows what kind of guy you are. Even if she didn't say, she'd have seen it. She'll message you back, Mack."

I joined him on my feet, shook his hand before walking him out. I had no doubt that by the time he got back to Brooklyn, at least one of us would be having a better night, and I'd assumed it would be him.

It was only after I'd settled back onto the couch, deciding whether to reheat the leftovers I had in my fridge or order out when my phone buzzed. Not sure why I bothered to look, the alerts had been coming all night and none of them were worth reading. But whether it was instinct or dumb luck, my hand wrapped around my phone seeing her name on the screen.

Finally.

Didn't even think twice, clicking open the message as fast as my thumb could swipe.

Hey Mack,
Not sure about Saturday, will have to check my schedule but hoping you'll still go and be judgmental enough for the both of us.
Hayden

I knew a brush off when I saw one, and that one was fairly clear. But because I had nothing much to lose, I figured I'd respond anyway.

Doesn't work like that, Hayden. Team effort is required for judgment, it's no fun if you don't have a wingman. Will take a raincheck for when your calendar is free. How was work? Hasn't been any reports of stray bodies circulated on any news agencies, always a good sign.
Mack

How she responded would dictate my next move. If she came back with the same lukewarm bullshit, then I'd let it go. But if she cracked open that door just a little, I was going to take it.

No bodies but it was a close call. How about you? Many fires?
Hayden

And there it was. She wanted to know how my day went. All I needed to hear.

We work 24 on, 48 off, so whatever fires there were, were dealt with by someone else. You do have me curious about this close call though. You should probably talk to management about hazard pay, I can help you negotiate a good rate.
Mack

You moonlight as a negotiator? What other skills do you have that I don't know about?
Hayden

And P.S. A club? I thought we agreed we were anti clubs. Unless this is a cry for help? If this is really *Mack*, what band recorded their highly successful album *The Downward Spiral* in the house Sharon Tate was murdered? Don't Google.

Please. That was too easy. Nine Inch Nails. And I feel there should always be an exception to every rule, was willing for Club Retro to be mine. As for my other skills, only disclosed on a need-to-know basis. And I'm not interested in giving you any more cheesy one-liners. But if you give me your number, we can discuss it.
Mack

There was a chance I'd pushed too far and should have continued with the back and forth a little more. But I also knew that every single time she sent a message, it could be her last and I wasn't repeating last night's mistake.

Come on, Hayden, just give me your number, sweetheart.

The phone was still sitting in my palm when it buzzed again, her number included. Didn't even give it a chance to settle, adding it to my contacts and dialing quicker than I probably should've.

"Hello?" She answered on the second ring, saving me from having to leave a voicemail. I never did well with those stupid things, preferring to talk to a human rather than a machine.

"Hayden, it's Mack."

"You weren't kidding when you said you were going to call," she laughed, the sound of it fucking magic. "I thought you meant tomorrow or next week."

"Didn't see a point in waiting. I already told you I wasn't working, and I assumed you were done too." I couldn't wipe the smile from my face, still surprised to be speaking to her on the phone. Hadn't seen that coming.

"Well, one job, yes. I was going to get some dinner and then do some transcripts." I could hear the weariness in her voice, hedging a bet she was probably dead tired. But as much as I should've let her go, relax and enjoy whatever was left of her night before she had to start working again, I didn't.

"Funny you mention dinner, I was just about to get some myself." I swallowed the rest of what I was going to say, wanting to ask her if we could eat together. "So why don't you tell me about your day."

She took a breath, hesitating a beat or two before launching into a story about a woman wanting a discount. She laughed, admitting that she called her ma'am just to piss her off and was surprised when her manager didn't wave the "customer's always right" card. Had to admit, I liked hearing her talk and from what I could work out, she was happy to share as long as it wasn't too personal.

There was a pause, her words of the day coming to an end and the air sitting still between us. I was about to say something when she beat me to it.

"Hey, so I guess I owe you an explanation about this morning."

Could hear the hesitation in her voice even over the phone, and knew it was something she didn't want to discuss.

"Actually, no you don't. You don't owe me anything, Hayden. So how about we leave that for another day and we talk about something else."

I swear I could almost feel the breath of relief. "Sure, so why don't you tell me more about these secret skills you have."

"Not a secret, just don't advertise them. Like to keep a bit of mystery." I forgot all about dinner, settling back into the couch as we spoke.

"Oh, like what? Now I'm really curious."

"Well I could try and impress you and mention I can bake a soufflé. From scratch."

"What kind of soufflé?"

"Any. Sweet, savory—the basic principle is the same."

"Sensing there's a story here. It's an odd thing to be good at."

"My mom owned a bakery, nothing flashy but it was fairly fancy considering she'd been self-taught. Anyway, when we were younger, she'd pay me and my brother to help out. She'd pay us more depending on how much we could do. For example, sweeping didn't get as much as measuring ingredients. So, because we wanted to earn as much as we could, it became a competition between me and Patrick. We'd try and outdo each other, and I always liked a challenge."

She gasped, probably guessing where the story was going. "Did you literally look up one of the hardest French dishes to attempt?"

"I sure did." I laughed, remembering I couldn't even pronounce it. "We were super competitive. Figured if I could do that, I'd out-earn him for sure. And I did, baked enough soufflés to buy my first car."

"I'm sure your mom was pleased."

"Yeah, think she assumed I'd follow in her footsteps, go to culinary school. But after I bought the car, I kind of lost interest. It was always only a means to an end."

"Do you still know how?"

"Oh yeah, was kind of burned into my brain. I make them for the crew at the station sometimes. They give me shit about it, but not one of those bastards complains when they're eating."

"Speaking of which, I am starving, and all this talk of soufflé hasn't helped. I should go and make some dinner."

"Or you could come over, and I could make you one."

It shot out of my mouth so fast, it barely had time to register. Not that I would be taking it back, refusing to make it sound like the invitation was anything but on purpose.

"Look Hayden, this deal has no strings attached. You can come, I make the thing to prove that I can, get to keep my bragging rights and you can leave. There are no expectations."

I didn't blame her for being hesitant, it sounded cagey as all hell. *Hey, come over to my place and let me cook you a fucking soufflé but I won't try and screw you.* But I *would* and *could* keep my dick in my pants and my hands to myself. And regardless of what we'd done the night before, I wasn't expecting a repeat. Hell, at this point I'd be happy just to see her again, and considering how things had been going earlier that wasn't a guarantee.

"I shouldn't, I have to work tomorrow and—" I waited for her to finish. Ready to hear all the reasons why it wasn't a good idea. It was late, she was tired, she had to get up early, she didn't want to travel to Midtown. But as we sat on the line, the sentence stalled out, she didn't finish it.

"I'll tell you what. I'll start and hopefully by the time I pull it from the oven, I won't be eating alone. See you later, Hayden." And without adding anything else, I ended the call.

There was no way of knowing which way it was going to go. There was a better-than-average possibility I was going to mess up my kitchen and be sitting at my table like a moron, eating soufflé by my damn self. But I didn't care, there was a chance. And at that point, a chance was all I needed.

Chapter 10

Hayden

GOING TO SEE him had not been the plan.

Hell, I wasn't even sure talking to him on the phone was a good idea, but when he asked for my phone number, I only hesitated for a second. I didn't even understand why I'd done it, having been so careful to keep myself at a distance. But Mack was a guy who wasn't easy to ignore.

He was like a planet, his own gravitational force pulling you into orbit. And even though I had no reason to trust him, there was a part of me that wanted to. Maybe it was because of his kindness with Riley, maybe it was because he hadn't demanded to know why I'd left, or maybe it was his calm, yet commanding voice. There was something innately good about him. Which was why I'd made two lapses in judgment.

One had been the phone call.

The other . . . getting into my car and driving to his condo in Midtown.

It was crazy, tearing through my wardrobe trying to find something to wear. But unless I recycled my new jean/knitwear combo, I was coming up empty on suitable date attire.

Was it even a date?

I thought I'd already agreed I wasn't going to date. Intent on steering clear of messy complications and just enjoying being by myself for a while.

It was a blurry line. And considering how our last one had kind of dissolved into less date and more sex, I wasn't sure whether or not it fell into my own loophole. And if the second time would follow the same path.

Did I want it to?

Of course I did.

Did he?

I literally had no idea.

Clearly—for reasons I didn't understand—he was interested in seeing me again. Although he'd made it clear that it wasn't about sex and having no expectations. But what I couldn't work out was if that was for his benefit or mine.

It wasn't until I was stopped in front of the grated metal door of the parking garage of his condo that I realized I didn't have the code or a way to get in. I'd driven the entire way on autopilot, lost in my own head.

My fingers shook—a mixture of nerves and excitement—as I dialed his number, leaving the car idling.

"You downstairs?" he asked, not bothering with a greeting.

"Yeah."

"Good, I'll be down in a minute to let you in."

Click.

That was it.

The phone was still pressed to my ear when the call ended, the briefness of it catching me off guard. He hadn't been surprised, or asked me why I'd changed my mind—nothing, he'd just told me he was on his way.

I hadn't waited long, my fingers nervously drumming on the steering wheel as the grated door slowly rose allowing me access to the parking garage. I drove in slowly, circling the rows and looking for a vacant spot near where I'd parked the day before. Thankfully I found something, easing my car into park and stepping out.

"Oh fuck." I grabbed my chest, finding Mack standing behind me, appearing out of nowhere. "You scared me."

"Sorry," he grinned. "Not exactly light on my feet, I assumed you saw me."

If I hadn't been running through a million scenarios in my head, he probably would have been right. But I still hadn't worked out what—other than it *wasn't* for fucking soufflé—I was doing there.

"You okay?" he asked, genuinely concerned. "Let's get you up to my condo." He held out his hand but made no other moves, keeping the physical contact ridiculously platonic as we walked toward the elevator.

The air between us was thick in the confined space, the scent of his cologne surrounding me and infecting me in ways that challenged my logical thinking. I wanted to kiss him. Wanted to touch him. And wanted him to do all of that to me and more.

Without thinking, I leaned forward, wrapping my hands around his neck and pressing my mouth to his. It was an echo from my past self, the girl who would kiss a man with a lip ring before even knowing his name and make out with him in a dark smoky corner. I wanted to be *that* girl, and take what I wanted.

He hesitated for a second.

Probably less, his arms wrapping around me and pulling me against his body as the kiss intensified. He didn't ask, demanding more from my mouth as the door flew open as we reached his floor.

"Hayden," he moaned into my mouth. "You're going to make me burn my soufflé."

I laughed, unable to stop the giggle as I pulled away. "That's something I've never been accused of before."

He brought our joined hands to his mouth, kissing my knuckles before leading me out, his front door ajar as he pushed it open and walked us in.

It was the funniest thing, the delicious smell of butter and cheese floating through the air at odds with his hard, masculine taste in furniture. I hadn't really paid attention the night before, the dark woods, the black leather of his couch, and light gray walls very much advertised I was in a male-dominated space.

He was dressed casually, a pair of jeans and T-shirt, and unlike the night before when he'd been clean shaven, stubble tickled his jaw. He looked edible, more inviting than what was baking in the oven.

Dark brown restless eyes roamed over my body, my black leggings and a long fitted top hugging my figure more than I would have liked. I hadn't even worn a coat, so absent minded when I left the house, I'd shivered my way to the car hoping I didn't get hypothermia before my heater kicked in.

"You look amazing," he leaned forward catching my lips with his before pulling away. "But I told you I was feeding you and that's what I'm going to do."

"Kitchen." He tipped his head to the hall. "Sit down at the breakfast bar."

He waited for me to go ahead, feeling the weight of his eyes on me as he walked slightly behind.

The move was totally sexy, making me feel more attractive than was probably right. But I didn't care, swaying my generous hips a little more until I lowered my butt on a stool at his kitchen counter.

My eyes closed, taking in a big breath. "It smells amazing. I can't believe you went to all this trouble."

"Wouldn't want you thinking I was making false claims," he grinned, grabbing a tea towel and draping it over his shoulder. "It's got about five more minutes."

There was a lot I could do in five minutes.

Namely find out some of his other skills.

"So this how you get women? Lure them to your condo with the promise of decadent baked goods?" Instead I went with talking, trying to act nonchalant about returning to the scene of the crime of my one-night stand.

His eyes simmered, not breaking contact with mine as he spoke. "Thought I made it clear yesterday that I wasn't in the practice of getting women."

"I wasn't sure if—"

"If I was feeding you a line or being serious." He cut me off, a small smile edging across his lips. "I get it. But no, I don't really date. I mean, there have been a few women since Melinda. Don't want to misrepresent myself like I've been some celibate saint, but nothing really stuck."

"How can that be?" I'd thought it as well as said it. "You're so great."

"Thanks, and I'm glad you think so. And I could say the same about you." He winked, turning to the oven and looked through the glass door.

Tempted to argue, I fought the urge. I hadn't come all that way, hungry and tired, to convince him I wasn't *great*. "Thank you." The words felt weird in my mouth, but not uncomfortable, a lot like how I was feeling.

"We should be just about there." He popped open the oven door, taking a look before lowering it even more. "Perfect."

He wasn't kidding, using two tea towels so his fingers didn't burn he pulled out a large round soufflé dish, the pillowy top bobbing gracefully above the edge. It was perfectly golden, impressively tall, and wouldn't have looked out of place in *Gourmet* magazine.

I held my breath as he lowered it onto a trivet, waiting to see if the top would collapse but it didn't. Like the rest of him, it remained impressive and unshaken. It was a contradiction of everything he was—this rugged, manly man who fought fires, creating something so soft and delicate.

"We can look at it all night, Hayden, but eating it is more fun," he chuckled, grabbing a couple of plates and some forks and dishing it out.

It smelled delicious, my fork sliding through it effortlessly as he watched me take my first mouthful. I didn't even care he was watching, too hungry to stop. "Oh my God," I moaned, my tongue curling around the fork to capture every last bit. "This is amazing. Wow, no wonder you earned enough for a car."

"Good, eat up. I'll grab us some drinks."

He went to the fridge and grabbed a couple of beers while I took another bite, the second taste just as magical as the first. "Seriously, Mack, screw the car, you should sell this. You'd have a private jet in no time."

"Don't have any need for a private jet, and I like my regular job just fine." He winked, helping himself to some of his handiwork. "But good to know I have something to fall back on if it all goes to shit."

We ate in a comfortable silence, him standing on the opposite side of the breakfast bar. He didn't ask questions, nor make me feel like I had to say something, refilling my plate without asking when it was empty, smiling at me while I tried to stop shoveling it into my mouth so fast.

It was only after we were done, stuffed beyond belief that he spoke. "You want some dessert? I have some ice cream tucked away in the freezer." He cleared the plates, rinsing them in the sink before loading them into the dishwasher.

"Mack, if I eat another thing, I'm probably going to explode." I groaned, thankful my leggings had a stretchy waistband so I wouldn't have to worry about popping out of my pants. "But thank you, it was one of the best things I've ever tasted."

It wasn't a lie either, between his delicious meal and amazing company, I couldn't remember the last time I'd enjoyed dinner so much.

"I really like hearing that, Hayden." His smile edged wider, folding his arms across his chest before settling back on his heels.

He looked powerful, his strong arms contained against his massive, muscular body, an explosion just waiting to happen. But he didn't move, the breakfast bar between us as he kept his distance.

It was intentional.

Ignoring the barrier, both physically and mentally, I slipped off my stool and walked to where he was. He hadn't moved, letting me come to him. "Thank you for dinner." My head tilted, bringing my lips closer and hoping he'd meet me halfway.

"It was my pleasure."

His arms unfurled, wrapping around me as his mouth met mine, the kiss just as intense as the one in the elevator. I could feel him hard, the ridge in his jeans and my body pressed against his, my hands unable to help themselves as they roamed over his impressive chest. I loved how he felt, so raw and strong, yet so beautiful.

I couldn't stop—kissing him, touching him—my mind fighting its own war while my body did whatever the hell it wanted. It was both wrong and right, and I couldn't decide if I was going to regret it in the morning.

Without missing a beat, he picked me up like I weighed nothing and lifted me onto the countertop. I gasped, parting my knees, his hand in my hair as he filled the gap. I loved it, loved feeling the way his mouth moved over my skin as I rocked my hips against his erection. It was dirty, and hot, and in that moment I felt like I was twenty-two in a club.

"Fuck, you're beautiful." The words vibrated against my skin, his lips moving to my neck.

And God, did I believe him.

My fingers clawed at his T-shirt, peeling it off him so I could touch his skin, exploring every curve and dip like it was the first time. Seriously, his body was addictive and I wasn't sure I'd ever get enough.

"Hayden," Mack warned, holding me still. "There is nothing I want more than to take you to my bed right now. I want to lay you out and make you come so many times you can't make out where one orgasm ends and the other starts. But I think you should go home."

It was confusing, hearing those words and unable to work them out. "You want me to go?"

"No, I don't." He kissed me again. "I don't want you to go anywhere. But it's probably the right thing to do."

Probably. Pity I didn't want to do the right thing.

"Take me to bed anyway," I moaned, shamelessly rubbing my body against his.

He chuckled against my throat, taking a few steadying breaths before taking a step back. "Not tonight, sweetheart. Deal was I give you soufflé and then you leave, and I'm a man of my word. But you let me know if your Saturday becomes available."

Groaning in frustration—and slightly embarrassed—I pulled myself together.

As weird as it sounded, sex would have been the safer option. It would reaffirm—if only to me—that what we had was purely physical and I wasn't going against my own rules. And even though I knew the connection could easily be more, I was hesitating opening that door.

But damn, he was making it difficult. Probably something I should have considered before hauling ass to his condo when he made it clear it wasn't going to be a booty call.

And shit, I wasn't sure how I felt about it.

Of course he was right. But even though he'd made assurances that all it was going to be was dinner, I couldn't help but be annoyed at his integrity. It would have been the one time I'd have been totally cool with him going back on his word. Pity Mack didn't see it the same way.

"Okay, okay, I'm leaving." I shuffled my butt forward, sliding off the counter. "Guess we'll have to wait until Saturday."

"Is that a yes?" He tipped his head to the side, not bothering to hide his huge grin as his hands settled on my waist.

I shook my head, pushing lightly on his chest. "Yes, send me the details and I'll meet you there." My mouth agreeing to a date I'd been positive I'd turn down.

What the hell did he put in that soufflé? A few hours ago I'd been determined to cut him off entirely, and yet there I was, belly full of his delicious baked goods, agreeing to go to a club. If he wasn't such a great firefighter, he'd make an excellent agent developing new compliance techniques for the FBI.

"Or I could pick you up," making it sound more like a statement than a question as he lightly kissed my forehead.

"Let me think on that."

Or at the very least, let the delicious persuasive measures he'd taken wear off so I could be sure I was making my own decision.

He didn't fight me, letting me grab my handbag and then walking me back down to my car. Holding the door open for me as I slid into the driver's seat, he waited until I was buckled in. "The code for the gate is 2727 in case there's another night in the future you need a soufflé, or something else."

I nodded, starting the ignition as I gave him one last smile. "I'll see you Saturday."

"Yeah, you will." He tapped on the roof of the car and closed the door.

My hands hesitated on the wheel, looking at him through my side window as I rolled it down. "My last name is Green. Hayden Green." I wasn't sure why I felt the need to tell him, the extra information completely at odds with my initial plan.

He lowered his head, kissing me gently on the lips. "Well Hayden *Green*, drive safe."

Never had a rejection ever felt so good, my body tingling from an unanswered need while my head appreciated the consideration. My overused vibrator was going to get a workout tonight. And on Saturday, he wasn't going to be able to turn me down.

Chapter 11

Mack

"COOKIES?" LEIGHTON SHOVED two of them into his mouth, chewing around the words. "I swear Rev's wife is the best."

Leighton was right in that Rev's wife was pretty great. The woman could take roadkill and make it taste awesome, and cookies were her specialty.

"She didn't make them, I did."

He coughed, holding his chest, sounding like he was hacking up a lung as he gasped for air. "Jesus, Leighton, chew before you swallow them for Christ's sake." I stood up, slapping his back in between his shoulder blades.

"Everything okay?" North popped his head around the doorway, having just walked in and heard the commotion.

"Chief." Leighton gasped between breaths. "Baked."

Oh for fuck's sake.

It was no secret that I knew my way around a kitchen, the byproduct of my mom's bakery. And while I usually left it to Nora—Rev's wife—to spoil us, every once in a while I got in touch with my inner Martha Stewart and broke out the Toll House.

"Chief baked?" The moron grinned. Not Leighton—he was still trying to regulate his CO2—the other one, North.

I rolled my eyes, wondering how much of a pain in my ass he was going to be for the rest of the day. "Yeah, thought I might do something nice for you guys, show you my appreciation. But considering the reaction, I might rethink any future displays."

Of course I wasn't being entirely honest.

Hayden had left me with a hard-on that didn't have a hope and a prayer of leaving. And after jerking off in the shower had only been a temporary fix, I needed to find another strategy.

Nothing killed an erection quicker than childhood memories with your mother.

So cookies were baked, my balls were saved, and I eventually got a few decent hours of sleep.

Pity the remedy had led to a whole other set of problems.

Riley picked up one of the cookies, inspecting it before putting it into his smug mouth. "Not as good as Rev's wife, but it's a solid B-minus. Your ratio of cookie to chip is a little off though, must have been distracted."

I eyed him hard, a silent warning that if he knew what was good for him, he'd keep his mouth shut. "Going to my office. Let me know if you don't have enough to do."

Taking my coffee and a few choc-chips—he was full of shit, there was nothing wrong with my cookies—I headed into my office. We'd already done the changeover, and I had a pile of paperwork I needed to get through, and the less time I spent thinking about Hayden, the quicker the day was going to go.

It was times like these that I missed being out on the engines. Wasn't time to think when you were out on a call, it was you and your team and whatever chaos you faced when you turned up. Not that I didn't love being a chief. It was rewarding in other ways—leading these men at the very top of that list—but the surge of adrenaline was MIA.

"Chief," Tibbs rapped on my open doorframe, his backpack still strapped to one shoulder. I'd half expected North, looking to ride me some more about Hayden, my body relaxing a little when it wasn't.

"What's up, Tibbs? Cutting it a little close." I tapped my watch, only a minute until his shift officially started.

"Yeah, I know, sorry. Issues with my sister, had to stop by and take her to my parents' this morning." He took a seat opposite my desk. "Which is what I wanted to talk to you about."

Justin Tibbs was twenty-six, and when he wasn't fucking everything that moved, he was an incredible firefighter. He came to us as a rookie, fresh faced right out of the academy, full of testosterone but without the smooth confidence of North. But when shit got critical, he left the cocky bullshit on the sidelines and brought his A game. So if he was coming to see me with personal problems, I knew it had to be pretty serious.

"What's happening? Presley okay?" I lowered my coffee giving him my attention.

In the time Tibbs had been with us, we'd seen Presley go from a cute college kid to a gorgeous woman who turned almost everyone's head when she walked into the stationhouse. Smart, beautiful, and as fearless as her older brother, it was a huuuuuuuuge pain in the ass for Tibbs. The warning thrown down that his sister was off limits made more than once.

He tipped his chin, the tension rolling in his shoulders. "Well, depends on your definition of okay. Her ex-boyfriend broke into her apartment last night when she was at work and trashed the place. Presley ended up staying with a friend, so didn't notice until she got home around six."

"You call—"

"Yeah," he nodded, not letting me finish. "NYPD were down there this morning. That's how we knew it was him. Asshole fucking left his ballcap in the kitchen, like a complete idiot.

The same ballcap that has his DJ logo and name." He shook his head. "Anyway, I took her to my mom's till we can get the locks changed. And before you say anything, he wasn't home when I went looking so I didn't do anything."

Tibbs was also a hothead, that extra testosterone not doing anyone any favors. And I was positive that if he had found Presley's ex, I'd have already gotten a call to bail him out.

"Good. Not saying the cocksucker wouldn't have deserved it, but last thing your sister or your parents need is you getting your ass hauled to jail on an assault charge. Let the law handle it. I can call my friend at the courthouse to help her with the restraining order, and I'm positive we can have a unit do a drive by for a couple of nights."

We were a family and took care of our own, and if some asshole was terrorizing Tibbs's sister, then he was going to be on a lot of people's shit lists. I almost felt sorry for the guy, except I really hated shit-for-brains jerkoffs who abused women.

"I guess." He shrugged, his jaw so tight I was surprised it hadn't cracked. "But this guy is a real piece of shit. He pulled a gun on her once. Can you believe that? What kind of man does that? She didn't even tell me, I only found out because I was there when the cops interviewed her and they asked if he'd ever been violent. I swear to God if he goes anywhere near her or so much as breathes in her direction again—"

"You will call me," I warned, leaving no room for interpretation. "And the two of us will sit him down for a discussion. No vigilante bullshit, okay?" Not saying I wouldn't let him rough him up a little. Hell, not a lot I could do if my back was turned, was there? But at least if I was around, I could keep a handle on it. Make sure the asshole didn't end up in a body bag and Tibbs didn't end up in cuffs. "I mean it, Tibbs. Whatever you or Presley need, we'll get you. But I need your word you will not go off on a solo mission."

He nodded, not liking the directive but not dumb enough to disobey it either. "You good for work today, or do we need to call in cover?" I asked, respecting him enough to make the call himself. "If your head is somewhere else then go home and cool off. I need you on all cylinders."

"I'm solid, Chief. A little edgy but nothing a session in the weight room won't fix. Not going to let you down."

"Good, exactly what I wanted to hear." Pushing away from my desk, I walked around to him. "If anything changes, I'm your first port of call."

Tibbs rose from his seat, joining me on his feet. "Thanks, Chief. Hey, if you're not doing anything, maybe we could go out tomorrow night. It's been a while since you've been to Presley's club."

I knew what he was hinting at, and shooting the shit with me wasn't it. He wanted to check out the club his sister worked at, see if their security was up to par or if the lowlife might try something in a public place. But he wanted to keep his little recon mission under the guise of a night out so his sister didn't chew him out for hovering. Presley might be female, but she was still a Tibbs, and being a hothead was genetic.

"It's been a while because I don't like hanging around with teenagers and paying thirty dollars for a beer. But if you want to make it a team effort, I'll tag along."

"Great, thanks," he gave me the first real smile since he'd walked in. "Hey, maybe we can find you a girl. Improve your mood a little." The grin got a little wider.

I rolled my eyes, the discussion of my sex life not one we'd be having. "First off, I have no interest in girls. I date *women*, something you might want to try before your dick falls off. And there's nothing wrong with my mood. I even baked you assholes cookies, so you might want to get out there before they're all gone."

"You baked?" A mixture of surprise and shock flooded his face. "Did someone die?"

"Get out of here," I laughed, slapping him across the shoulders.

He didn't linger, not bothering to hide the smile as he tipped his chin goodbye and left.

There was no telling how the day was going to go, and since I was already debating whether or not to call Hayden, it was probably for the best that I got myself busy.

Hayden.

Should have baked more cookies.

It was a surprise to everyone that Riley was joining us at the club.

With Quinn ready to go into labor any day, we expected he'd be home, checking the tire pressure of his truck and plotting fifty different contingencies for when the big day arrived. Which apparently he'd already done. It prompted Quinn to beg me to take him off her hands for an evening, the need for sleep more important than having her husband home.

"You sure I shouldn't stick around?" North lingered at the door, the decision to spend the night at a club not his own. "What if something happens and I'm not here?"

"Karli and Brad are right next door." She pushed playfully against his chest. "Besides, how do you think I manage when you're at work? Go, have a good time and find out more information about Mack's new girlfriend."

I raised a brow, giving Riley the *look*.

"What? We're married, I *have* to tell her," he had the nerve to laugh.

Quinn nodded, holding up her ring finger. "It's true, a contractual obligation."

"Nowhere in your marriage vows does my business come into it. Love, honor, cherish—not discussing Mack."

It was a waste of breath when both of them were involved, neither of them listened. But if talking about me meant distracting Riley enough to let Quinn get some R and R, then I'd take the hit.

"Your business, our business, it's kinda the same thing. Besides, we love you and want you to be happy." Quinn threw her arms around me in a hug. "And you're welcome."

"Funny, I don't remember saying thank you." I hugged her back, her belly making it difficult.

"Awww it's okay, Riley mentioned you've been forgetful lately," she chuckled.

Hell, soon there was going to be another of them.

"And on that note, kid, let's go."

After more minutes than was actually needed to say goodbye, Riley was satisfied Quinn would call if she so much as felt a muscle out of place. And we were on the road back to Midtown. It didn't really make sense for me to drive to Brooklyn considering the club was literally in my neighborhood, but unless I turned up on North's door and dragged him out, there wasn't a chance he'd leave. So we'd compromised. He took his truck, I took mine, and if he had to make a hasty exit, he didn't have to rely on my "old man driving."

I'd reached for my phone on more than one occasion, the itch to call Hayden crawling up my skin. But it had taken some work to get the number in the first place and I didn't want to overplay the card. Plus, she had sent me—unprompted—a text telling me she was looking forward to tomorrow night, and I knew she was gun shy. Last thing she'd want was twenty questions from me. So instead I played it cool, sending her a few casual text messages during the day but keeping my need to speak to her to myself.

It was just as well I was going out.

No way I'd do it with an audience, so less likely to cave if I kept myself social. And while the last people I'd ask for dating advice would be the rocket scientists in my company, it would at least serve as educational. Possibly on what *not* to do, sure as shit couldn't hurt considering I'd been out of practice for a while.

By the time we got to *Diablo*, Tibbs and Leighton were already there.

"Well, well, well." Presley looked anything but surprised when we walked in. As the club's manager, not much got past her even if Riley and I weren't over six foot.

"Chief, to what do we owe this pleasure?" She gave me a small kiss on the cheek. "And North, really? Don't you have better things to do?"

"You and I both know that it takes a full crew to stop your brother from making a fool of himself," he grinned, leaning down and giving her a hug. "You should be thanking us, saving the female population of your fine establishment from his hideous pick-up routine."

She planted her hands on her hips, not buying it for a second. "Just keep him out of trouble. Lewis wouldn't be stupid enough to walk in here, and if he did, I have enough security to take over a small country."

Didn't doubt it either. Presley was beautiful, but she wasn't running one of the biggest clubs in New York because of her pretty face. Still, smart or not, if it were my sister, couldn't say my reaction would be any different. "Heard he pulled a gun? Can't say I blame Tibbs for wanting to be extra sure."

"That was a few months ago and the reason I kicked him out in the first place." Her gaze didn't faulter as she met mine. "And I've got it handled. But you should be less worried about me, and more concerned about your ex-wife."

And to think I'd planned on having a decent night.

Just the mention of Melinda could ruin even the best of days. "And why would that be?"

Presley tipped her head to the bar. "She's turning into a

regular, been here every night this week. And tonight, is three cocktails in."

Great.

Just fucking great.

My jaw tightened, every muscle in my body tensing even though I hadn't seen her yet. Of all the places she could be, she had to pick the one I was at. "Thanks for the tip off. And sorry if she's been any trouble."

"Oh Mack, when are you going to stop apologizing for her? She is her own disaster, and you were waaaaay to good for her. And as much as I'd like to toss her out, she hasn't given me a reason to. Yet. But trust me, if she steps out of line, she'll be gone."

"Well, sounds like a fun night." Riley had the nerve to laugh. "Should we go over and say hello, or slip the bartender a fifty to put hot sauce in her drink?"

"Enjoy, gentlemen. And Mack, it was great seeing you. Forty-five looks good on you." She gave me a friendly tap on the chest and then disappeared into the crowd.

Riley's eyes cut to me, and I figured he'd have something to say. "You know she's doing this to get your attention. She *knows* this is Presley's club, *knows* eventually one of us will turn up."

"She's called a couple of times. I didn't answer."

It was unlike me to ignore her, usually figuring it was easier just to talk to her and get it over with. But after her latest request, I was less enthused to have further conversations. Didn't want to scratch that old wound, even if it made me feel like a pussy because it still kinda hurt. Then meeting Hayden had pretty much put a nail in that coffin. "Let's go find Tibbs and Leighton. Like Presley said, she's not my problem anymore."

Riley's eyes peeled back in surprise, not expecting my response. "Wow. Yeah, we should definitely go find Leighton and Tibbs."

Avoiding the bar entirely—and whoever was sitting there—we moved to the back part of the club. Tibbs and Leighton had commandeered a table and were entertaining a couple of ladies.

"Chief!" Leighton stood, slapping me on the back. "Can't believe Tibbs talked you into this."

"Yeah, I can't believe it either." I shook my head, tipping my chin to Tibbs who was getting the number of one of his female friends. "We can go find another table," I suggested, not wanting to cramp their style.

I was happy for them to continue *entertaining* if that was what they wanted to do, just didn't want a front-row seat for it. Figured Riley would probably feel the same, preferring to sit with the *old man* than watch his two buddies create a floorshow.

"Not necessary." Tibbs kissed the brunette—who incidentally was not the girl whose number he got—both of the ladies vacating their seats and waving him goodbye.

"Two?" North laughed. "Jesus, Tibbs, you've got to stop using my deodorant. Not sure you can handle the pace."

He flipped North off, shoving the number/numbers into his pocket as he grinned. "Laugh all you want, North. But since you met Quinn, you left a big gaping hole in the market. And I'm more than happy to fill it."

"Not the best choice of words, Tibbs," I cringed. "Just try and be respectful. And what about you?" I looked to Leighton, surprised we hadn't caught him mid dry hump as well.

"I . . .er . . . figured I'd didn't want to be distracted. You know, in case I'm needed." He rubbed his chin awkwardly, not convincing me there wasn't more to his lack of female company. Still, I wasn't there to argue, willing to buy into his BS if it made the night easier.

Riley and I each took a seat, a waitress with some beers making her way over. "These are from Presley." The waitress smiled, laying the four cold longnecks on the table. "Said it was to save you from having to go to the bar."

Tibbs grabbed his beer, toasting Leighton before taking a swig. "Tell Presley thanks, but if this is her way of keeping me at my table, she'll have to be more creative than that."

North laughed, thanking the waitress and tipping her, but leaving his bottle untouched. "Your ability to think everything is about you never ceases to amaze me. Melinda is at the bar."

Riley and his big fucking mouth.

Waiting until after the waitress left, I took a pull on my beer before elaborating. "Apparently she's been a frequent flyer lately."

"What?" Tibbs screwed his face up in confusion. "But she knows this is Presley's club, why would she come here?"

Melinda and I had still been married on *Diablo's* opening night. We'd been guests of Presley, with Melinda complaining she was bored only thirty minutes in. We stayed despite her protests, getting into a huge argument later. It was the beginning of the end. And any other time I visited *Diablo*, I did so alone. So other than her recent patronage, opening night was the only time she'd been in the place.

"I haven't answered her calls. Guess it's her way of making a point." I shrugged, not qualified to work out what went on in her head. "Ignore her. She'll eventually get tired of whatever game she is playing."

"No offense, Chief, but I'm not even sure how you guys stayed married for so long. She's fucking beautiful, but Lord, she is batshit crazy." Leighton's eyes widened, tipping his drink back.

"We done talking about me? Surely you have better topics of conversation?"

The failure of my marriage wasn't something I liked to think about, especially not around men whose respect I demanded. But whether I wanted to admit it or not, Leighton had a point.

"Hey, I need to make a call." I excused myself, taking my beer and moving away from the table. Guess having an audience wasn't going to be as big a deterrent as I thought, pulling out my phone without bothering to wait.

Maybe it just took seeing what I didn't want, to know what I really did. And whether I was playing it cool or not, I wanted to call Hayden.

And that was damn well what I was going to do.

Chapter 12

Hayden

WHEN PENNY HAD suggested a night out with her friends on Friday night, I'd assumed maybe dinner and cocktails. A movie?

Not a nightclub in SoHo.

Because that was apparently my life now. Clubs—something I'd actively avoided for years—had somehow become a cornerstone in my freaking emotional development. Still, it could always be worse. I heard women these days were steaming their vaginas and doing Kegels in organized groups. Not sure I'd be so down for that kind of girls' night out.

It was trendy, loud, and filled with so many beautiful people that I felt like I was in a bad dream. The kind where you realize you're standing in front of a large crowd about to make a speech and you forgot to wear pants. Thankfully, being naked was about the only thing I didn't have to worry about.

"Come on, Hayden, dance with us." She swirled her long blonde hair while simultaneously taking a shot of tequila. "Here, have this, it'll help loosen you up."

I shook my head, waving off the offer of yet another shot. "Penny, any more and I'm not going to be able to stand, let alone dance."

As promised, her friends were great. Welcoming and kind, but ten to fifteen years younger than I was. And while I wanted to live in the fantasy that I could still keep up with people in their late twenties/early thirties, my body had other ideas.

Leaving them to dance with apparently no regard for their feet, I hobbled—my new heels killing me—to find a place to sit down. There wasn't much available, a stool I could barely get my ass on, my only choice.

Despite originally wanting to keep things with Mack casual—and possibly date other men—I had been unable to stop thinking about him. He'd been on my mind when I slithered into the only sexy bra and panties I owned. A smile on my lips as I poured myself into a fitted dress that I was positive made me look too curvy. Not that I understood it, but he really seemed to like my body, putting his hands all over it like he couldn't get enough.

It felt good.

Not that I wanted to be the kind of woman who needed external validation, but having someone appreciate me didn't make it a bad thing either.

And what a someone he was.

So good looking, so sexy, so . . . everything, and I could barely wait to see him again. I'd messaged him earlier in the day, but it hadn't been enough, about to get another fix and text him again when my phone rang.

Mack.

It was ridiculous how much seeing his name pleased me, the alcohol and the heat from the club no longer responsible for the tingling of my skin. And since being out of character was the theme of the night, I decided to continue, answering the call before it had a chance to go to voicemail.

"Hello." I smiled so wide my cheeks hurt. "I was just thinking about you, let me just get somewhere I can hear you better."

Shuffling off the stool, I moved toward the bathrooms. The hall wasn't private—people lining up to use the toilets—but at least the music wasn't so loud. "That's better."

"You at a *club*, Hayden?" He laughed, his voice sounding sexier than should be allowed.

I rolled my eyes, willing to come clean even though it made me look like a hypocrite. "Yes, yes. I know. But I still maintain my position, even if I'm willing to concede they aren't *always* terrible. I'm with my manager, if you can believe it. Not as good an idea as it originally sounded, my feet are killing me." I leaned up against the wall, the tequila and my shoes not helping the situation. "Where are you?" I was trying to make it sound sexy but wasn't sure if I was managing, concerned I sounded clingy and possessive.

"Not with you," his response came without hesitation. "Any chance we could change that?"

My heartbeat quickened, my body getting hot as I grinned on the phone. "I thought we were seeing each other tomorrow?"

"We are. Doesn't mean I don't want to see you right now as well."

He said all the right things, *things* I hadn't even realized I wanted to hear. Like he innately knew. I took a deep breath, already feeling the regret. "It would be rude if I left. I don't have many friends, Mack. Probably wouldn't be a good idea to ditch the ones I've just made."

The alcohol was making me more honest than I'd intended, but I couldn't help but feel like I was between a rock and a hard place. Penny had been so generous to include me, it felt wrong to leave because I had a better offer. Even if that offer was one I *really* wanted to accept.

"Why don't you have many friends?"

He'd always been careful never to push. To let me volunteer as much or as little as I'd wanted, but I knew he had to be curious. And whether it was because my defenses were down or I just believed he wouldn't hurt me, I wanted to tell him.

"The divorce. I was the one who asked for it, so they all sided with him. It doesn't matter that he moved on and I'm still alone, they still chose him."

"Are you still alone, Hayden?"

I felt dizzy, worrying it was the wrong time to have the conversation. I hated that I couldn't see him, couldn't look into his eyes and try and work out what he was thinking. But deep down I knew that if he'd been in front of me, I'd probably not have said any of it.

"I don't want to be, Mack, and that scares me a little."

"Do *I* scare you, Hayden?"

"Never."

There didn't seem to be a scenario where Mack could scare me, the possibility almost laughable. But I wasn't laughing, knowing it was too soon to be having feelings that weren't just sexual.

"I should go." I fumbled to think of an excuse. "I'm sure you want to get back to doing whatever it was you were doing."

"Hayden, wait. I need you to listen to me and know that none of it requires a response, okay?" He waited for me to agree before continuing. "I'm deleting the profile, the app and tossing out all the other messages, and I have no expectations from you. Not unless you decide you want to do this with me, then I'll have a few. One of them is getting to know you, not just fucking you. And I understand that might not be what you want right now. And if that's the case, fair enough. But I think you owe it to yourself to work it out."

I felt my throat tighten, the inexplicable urge to cry prickling at my eyes while my skin heated. It was both beautiful and soul destroying at the same time, and all of it felt too much.

He was right.

I didn't know what I wanted.

I'd thought I'd wanted just sex, but I wasn't so sure anymore, and giving him up felt impossible.

"They thought I was a boy."

I should have ended the call. He'd said he didn't need a response and I should have listened to him, said goodbye and seen him tomorrow.

But I didn't.

"Who thought you were a boy?"

"My parents. It's why I'm called Hayden. They were so convinced I was going to be a boy they didn't even have a girl's name picked out for me. When I arrived, they figured they'd go with it anyway. And a few years later, they eventually got their son when my brother was born." I took a breath, knowing if I stopped, I'd never go through with it. "Don't get me wrong, they loved me, and other than reminding me how much of a screw-up I am, they've never done anything to hurt me. But it kind of stuck, you know. That I was a replacement. There by default. And ironically, it's how I'd felt in my marriage. Cooper was everything they'd hated initially." I laughed, remembering my mother's face when I'd brought him home. "I think that's why I was with him. I mean, I had feelings for him, but I guess I wanted someone just for me. And at the start, it was so good. But things changed, and I think deep down I've been fighting my whole life, you know? First to prove that I'd earned a right to be born, and then with Cooper that I could make him happy. So you see, I'm not even sure I *remember* what I want anymore."

It was sooooo much.

So much to dump on a guy I'd met less than a week ago on the Internet, who wouldn't have signed up for the drama if he'd only known. But about the only thing I was positive about was, I was tired.

Tired of fighting.

And tired of battling an invisible voice that told me I wasn't enough.

"Hayden?" My name broke the silence.

"It's okay, Mack. I've just had too much to drink and should have known better than to answer the phone." I closed my eyes, cursing the tequila. Why couldn't I have rambled about how hot he was?

"Tell me where you are."

"Why?"

"Because there are a lot of clubs in New York. And while it will be quicker if you just tell me where to go, don't think I won't look through every single one until I find you if that's my only option."

And boy, I didn't doubt for a second he would too. Stomp through every door, breaking down any barriers until he found me. But hearing me teary and vulnerable was one thing, seeing it was entirely worse. And I wasn't sure I could do that.

"Mack, it's late and I'm a mess and—"

"And I don't care about any of those things. What I *do* care about is seeing you tonight. You don't even have to talk to me. Just let me come get you and drive you home. Pretend I'm your Uber driver."

I laughed, the idea of Mack as an Uber driver—hilarious. I bet his rating would be awesome though, all his women passengers taking sneaky shots of him to share with their friends. Maybe even some of them trying to seduce him, and give him a tip of a different kind. Like bad porn. Which just made me laugh more.

"What's so funny?" he asked, not having the benefit of my internal dialogue.

I chuckled, deciding that even though I was messier and emotional than I would have liked, I wanted to see him too. "Nothing, I'm at Chase in SoHo, do you need the address?"

"Nope, I'm in Midtown, see you soon."

And with his last goodbye, the call ended. Me still standing against the wall for support, the phone still pressed at my ear. And my feet still hurting.

"There you are!" Penny's face was flushed but still magically sporting perfectly smoky eyes. "I was worried you'd left without saying goodbye."

"No, I just needed the bathroom and got a call." I held up the phone, shaking it in my hand. I didn't bother to mention I'd never made it to the bathroom.

She grabbed my arm and yanked. "Cool, so come back out on the dancefloor. I promise, no more shots."

As tempting as her offer was, even if Mack wasn't on his way, I'd already decided to call it a night. Not sure if it was my feet, the drinking, or the emotional retrospective, but I needed to go home.

"Actually, I am probably going to go." I winced, knowing I was punking out way too early for Penny's liking. "I really appreciate you inviting me out, and I did have a good time. But honestly, this just isn't me anymore. And I'm okay with it."

Her brow furrowed in disappointment, like she was genuinely sad. "So you're going?"

"Yeah, I called . . . an Uber." I grinned, trying not to laugh. "But seriously, I can't thank you enough. Maybe keep me as an alternate or if you have a movie night or something. I'd totally be down for that."

She laughed, probably thinking she'd rather be dealing with shitty customers at work than having a movie night. "Okay, so come out and wait with us until your Uber gets here."

Agreeing, I followed Penny back out to the main part of the club, the music still thumping uninterrupted. Her friends had momentarily stopped dancing, hydrating at the bar before their next session. We ordered some drinks. Water for me, and vodka and soda for Penny—because while she said no shots, mixed drinks were apparently still okay—and chatted while I waited. I wasn't even sure what car he drove or if he would walk in, checking my phone a couple of times for a message in case he texted.

"Whoa," one of Penny's friends, Laura, coughed out. "He's so hot."

I didn't even have to look to know it was Mack, but turned all the same. There he was, striding toward me with purpose and looking so sexy I wasn't sure I'd be able to talk.

Dressed completely in black, his gaze didn't move from mine as he got closer. God, Laura was right. He was sooooo hot. "Hey, do you have a coat?" His hand went around my waist. "It's freezing outside."

"Wow, is that your Uber driver?" Penny laughed, her eyes getting wide. "I am definitely using your app next time."

Mack's lips edged into a cheeky grin. "Hi, I'm Mack."

"No, you're gorgeous," Laura crooned, sliding to his side and rubbing his pec muscles suggestively. "Are you available later to drive us home? I'll pay double."

"Actually, he's . . .a friend. My friend." I straightened my shoulders, ready to peel her fingers off him one by one if it was necessary. Turns out, it wasn't necessary with Mack having already removed her hand. "And we should go. My coat is checked up front."

Penny leaned in, attempting to be discreet but failing miserably. "Go you! I want to hear all about it on Monday."

I shook my head leading Mack away from the giggling circle, feeling like I should be embarrassed, but not able to care. "They're drunk, ignore them."

"You're assuming I give a shit," his grip around my waist tightened. "Or that I could pay attention to anything when you're around."

All the right things.

My body snuggled against his, matching his strides until we got to my coat. And even though I was more than capable of doing it myself, he helped me get into it. "I'm parked around the corner."

"So you never told me where you were before. Were you out with friends?" I hadn't even noticed that my arm had snaked around his back, holding him just as tightly as he was holding me.

He pressed his lips to my forehead, kissing me gently. "Ironically, I was at a club myself. In Midtown with some of the guys from work. Seems like we *both* might have to reevaluate our stance on hating clubs."

"Oh, did you want to go back? You don't have to take me home."

We stopped walking, his hands settling on my hips. "Hayden, I'm here because I want to be here. So no, I don't want to go back."

I nodded, knowing we'd eventually have to talk about what I'd said on the phone but wanting to prolong it a little more. "Thanks for coming to get me."

"Don't mention it."

He drove exactly the kind of vehicle I'd expected, a big black truck. It was relatively new, the headlights lighting up as he hit the fob as we stopped in front of it.

"You know, you still haven't told me where you live." He opened the door, waiting until I was settled into my seat before walking around and climbing into the driver's seat. He buckled in and started the ignition, reaching out for my hand. "I can just take you home, Hayden. I don't have to come in if you don't want that."

"I want you to come in," I squeezed his hand. "And I live in Inwood, near the park."

I rattled off the rest of my address, easing back into the seat as he put the car in drive and pulled away from the curb. It was hot, the heater blowing warm air through the cabin as I unbuttoned the top of my jacket. He was the first man I had ever brought back to my new condo, and I was both excited and nervous at having him in my space.

Like he'd sensed my tension, he turned up the stereo, the familiar sounds of Stone Temple Pilots making me laugh. "Is that the radio?"

"Hell no," he grinned. "I made a playlist on Spotify."

There was no way of knowing if our planned date had inspired his collection of tunes or it was something he already had. But I liked it more than I cared to admit that I might have something to do with it, or that he knew playing it would make me feel more comfortable.

Getting all the way back uptown in Friday night traffic was going to take some time, it was bumper to bumper with a sea of brake lights in front of us. I didn't care though, happy for it to take all night as I rolled my head to the side and looked at him. "Were you serious about deleting the profile?"

He turned, nodding without hesitation. "Hayden, you're the only message I ever answered, and the only reason I didn't delete it immediately was because you hadn't given me your number that first night. It was the only way I could contact you."

"That was intentional," I admitted. "You were only supposed to be a . . . well, I'm not sure what the hell you were supposed to be, but I wasn't supposed to see you again."

"Why?"

"I just figured I'd meet someone, have meaningless sex and then move on. I wasn't supposed to like you. You're not easy to forget." I had kept away for what? A few hours before I caved and answered his message? Clearly I'd been terrible at keeping up my end of the bargain. Not that I regretted that night, or answering that message later.

He laughed, "I'm not apologizing for that. And I never intended to sleep with you that first night. Hell, maybe I did? All I know is that I'm not a one-and-done kind of guy, especially not with you."

It was weird to hear him talk about it. Not really saying exactly what he wanted, just that he wanted more. I wasn't sure if it was intentional, or if he was genuinely willing to work it out along with me. But what I did know was there was no pressure. No anxiety building in my throat, needing to have it all planned out. And that was so liberating I was almost giddy.

Inwood was a world away from Midtown. It was still busy, but less congested, missing the insanity of the inner city. I loved my home, glad I could still be in Manhattan, but far enough so I didn't feel like a tourist.

"I haven't been out here in years," Mack pulled up to my apartment building, bowing his head to see out the windshield. "My brother and sister-in-law had an investment property out here for a while, but sold it when they moved to Florida."

"Your whole family lives out there?" I asked, wanting to keep him talking. Partly to know more, and partly because I didn't want the night to end. I had no idea if he was going to try to be a gentleman, or give us what we both seemed to want.

"Yep. My brother and his family moved first, my parents followed soon after. Just me here now. Some extended family, and Riley and Quinn of course."

He looked so beautiful.

The light reflecting off the glass of the windshield sharpening his features, his eyes darker and everything else more rugged. He looked huge, his broad shoulders and looming frame took up so much room in the truck, it would be easy to be scared. He could break me into a million parts if he wanted to, and there would be little I could do.

But even knowing all of that, I saw something else. A tenderness that contradicted all those hard edges, a kindness in his eyes I wasn't sure I'd ever seen.

If Mack had some kind of agenda, then I had no idea what it was. But I couldn't believe that the man I saw in front of me was anything other than perfection.

"What are you looking at?" He smiled, his finger tracing the edge of my chin and reminding me I'd been staring.

I shook my head, not sure if it was the alcohol or something else making me so philosophical. "Nothing."

His smile got wider as he leaned closer. "You know I don't believe that, but I'm not going to push you if you don't want to tell me."

God.

Who was this guy?

"I'm worried you're too perfect," I answered honestly, wondering if there wasn't something dark and terrible headed my way. "But right now I'm more worried about getting out of your truck and walking up to my condo alone."

"Because you're scared?" His eyes met mine and I couldn't read them.

"Terrified. But not of being outside alone in the dark."

His mouth was on mine before I was able to process another thought, his hands holding my head while he kissed me. For every ounce of restraint he'd shown before, he became unhinged, that gentleness turning to demand.

I wanted him, wanted to take him up to my bed and—

"Come with me," I moaned as he continued to kiss down my neck. "Come upstairs with me and spend the night."

My fingers clung to him desperately, needing the connection more than I cared to admit. But I knew better than to know it was a sure thing.

He blew out a long breath, his lips breaking contact on my skin by barely an inch. "Hayden, you have no idea how much I want to. But I need you to understand what me coming to your bed means. I can feel your head is in two different places, and I won't let myself be what sways you."

Oh. God.

Never in a million years had being turned down ever felt so good, and yet the consideration he was showing me, almost infuriating. Sure, I understood it, but my hormones were also running riot and knew of the orgasms he promised.

"Just come with me and we'll work out the rest later."

He laughed, holding his mouth just out of reach. "Yeah, that sounds like a recipe for disaster. And you're adorable for thinking we're going to do anything other than screw each other's brains out if we go to bed together. You keep thinking I'm this perfect guy, Hayden. But I can promise you, I'm not. I have flaws just like the next guy."

"Uhhhhhhhh," I groaned in frustration. "Obviously you have flaws. Like now, and your inability to just be irresponsible."

It was childish, bratty and selfish, but I didn't care how it sounded. How *I* sounded. Tempted to see if I could just seduce him into changing his mind.

"You *really* want me to be irresponsible?"

It was a dare, a challenge, a flashing button waiting to be pushed. His eyes heated, the sweetness of his smile lost as his expression got darker. "I asked you a question, Hayden. You sure that's what you want?"

My head nodded, the words getting caught in my throat as I all but begged.

"Yes, Mack. I am positive it's what I want."

Chapter 13

Mack

HAD NO idea what the hell I was doing, my balls and my head championing their own fucking agendas. And while I wasn't sure I knew what was *right*, I knew what I *wanted* to do.

Her.

Fifty ways to Sunday.

But she'd been drinking and was emotional, and I didn't want there to be any misconceptions. And if I took her to bed, she wasn't going to be fucking anyone else. Those grand plans she had to play the field—no longer an option. And Hayden and I—we were going to be dating. Not none of this swipe left and hook up, not playing it casual and working shit out as we went. So unless she was on the same page, having sex probably wasn't a good idea.

Pity the rest of my body didn't get the memo.

We were out of my truck and into her condo before I'd even had time to reconsider. Fumbling first to open her front door, and then the lock to make sure it was shut. All the while keeping my hands and my mouth firmly pressed on her.

"You can't cancel the date tomorrow," I warned her, sliding

my fingers down her body and anchoring on her hips. "You don't get to wake up in the morning and ghost me either, Hayden."

She chuckled, yanking my shirt and pulling me closer. "Well it's not like I can sneak out, it's *my* condo."

"Good point. And as sexy as you look in these clothes, I want you out of them." I stopped talking, putting my mouth to work kissing her while my hands got busy.

Her eyes flashed open, gasping as I roughly yanked on the zipper of her dress and shoved it down to the floor. Underneath was a whole bunch of black lace—and just like the dress I'd removed—I had no interest in.

"Who was this for?" I asked, my hands following the curves of her tits and pulling down the cup of her bra. "Were you planning on bringing someone else back here?"

"Nn-oooo," she shuttered, taking another gasp of air while my tongue swirled around her nipple. "I did it because it makes me feel sexy. And I kinda need all the help I can get."

My mouth moved to the other nipple, my fingers twisting the one I'd just left while my lips closed on her tight peak. "Honey, trust me, you don't need any help."

She moaned, tipping her head back while my hands and tongue stayed busy. I loved kissing her, touching her, and preferred to do it without the restrictions.

With not much patience and/or coordination, I flicked the hook at the back of her bra and pulled it from her body. Her tits were beautiful, round and full, with tight pink tips that were hard and ready.

Next were her panties, my fingers snaking down her belly, breeching the top of the lace and diving inside to find her wet and warm. "You want to show me where your bedroom is, Hayden? I'm not fucking you here on the floor."

She bobbed her head, closing her eyes as the pads of my fingers swirled against her pussy, feeling the needy and desperate buck of her hips with every pass. "Down the hall. Door is open."

And they were all the instructions I needed, pressing her mouth to mine as we walked—my hand still teasing her—down the hall to the first open door I found. Didn't care if it was the bathroom, those noises she was making driving me crazy, resigned to making her come in the tub if that was my only option.

"Take them off," she begged her hands too busy unbuttoning my shirt to get rid of the lace that had apparently made her feel sexy. "Just take them off and touch me more."

I knew what she wanted, my fingers teasing her entrance while keeping themselves outside. But that would have to wait, my shirt hitting the floor around the same time as the backs of my legs felt the mattress. And since we'd reached our destination, I wanted to do what I'd been desperate to all night.

Kissing her, I spun her around, lowering her onto the bed as gently as I could manage while rocking a hard-on that could drill concrete. It wasn't easy, the urge to toss her onto the mattress and fill her with my cock so overwhelming I needed a minute just to take a breath.

She gasped, the heels she'd been wearing dropping to the floor as she shuffled herself further up the bed, her eyes on me as I utilized the short timeout to get the hell out of my clothes.

Everything was dropped to the floor in an unorganized pile as I stripped as fast as I could. I liked the way she was looking at me, her eyes roaming over my body while I stalked onto the mattress and gripped her thighs. "Now, I'll take them off."

My fingers moved to the edge of her panties and yanked them down her legs. Her mouth opened, a satisfied "ahhh" spilling from her lips before a more desperate "yes" took its place.

No, I hadn't put my fingers inside of her like she'd wanted, instead replacing my hand with my mouth, my tongue savoring every last inch.

"Mack," her back arched, her head easing back on the pillow while I continued to taste her. As much as I wanted to feel her pulsing on my dick, my mouth was going to get the privilege first.

I loved to watch her writhe, those uncontrolled noises escaping from her mouth while her eyes struggled to stay open. It had clearly been a long time since a man had done it properly, the look of surprise flashing across her face as I took her to the edge and had her exploding on my tongue.

"Oh my God. Oh my God," she panted, her tits heaving with hard breaths as her body shook. "I—that—I—"

"You're so fucking beautiful when you come. I'm going to enjoy watching it happen again." I kissed the inside of her thighs, sliding higher up the bed.

She nodded, not letting me know which statement she agreed with as my mouth went back to her tits. "Remember what I said, Hayden, no second thoughts."

"None. I want you." Her hand snaked down between us, gripping my dick. It was rock hard and throbbing, a hiss coming from my clenched teeth as she gave me a firm slow stroke.

It was difficult to concentrate, the hand action feeling so good I almost forgot her beautiful tits were in my hands. Everything about her was a wet dream waiting to happen, and I couldn't believe she was mine.

"Condom," I gritted out, wanting to get suited up before I did something stupid. I was desperate to fill her, needing to be inside of her more than made sense. "Hayden, please tell me you have a condom."

Thankfully, she nodded, letting go of my cock for a few minutes while she pulled open the bottom drawer of her nightstand. "Not sure what the shelf life is on these things, I've had this pack for about a year."

I didn't bother checking the expiration date, trusting science and her hopefully cool, light-tight bottom drawer, in knowing we were fine as I reached for the box. "Longer than a year, sweetheart. And I'll try not to use the whole box."

That wasn't a promise, my intention to stay the night left unspoken as I opened the foil package and rolled the latex down my shaft. I tried not to think of the significance of how long she'd had that box, knowing without being told what big a deal it was that I was even in her bed.

"You're so hot." Her eyes followed my hands, giving myself a quick jerk as I made sure the base was secured. "Your body is so incredible."

"Funny, those are the same thoughts I have about you." I kissed her, easing her back onto the bed before shuffling to my knees. I wanted to enjoy the view, see as much of her as I could while making us both feel good.

I took each of her legs in my hands, parting them and settling in the middle. She craned her head, watching me as I teased her opening with the head of my cock, staying upright so she could see exactly what I was doing.

"Watch me, Hayden." Our eyes connected. "Watch me worship your body the way it should be worshiped."

Her teeth bit her bottom lip as she eased out a shaky breath, the head just barely pushing into her. It wasn't a lot, the restraint needed to bury myself almost impossible to maintain as I pushed in a little more, feeling her squeeze around me.

"More." It was both a plea and a demand, her hips tipping to try and get me deeper. But my hand held her still, not letting her control the pace as I slid in an inch at a time.

It was madness for both of us. Each agonizing second feeling like an eternity as she whimpered. She wasn't the only one desperate, my plan to go slow tossed out the window halfway when I sank all the way in.

"Jesus, Hayden." I rocked my hips, dragging myself out and then pushing back in. "I keep wanting to do slow with you, but I keep losing control."

She flashed me a smile, matching each one of my thrusts with one of her own. "Good, I like that I do that to you. And slow is overrated."

Wasn't that the truth, the original tempo all but forgotten as I plunged into her, again and again, harder and faster each time.

It felt amazing, her grip around my length tight as we rocked, and I could feel her getting closer. Slow was definitely *not* the way to go.

"Beautiful. You're so beautiful." I couldn't stop looking at her, reaching down between us and rubbing her clit. It was swollen and needy as the rest of her, my thumb circling her as I continued to pump.

She bucked, her body shaking as she screamed out, "yes." The roll of her hips slowed as she came unhinged, the pulsating against my shaft enough to do me in.

"Hayden." I gritted my teeth, unable to stop as my balls rose up and I exploded.

It was intense, every single muscle in my body tensing before releasing, my mind feeling like a jigsaw puzzle as I spilled my load.

Romantic, it was not—our hot bodies still fused as I tried to slow down. It was almost impossible when I was with her, that look of satisfaction on her face making me feel like a superhero.

Her chin tilted, my mouth finding hers whether that was her intention or not, pressing heavier on her body than I wanted as we both collapsed on the bed. I didn't want to move, loving the way she felt underneath me even though I probably weighed a ton.

"No, you don't have to move," she wrapped her arms around me, holding me still. "I like it. I won't break."

And as much as I wanted to test her theory, common sense finally showed up as I lifted myself off her. "How about I take care of the condom and then we can see what else I can do that you like."

Reluctantly I pulled out, easing out of her and shuffling off the bed. I had no idea where the bathroom was, my feet hitting the floor before she pointed to the bedroom door. "It's opposite. And I'd really like to come with you."

Even though I had no idea why—whether it was to use the facilities herself or just watch me—I agreed, reaching out my hand and helping her out of bed. It was unreasonable how much I liked being with her, not the least bit concerned at having an audience while I took a piss.

She led me across the hall, the flick of the bathroom light blinding us both as she walked over to the combination shower tub. It seemed I wasn't going to have an audience after all, leaving me to lose the condom while she turned on the faucet.

I watched as the showerhead sprayed out water, the jets hitting the plastic curtain. She looked over her shoulder, climbing inside but not pulling the shower curtain closed as she disappeared from view.

It couldn't have been a clearer invitation, the condom tossed into the wastepaper basket as I followed her in, the hot stream of water hitting my back as I pulled the plastic closed across the tub.

"If you're thinking of shower sex, Hayden, I can tell you right now that's a bad idea." I laughed, pulling her body flush against mine. "You don't have those non-slip adhesives and I couldn't lay down in this tub if I tried."

She arched against me, resting her head against my shoulder as I bent down to kiss her. "Mack, even I have my limitations. No sex, just washing."

Taking a faded pink fluffy thing that looked like a pom-pom, I picked up some shower gel and squeezed some on. It had been a really long time since I'd been in a shower with a woman and was surprised by how much I liked it.

Without asking, I moved the soapy fluff ball down her arms and across her back, angling myself so she could be under the water and not get cold. Careful not to slip or worse fall right out of the tub, I maneuvered myself around so I was facing her, her wide gray eyes open as I washed her.

She didn't say a word, watching me with interest as I knelt down and soaped up her legs, taking extra care to lift each foot and then rinse off the pink thing before gently wiping between her thighs. Even though I'd been inside of her less than half an hour ago, touching her like that felt more personal.

Desperate to kiss her but not wanting to make it sexual, I turned my attention to her collection of shampoo bottles perched on the ledge of the tub. There were about six different colored and shaped bottles, and I had zero idea which one to use. But instead of asking, I picked up one and smelled it, not settling until I found the one I thought smelled the most like her.

It was sweet, like peaches and cinnamon, and the same scent I'd buried my nose in the first night I'd met her. "That one is my favorite." Her eyes lit up as I squeezed some out of the bottle into my palm and lathered it up. "How did you know?"

I smiled, my hands going into her hair as the scent got even stronger. "I didn't know, but it's what you were wearing the night I met you."

She was skeptical, her eyebrow hitching as she tried to figure out what my angle was. "How can you remember what shampoo I was wearing?"

"If I told you I remembered everything about that night because you were so beautiful, it wouldn't be a lie." My fingers massaged her scalp, her hair covered in white soapy bubbles. "But being a fireman, you literally depend on the details. Everything from airflow to the furniture around you. What's going to be an accelerant, what could collapse and hinder your exit, and where your backup is. You need to know where you are, what you're doing, and who you're with at all times. Your head needs to be in the game, and I have a hard time switching it off. And with you, I wouldn't want to even if I could."

And regardless of my intentions of keeping my lips holstered and it not turning sexual, I kissed her anyway. Pushing her gently into the water as the shampoo washed out of her hair and pooled around our feet. She closed her eyes, tipping her head back as she let me kiss her, her arms wrapping around my chest as we stood under the spray.

"Will you stay the night?" Her eyes blinked as I moved her hair to the side.

I laughed, wondering if I hadn't made myself clear in the truck before coming up. "Just try and make me leave, sweetheart."

Chapter 14

Hayden

IT WAS A weird sensation having a man hold me while I slept.

I'd never thought I liked it, Cooper and I both preferring to sleep on our respective sides with an invisible wall in the middle. Over time the wall got bigger, and it wasn't just the space between our bodies that was the problem.

But Mack holding me felt so good I almost didn't want to close my eyes, wanting to absorb every last drop of the sensation and not waste it on being asleep. It was like he knew the exact amount of pressure to apply, the right way to position himself so I didn't feel smothered or overwhelmed, his arms around me keeping me close to him while not trapping me in bed. And as much as I had really—and I mean *really*—enjoyed the sex, being held by Mack was pure bliss.

A soft pair of lips kissing my collarbone woke me, making me smile before I'd even opened my eyes. It was crazy to think I'd tried to push him away, even though in my head, getting involved with a guy made no sense.

My mother had always accused me of making shitty decisions.

What was the harm in another one?

"Want me to make some breakfast?" I rolled toward him, not getting to ask any more questions as he kissed my mouth. It wasn't the sweet kind of kiss he'd been giving my collarbone either, his tongue sliding into my mouth making me think how many more bad decisions I could make.

"I wish I could, but I can't." His lips moved back to my neck before shaking his head. "I left a bit of a situation last night and I need to make sure it's squared away. My phone has been blowing up all morning, and if I don't answer it soon Riley will probably send out a uniform to find me."

We hadn't really spoken about his night when he'd called. I knew he'd been out at a club, and he'd said he'd been with friends. But other than those sketchy details, I had no idea what he'd been doing. Hell, not sure I remembered much other than being a big ball of emotions. Then there was mind-blowing sex when we got to my place.

"Was something wrong? You know you didn't have—"

"Stop that." His finger rested on my lips. "I absolutely had to see you last night. And it wasn't only the right choice, but the best choice. For me, Hayden. I wanted to be with you. And the guys had it handled, but I need to check in this morning."

It was hard not to believe him, his eyes so intense and decisive that I didn't know if Mack was capable of doing something he didn't want to. So leaving his friends, and being with me, had most definitely been his choice.

"Is it Quinn and the baby?" I asked, still not knowing what the emergency was.

"Nope. If it was Quinn and the baby, Riley wouldn't have been so patient." He kissed my shoulder before sitting up. "One of my other guys, Tibbs. His sister Presley has an ex-boyfriend, who on top of being an asshole, isn't very smart. We were at her club last night making sure he didn't turn up and start trouble."

There was so much in that, I wasn't even sure how to process. And sadly—because I'm clearly messed up—was wondering what *kind* of club. If maybe Presley was a stripper. Surely her brother wouldn't have been sitting in the audience if she—"Was she hurt?" I finally asked a logical question, and what I should have been most concerned about.

"No, he broke in when she wasn't home. She's tough, and can handle herself, but we don't like to leave that shit to chance. And Tibbs isn't the kind to let someone mess with his sister and let it go. Not that I blame him, and off the record, I'd do the exact same thing."

He didn't even have to tell me the last part, knowing exactly the kind of man he was. I had no doubt that if anyone hurt someone he loved, he'd tear them limb from limb. And as much as I hated to admit it, I was a little jealous of Presley. Not sure I'd ever had *one* person willing to do that for me, and she had a whole team.

"Coffee. I'll make you coffee then." I pushed down the covers and got out of bed. As much as I wanted to selfishly keep him, he was too kindhearted to turn his back on a friend in need. And I didn't want to be the reason he started. "Get dressed and I'll get the coffee started."

He leaned forward, stopping me from getting too far. "Don't forget about tonight. We still have plans."

"Of course. 90's night. Club Retro. I promise I will be there." I crossed my heart, not needing the reminder. I couldn't think of a better way to spend my night, probably spending the rest of my day counting down the hours like a lovesick fool.

He nodded, letting my arm go. "Good, I better go get my clothes and my phone."

Like it had been summoned, a faint ringtone echoed from my living room. I assumed it had been in his pocket, discarded with the rest of his clothes when we walked in and attacked each other like animals. Not that I was mad, happy my night had ended as amazing as it did. I probably had a few missed calls myself, Penny probably looking for the scoop with my *Uber driver*.

"Better go get that." He winked, planting his feet on the floor and walking out of my bedroom completely naked. I'd probably do the same if I had his body, silently wishing I had that kind of confidence. The light of day didn't do wonders for my jiggly bits, settling for only getting half-dressed and shoving a long sleep shirt over my head before heading out to make coffee.

He'd pulled on his boxer briefs, scrolling through his phone when I emerged. I could get used to that view giving him a playful wolf-whistle as I walked past. "It's even more impressive in the daylight. Seriously, Mack, your body is crazy."

"So that's why you're with me." He chuckled, picking up his pants and putting them on. "Glad I know where I stand."

"Yep, just the body." I lied, heading to the kitchen and turning on my coffee machine. I let him finish getting dressed, hearing him go into my bathroom while I waited for the coffee to brew. It had just finished when I felt the weight of his stare on me, turning to see him leaning against the counter, watching as I reached for a cup.

"Okay so this is probably a terrible idea." His eyes fixed on mine. "But how would you feel about coming with me?"

I froze mid task, the gurgling of the coffee pot reminding me why I had a cup in my hand. "With you? *Where*?"

"To check on Tibbs and Leighton, make sure neither of them is in a holding cell somewhere. Look, I know the idea of tagging along while I run errands sounds terrible, and as far as being fun, it probably won't be. But the last time you left before we got to have breakfast, and this time, I'm doing it. It just doesn't sit right with me. I'm hoping we can get something on the way. And while it's not the romantic morning after you deserve, I'll feel less like a low life."

He was adorable and thoughtful, and I wasn't sure what to feel. "Mack, you couldn't be a low life if you tried. But I'm sure you need to go soon and I'm—" I looked down at my sleep shirt, thankful I couldn't see the disaster that was my hair. "It will take me a while before I'm ready to leave."

"Why? Just put on some clothes and we can leave. I can wait a few minutes." He looked genuinely perplexed why it would take so long. Like we were all blessed like he was, and could throw on yesterday's clothes and look great.

"Mack, I'm going to be meeting people you work with *and* your friends for the first time." I poured the coffee, needing a strong hit of it myself. "It's gonna take a little more than a couple of minutes."

He shook his head. "Just answer me this. Do you want to come? Or not?"

"Of course I want to come. As tragic as it is to admit, I don't want you to leave. Even though I know I'm seeing you tonight. But if you don't have time for breakfast, you won't have time for me to get ready. And I don't want to make you late." *Or turn up looking like a hot mess and have your friends wonder what the hell you're doing with me,* I didn't finish out loud.

I had no idea what feelings I had for Mack. If it was infatuation, or appreciation or I was just so drunk from so many orgasms I couldn't see straight.

But I liked him.

I liked him more than I wanted to.

So naturally I cared what his friends thought of me, and wanted to make a good impression. Surely that wasn't such a hard concept to understand.

"Hayden." He moved closer, taking the cup out of my hands and resting it on the counter. "I don't want to leave either. And if we both can agree on that, then go get ready and come with me. I'll wait."

It was tempting to argue, or just be honest and tell him that I didn't have time to make myself look the way I wanted to. But part of me didn't want to, instead push those feelings to the side for a minute and just go.

I wanted to go with him.

Wanted to spend the day together, and as much as I wasn't ready to meet his friends, it was either get over it or sit at home by myself. And if I could remember back to the last fifteen or twenty years, there was a time I wouldn't have even thought twice. I'd have met his friends just wearing the sleep Tee I had on and not cared what they thought.

God, I missed that girl.

"Okay, but I'm going to need a few minutes. I promise I'll go as fast as I can but I'm not walking out of here with unbrushed hair and morning breath." I pushed playfully against his chest. "And clothes. Proper clothes, so if it's going to take too long, you should probably leave now."

He laughed, "Not leaving. Go get ready and I'll get *myself* the coffee you promised me."

I ran to the bathroom, trying to tame my hair while brushing my teeth. It didn't look good. My night of reckless abandon didn't help my cause, my rebellious curls giving Medusa a run for her money. Doing the best I could—with some anti frizz serum and a heated styling brush I bought from a Facebook ad—I threw on some foundation, a lashing of mascara, and some lip gloss. It was nowhere near good enough, but I didn't look downright scary either. And, it had only taken me ten minutes, sprinting to my bedroom while mentally going through my wardrobe choices.

I'd decided on those new jeans and a top, Mack sitting on my freshly made bed while I pulled open my closet doors and tried to go faster. "You made my bed?" I threw one leg into the skinny jeans and then the other, hopping in place as I shimmied them up my thighs and hips.

"Seemed fair since I helped mess it up." He watched with amusement as I zipped and buttoned my jeans and then ripped off my sleep shirt. "And if I get to see you bouncing around while you get dressed as a thank you, I'll come make it every morning."

I rolled my eyes, slipping on a bra before pulling on a fitted shirt. "I need to work these jeans over my ass, trust me, bouncing is the most efficient way."

Grabbing a pair of boots and socks, I joined him on the bed. It was quicker than I'd anticipated but still longer than I'm sure he wanted to stay, the digital numbers of my clock seeming to change faster than usual. "I'm almost done."

"It's fine, I've checked in with North and Tibbs and they're meeting us at a coffee shop. No one has heard from Leighton yet, but apparently he didn't come home last night."

Trying to digest all those names and finishing putting on my boots, I tried not to be concerned I was going to be meeting them all for the first time. Nor did I worry about how inappropriate it was that I turn up—a stranger they'd probably never heard of—to a meeting to discuss something private and personal. Okay, so maybe I was worried about that, but maybe men didn't think like we did. And if Mack thought it was fine then I was going to trust him. After all, he knew these guys a lot better than I did.

"Ready?" he asked, standing up and holding out his hand. "And in case you're wondering, you look amazing."

"Well you're delusional. But we're already running late so let's get out of here." I motioned to the door.

He laughed, taking my hand as we left my condo and walked to the front door. "If there's anyone who's delusional, it's you, but you're right. Let's get out of here."

Chapter 15

Hayden

IT WAS STILL early, joggers out on the sidewalks as we got into his truck and drove back to Midtown.

It should have felt weird, me being in a car with a man I had unexplained feelings for, going to see his friends I'd never met. It was well and truly not what I'd envisioned when Gayle and I had signed me up for that dating site. And wasn't even close to the casual one-night stand I'd planned. But it didn't feel anything but amazing, my body relaxed as we drove to the inner city.

Gayle had texted me, checking in to see how my "fun" night out with the youngsters had gone. I had begged her to come with me but she'd told me she wasn't crazy enough to try and keep up. I still needed to tell her everything that had happened with Mack, the quick response I sent while in the car not enough to catch her up on the happenings of the last few days.

"All good?" Mack smiled, watching as I shoved my phone in my pocket. He hadn't even asked me who it was, or given me any suspicious sideway glances. He was clearly secure in himself or really trusted me. I liked he didn't crowd me, those small gestures of kindness making me feel so incredibly special.

"It was my sister-in-law, Gayle. My two nephews take up a lot of her time, so we don't get as much girl time as I would like. But she's probably my best friend. It feels weird that she doesn't know about you, she's the one who helped me put that profile up in the first place. We'll have to set up a meeting."

She knew I'd gone out with Mack—and consequently slept with Mack—and had even argued with me when I'd initially decided not to see him again. But since I hadn't worked out what it all meant in my head yet, I hadn't given her an update.

Shit.

I hadn't meant for it to sound like that, turning to Mack to see if he was looking at me like a crazy person who was inviting him to Sunday dinner.

"Not that I'm asking you to come meet my family or anything like that. I mean, as a friend. It's just a coincidence she's my sister-in-law. Trust me, you don't want to meet the rest of my family."

He laughed, clearly amused I was stumbling over what was obviously not what I'd meant to say. "Hayden, I'm happy to meet any member of your family. I'll meet any of your friends too. You're the one who is trying to keep her distance, sweetheart, not me."

"Just drive," I chuckled, not willing to admit he had a point. Hell, I could gather everyone I knew and/or loved into a room and form a reception line to greet him, and it *still* wouldn't faze him, his ability to roll with the punches more than apparent. But even if he didn't have a problem with it, it didn't mean that it would be happening.

It was only after he parked the car that he turned to me and his casual look turned serious. "Hey, before we go in there I want to tell you something. Probably something I should have mentioned earlier but I wasn't sure how you would take it. But we said no games, and that means I need to tell you anyway."

Panic set in, every single bad scenario I could imagine being played in my mind and then amplified to a million. "What is it?"

"My ex-wife was at the club last night. Not with me, and we didn't even speak. But I don't want you to think I didn't mention it because I have something to hide. Melinda and I are ancient history, I have zero feelings for her and I don't want you to even entertain the idea that I might want to revisit that with her."

I swallowed, wishing he'd told me back at my condo where there would've been time to think. "It's none of my business who you see and who you don't. You don't owe me any kind of explanation."

He took my face in his hands, not letting me turn away. "I didn't tell you because I owed you, I told you because I always want you to know where you stand with me. Trust me, Melinda has a way of screwing things up, and I won't let that happen here. I'm always going to be honest with you, Hayden, even if it's easier for both of us if I'm not."

Ridiculously, my eyes started to tear up. I was almost ashamed at how emotionally damaged I'd become, that something as simple as a man being honest and kind seemed like such a big deal. So unexpected. And even though he'd repeatedly shown me what a good man he was, I was constantly surprised.

"I won't lie to you either, Mack. Even though meeting you and feeling like this was completely unplanned, I promise I won't run."

He kissed me, gently at first but deepening into something more and I loved it. I loved that he innately knew when to speak and when to show me. And after admitting what I had, I didn't want to talk. "I didn't plan on meeting you either, Hayden. But I'm not stupid enough to walk away. And we'll go as slow as you want, we're not on any kind of deadline."

I couldn't describe how important those words were, knowing that he was willing to work with me until we figured it out. "So are we dating now? I feel stupid calling you my boyfriend."

Did it even count as a boyfriend when he was very clearly a man and both of us were over forty. Manfriend just didn't sound right, but neither did anything else.

"Yes, we're dating, and you can call me anything you like. Now let's go get this over with so I can give you that breakfast I promised." He winked, his hand popping open the car door.

He met me on the sidewalk, giving me a quick kiss before taking my hand. He always seemed to want to hold me, and I liked it, so I let him. The grin couldn't be wiped from my face as we walked into a little coffee shop not far from where Mack lived, three huuuuuge guys dwarfing the table they were sitting at, looking up as we entered.

"Chief!" One of them stood. He was incredibly good looking with brown hair and amazing brown eyes, and at least two to three whole inches taller than Mack. "And you must be Hayden." He held out his hand, his very cheeky smile getting wider.

"Riley?" I asked, assuming he was Mack's—adopted?—son. From the little I knew of him, the guy in front of me seemed to fit the bill.

"In the flesh." He shook my hand before turning to Mack. "But don't believe everything you've heard. Unless it was positive, and then of course it's all true."

He was charming, his warm smile welcoming as he released my hand and engulfed Mack in a one-armed hug. "And you've been totally holding out on us."

"Settle down, North. Don't make me regret meeting you here. You've already ruined our breakfast plans." Mack slapped Riley's back, pretending to be annoyed.

The two other guys stood, both looking incredibly pleased, wearing matching mischievous smiles I'm sure meant trouble.

"Justin Tibbs." The dark haired one with hazel eyes grinned.

"Jared Leighton." The fairer one with blue eyes added.

They all seemed to be in their mid-twenties—Riley a little older—but it was clear they saw Mack not only as a boss, but a father figure as well. It was in the way they looked at him, a cross between reverence and respect, that awed me.

I introduced myself, Jared and Justin not having the same wealth of information Riley apparently did, finding a seat at the already overcrowded table while Jared went and got everyone coffee.

"He show up?" Mack asked, casually draping his arm around my waist and ignoring the raised eyebrows he got from Justin. Riley didn't seem as surprised, leaning back in his chair enjoying the display.

"Nope. Took some convincing but Presley let Leighton drive her home. I'd have done it myself, but she flat out refused. He checked out her apartment before leaving. Got a hot tip last night though. One of the boys in Ladder 151 out in Queens spotted his Audi."

I had no idea who they were talking about, fascinated all the same.

"Nice to see you didn't follow up on that lead, Tibbs. Proud of you."

"Yeah, well, I said I'd tell you about it so here we are." He folded his arms across his chest. "But Chief, I'm not going to sit on my hands either."

Jared returned, a tray full of coffee and a selection of cookies. "Didn't know if you'd had time to bake, Chief," he smirked, handing out paper cups. "And wasn't sure how you took yours so it's black, but I got you sugar and cream."

I accepted the cup, thanking him while Mack shook his head. "You won't be getting squat if you keep giving me shit about it. And where the hell were you this morning? Tibbs said you took Presley home."

Jared nodded, taking a sip of his coffee. "Took her home, checked out the place and then left. Then I—" his eyes shot to me, grinning. "Uh-hum, I was just busy, Chief."

It was fairly obvious what he'd been *busy* doing, the need to elaborate it had been a booty call not necessary.

"And seems I'm not the only one in last night's clothes." His eyes flicked to Mack. "Funny that."

Justin chuckled, taking a sip from his cup. "All jokes aside, you free to take a ride down to Queens tonight? I just want to check it out."

"Hayden and I have plans tonight," he answered, eyeing him hard. "And I don't want you going out there alone."

While I didn't know the particulars—other than his sister's boyfriend being an asshole—I could tell it was important. And while the last thing I wanted was to spend a night alone, I knew Mack's mind would be elsewhere, feeling responsible if something happened.

"We can reschedule." I offered, everyone turning to me, looking surprised I'd spoken. "I'm sorry, I know this is none of my business, Justin."

Justin shook his head. "Tibbs, call me *Tibbs*."

"Okay, *Tibbs*. I'm really sorry if something bad happened to your sister, and I'm really glad you're all looking out for her." I turned to Mack. "We can go to Club Retro next week, maybe have an early dinner instead? This sounds like somewhere you need to be."

What I most admired about Mack was his unflappable integrity. He was ironclad, the kind of guy who didn't litter or steal a ballpoint pen from a bank. And exactly the kind of man these guys needed.

Mack looked at me, squeezing my hand under the table and leaning in. "Are you sure this is what you want?"

"Positive." I squeezed back. "Besides, we've probably both exceeded our limit for *clubs* for at least a week. Any more and

I think we're both going to need our heads examined. And you said it yourself. *Club Retro* is probably going to be crawling with millennials in faded T-shirts of bands they've never heard of."

"Hey, not all of us are posers. And for the record, I know my 90's grunge." Riley coughed under his breath. "Not that I had a choice."

Mack rolled his eyes, clipping the back of Riley's head. "You should be thanking me. Then it looks like it's all settled. We'll head out around nine. Leighton, have any other *business* this evening? And North, what are your plans?"

"Yeah, as much as I'd love to come see how it all plays out, I'm going to have to pass. Not leaving Quinn two nights in a row. No offense, guys." Riley raised his hands, clear he wasn't going to be swayed. It seemed he got more than just his knowledge of grunge from Mack, integrity would be a safe bet as well.

"Probably for the best." Mack cupped his shoulder, giving him a nod. "We'll keep you in the loop."

A silent dialogue passed between them that was incredibly sweet, the other two seeming to be in agreement that Riley should be with Quinn.

"Soooooooooo how did you guys meet? Please tell me he didn't pick you up in a grocery store?" Jared raised his eyebrow, edging the cookies closer.

Riley laughed, grabbing one of the chocolate chips and taking a bite. "Hayden, I should probably warn you that Chief is like catnip to strange women in grocery stores. I think it's because he looks like a deer in headlights. Those poor women just want to make sure he makes it out of there okay."

Mack shook his head, shooting Riley an irritated look. "Don't listen to them. I'm just polite." He turned to the rest of them. "And not that it matters but we met online."

"Online?" Tibbs coughed out. "You know how to do that?"

It was my turn to laugh, the look of bewilderment on Justin's face, hilarious.

"Yes, you moron. You've seen me on a computer, of course I know how. Any other questions?" He took my hand and kissed my knuckles in front of them, daring them to say something stupid.

It was like he didn't care. Wasn't concerned in the slightest what they thought or what they'd say, and wasn't going to hide his affection. Not that I thought he was going to whip out a huge PDA and kiss me on the mouth in front of them, but he wasn't backing down either. Like he'd said, he wasn't interested in playing games, and that included hiding me away. Amazing how special that small gesture made me feel.

"Nope. But I might head out if we're done here." Jared stood, picking up his coffee. "Got more *business* to take care of," he smirked before turning to me. "Hayden, it was a pleasure meeting you. Hoping we get to see more of you around, especially now we know why Chief has been in a better mood."

"Be respectful, Leighton," Mack warned. "And for Christ's sake answer your phone later."

Jared saluted, tipping his chin goodbye to the others before making his exit.

Tibbs pushed his chair back, grabbing his coffee and a cookie and standing. "I should probably call Presley, just to make sure. Will check in with you later. And Hayden, great meeting you." He gave me a nod before grinning.

Mack smiled, probably anticipating their silence on our relationship wasn't going to be permanent. They were saving it for when I wasn't around.

"Likewise. Hope everything works out with your sister."

"Yep, me too." He waved goodbye, walking out the same door Jared had earlier.

Mack's eyes swung to Riley who was still sitting across from us. "And you?"

"Kind of torn, Mack. Really want to get back home to Quinn, but this is just too fascinating to leave." He leaned forward, grinning as he stage-whispered. "Now I see why he ditched us so fast last night. Lucky for him, I'm married and completely devoted to my wife or I'd make a play for you myself."

It was utterly ridiculous that he was flirting with me. Mainly, because while I wasn't quite old enough to be his mother, he didn't look like the kind of guy that dated in my age bracket. And another thing, just like Mack, he was gorgeous. Before he'd put a ring on his wife's finger, he'd probably had a different woman every night.

But even though I knew he was just being polite, or playful, or just plain doing it to annoy Mack, it was kind of flattering that he even bothered.

"I'm sure Quinn is a very lucky woman, but you're not really my type," I joked nestling closer to Mack.

"What? Smart, good looking, and talented?" He snorted, pretending to look shocked. "You know he mainly sits behind a desk these days, right? I'm the one running into burning buildings and making the city a safer place."

"Jesus. Your ego gets any bigger, North, your head isn't going to fit through the exit." Mack laughed, shaking his head. "And I thought impending fatherhood would teach him some humility."

"Speaking of my impending fatherhood. I should get going." He checked his watch, pushing away from the table. "And thanks, Hayden."

"For what?" I laughed, wondering what reason he could possibly have to thank me.

He pointed to Mack's face. "Haven't seen a grin like that in years, and as much as I'd like to take responsibility, even I'm not that conceited. Behave, kids, see you soon." And with a squeeze of Mack's shoulder, he said one final goodbye, Mack and I watching him walk out.

I turned, facing Mack, wrapping my arms around his chest as I tilted my chin. "You really are amazing."

He shook his head, actually looking bashful at the compliment. "Why do you say that?"

"Because you raised one hell of a man in him. Not to mention, Tibbs and Jared."

He laughed, squeezing his arms around me and dropping a kiss on my forehead. "Can we call him Leighton? Every time you say Jared, it takes me a minute to work out who you're talking about."

"Fine," I rolled my eyes. "I'll call them whatever you want me to but it doesn't change the role you play in their lives. They depend on you, respect you, and that's all the proof I need to validate my claim of you being amazing."

He looked down at the abandoned cookies and our half-consumed coffees. "Whatever the reason, Hayden, I'm just glad you stuck around. Oh, but for future reference, or if anyone asks, it's because I'm amazing in bed."

I laughed, tossing my head back like a sorority girl. "Oh, you totally are. Now let's go get this breakfast you promised me. I have a whole day with you to myself before I have to share."

He stood, pulling me to my feet and pressing me against his chest. "Sweetheart, the one thing you're never going to have to do is share me."

Chapter 16

Mack

DINNER WITH HAYDEN had been great.

Determined for it to be a regular date, I dropped her home a few hours earlier so she could get ready, and then took her to a small bistro not far from where she lived. It didn't have the noise or craziness of *Gino's*, but the food was great and I got to hold her hand without some asshole picking up the phone and telling my entire battalion.

Not that I gave a shit what people thought, willing to hear jokes about me dating again until the end of time if it meant I got to be with her.

It fucking bewildered me she had no idea how beautiful she was. Or how much I wanted to be with her, looking at me doe-eyed and surprised when I whispered all the things I wanted to do to her the minute I got back.

That was the other thing, not many women would have been so understanding. She didn't know Tibbs or Presley, and other than giving her the basic rundown, had no idea what kind of cocksucker Lewis was. Would have been easy for her to dig in her heels, remind me it had been *my* idea to take her to that stupid club and not given two shits about anyone else. Probably would have been fair too, considering I'd been such a hard ass about keeping commitments.

But she hadn't even blinked, insisting I go and being completely cool about it. And not going to lie, initially I did think it might have been some kind of test. Melinda used to do it all the time, tell me she was "fine" with something only to throw it back in my face. To say it was confusing was an understatement. But Hayden was nothing like Melinda. And fuck me, was I into her more than I thought was possible.

"You sure it was the shit stain's Audi?" I asked Tibbs, my truck idling in the parking lot of the Cineplex in Flushing. While I trusted Lucas from 151's word, I wanted some kind of reassurance we weren't going to jack up some oblivious tool who would—quicker than shit—file a harassment charge.

Tibbs kept his eyes on the parking lot, cars filled with teenagers or couples on dates accounted for most of the traffic. "Yep, he said the plate numbers were different, but he has that stupid holographic sticker on his bumper. He thinks he's a fucking DJ, and it's his dumbass logo." He rolled his eyes.

Even if he had amnesia—forgetting Lewis brandished a gun in his sister's face *and* broke into her apartment—he'd been less than impressed with Presley's choice. I'd only met the guy twice, and that was enough for me to agree he wasn't someone I'd want my family around.

"How do we know it's not some other jerkoff's Audi with the same sticker?" I tapped the steering wheel, wondering what the chances were he was still in the neighborhood. He had to know Presley would have made a statement, and at the very least the police would haul him in for questioning.

"C'mon, Chief. Same make, model, color, *and* the fucking sticker? You and me both know there's no such thing as that many coincidences."

He was right about that.

Singularly, the Audi TT coupe could be anyone's. But add in that hideous Pulse Orange paint job, the unique sticker on the bumper, and the fabrication year of the car lining up—and chances were remote.

"You're quiet." My eyes landed in my rearview, Leighton sitting in the backseat like a boy scout. "Your afternoon activities wear you out?"

He coughed, squaring his shoulders before meeting my eyes. "You want to talk about ladies we're entertaining now, Chief? Because if that's what we're doing, then you should probably start."

I flipped him off, wondering if I'd been as big a pain in the ass when I was his age. Christ, I hope I wasn't, reminding myself to call my old captain to apologize, just in case. "We are not talking about Hayden. And I know I don't have to remind you that unlike the two of you, I don't fuck around. She's obviously important to me. But on the chance your memory is foggy, you'll be-fucking-have. And for God's sake, tell me you're being safe. A pregnancy is the least of your problems, and that's saying something considering you procreating is a goddamn nightmare."

Leighton laughed, satisfied he'd hit a nerve. "You're such an easy target, Chief. And you know I'm a saint. Wouldn't dream of messing with your woman, even as a joke. But, if Hayden continues to inspire the baking," the asshole had the nerve to chuckle, "I'd like to formerly request brownies. Double chocolate."

My fingers pinched the bridge of my nose as I groaned. "I swear you're worse than preschoolers. How you guys made it through the academy is a mystery."

"It's 'cause we're brilliant, Chief." Tibbs piped in from the passenger's side.

"Not to mention, fearless warriors," Leighton added from the back.

I shook my head, not able to honestly disagree. "And your own biggest fans too. Let's keep the appreciation society for later, like much later, when I'm not around."

Deciding we'd sat in the parking lot enough, we took a scenic drive of the surrounding area. Lewis apparently had friends in Queens, not that any of them admitted to speaking to him, let alone seeing him since last Saturday. And who even knew who his family was? He'd told Presley he wasn't on speaking terms with any of them. The kid was slick, I'd give him that. And because Presley hadn't filed any official assault charges, it was a standard B&E, and not a high priority for an already overworked force. Even as a favor for a fellow first responder, their hands were tied. Unless we found him, then they'd happily look the other way too.

"Presley working tonight?" We headed back to College Point Boulevard, keeping our eyes peeled for the bright douchey car.

"Yep, but she promised she's getting a ride home with one of the girls from the bar. We still don't know if he did it just to mess with her or if he was looking for something. And I don't trust the guy."

"Speaking of people we can't trust." Preferring to talk about anything else, but needing to ask. "Either of you two clowns see Melinda?"

Tibbs shot Leighton a look, making it obvious something had gone down, both of them remaining tight lipped despite me having outright asked.

"Spill it. What did she say? And don't try and tell me it was nothing because you're terrible liars."

"So, I saw her at the bar," Leighton started, fessing up to what I already assumed. "I swear I didn't say anything, but she walked up all the same and offered to buy me a drink."

"And?" I waved my hand, knowing there was more to the story.

He blew out a breath. "And . . . suck my dick."

Wow.

Hadn't been expecting that.

"Chief, I told her I wasn't interested. And I'd never—like *ever*—go there. But before she left, she told me to give you a message. Either you call her back and give her what she wanted, or she was going to make your life a living hell."

I shook my head, trying to remember a time when I'd loved her. God, I had to have at some point, right? But lately, she was making it hard to summon the recollection. "I'll take care of it."

Wasn't exactly sure how I was going to do that, but me meeting her demands wasn't happening. And I wasn't going to be extorted. She'd better have more up her sleeve than idle threats. And she could blow the whole battalion for all I cared, because if she was trying to make me jealous, she was shit out of luck.

"So what does she want?" Leighton asked, obviously not informed by my *charming* ex-bride of her plan to harvest my fucking seed.

I swear, even in my head it sounded batshit level crazy. What the hell did she think I was going to do? Get her pregnant and then walk away from my kid? Especially knowing how much I'd wanted one when we were together? There wasn't a chance I'd be a sperm donor dad, knowing that if or when I made that commitment there'd be a ring on their mother's finger and a promise I'd never leave. And that was ignoring the fact I'd never condemn them to the persecution of having *her* as a mother. Even if she was the only female on Earth and the survival of the race depended on it, I'd *still* turn her down.

"Nothing she can get from me."

We circled the streets a little more but didn't see the Audi or the dipshit, deciding he was probably laying low. Not to say that we wouldn't take another drive if we got more intel, but so far we'd come up empty.

Tibbs and Leighton shared an apartment in Hell's Kitchen, not far from my place on Tenth. So we drove back to Midtown, giving me a chance to drop them off before heading back to my place to pack an overnight bag.

As much as it would suck getting up early and fighting traffic from Inwood to the station in the morning, I wasn't spending a night away from Hayden. And not just because I promised her I'd stop by after I was done with Leighton and Tibbs. But because the idea of sleeping alone when she was an option was unthinkable.

"You hear anything, call me. See you both tomorrow morning on shift," I warned, waiting for them to get out of the truck.

Both of them nodded, giving me nonverbal grunts in the affirmative while Leighton swung his keys and headed to his car.

"Where are you going?" I left the car in park, not moving an inch until I got reassurances he wasn't channeling his inner vigilante and deciding to go out again.

"I'm not looking for him, I swear, Chief. Just want to go kill some time or something." He shrugged, pretending like he didn't know *exactly* what he had planned.

There was something cagey going on though, Leighton not usually one to hide his extracurricular activities. Had to be a woman, and judging by his need to keep things under wraps, probably one he thought we wouldn't approve of.

"You going too?" I tipped my head to Tibbs, about to get out of the car and handcuff them both to their kitchen sink.

It *wasn't* Leighton's sister. So unless the two of them had made some bullshit blood oath, I doubted he'd do anything without the say so of Tibbs. More likely he was looking to work off some steam, and not by running a few miles either.

"Nah, I'm going to get an early night. That six a.m. alarm sucks balls." Tibbs waved goodbye to his roommate. "And if you bring anyone home tonight, try and keep it down."

Satisfied they could keep out of trouble for a night, I said goodbye and headed back to my condo. If I'd had my mind right earlier in the day, I'd have packed the bag then. But being with Hayden made everything less of a priority, which meant, I hadn't thought of anything other than being with her.

Annoyed it was almost eleven and I was just getting home, I put the code into the underground garage, and parked in my usual spot. I cursed as I headed to the elevator anxious to get to my condo. The quicker I got in, the quicker I could get out, the metal doors opening on my floor and finding Hayden sitting on the floor in front of my door.

"Hayden?" I asked, wondering if I was tired and hallucinating or she'd somehow materialized. "What are you doing here?"

She looked up, her eyes tired but her smile happy. "I know you said you would come to my condo when you finished, but it was getting late. And you have to get up early tomorrow, but I have a day off. I figured it made more sense if I came here even if it did make me look sort of crazy. I promise I'm not one of those women who cruises by your house just to see if you're home."

I pulled her off the floor, wrapping my arms around her body while kissing her neck. "Sweetheart, the thought hadn't even crossed my mind but why didn't you call me? How long have you been sitting there?"

"Only half an hour," she mumbled against my chest. "When you didn't show up at ten, I got in my car and drove over. Your neighbors probably think I'm some scorned lover, waiting for you to come home so I can make a scene."

"Hayden, you're in *Midtown*. Short of setting yourself on fire in the hall, no one would give a shit," I laughed, thankful for whatever turn of events had her landing on my doorstep.

After kissing her again—once was never enough—I got us into my condo and turned on the light. I hadn't even noticed the small overnight bag she had beside her, my attention unable to deviate from her, and only her.

"I don't usually do this. I mean, *obviously* I don't do this since I haven't dated in forever. But you gave me your code and . . . well, I just wanted to." She dropped the bag at our feet, slinging her arms around my neck.

"Good on two accounts. One, I wouldn't have given you my code if I hadn't wanted you to use it, but more importantly, I'm glad you wanted to. I meant what I said, Hayden, I'm willing to take things slow."

She grinned, tilting her head back. "Not too slow, I hope."

"Tempo can be totally fluid, sweetheart. We'll set it as we go."

Leaving the bag at the door, I tossed my keys onto the coffee table and walked her back into my bedroom. It was still dark, not bothering with the lights as we kissed our way to my bed. The sexy dress she'd worn to dinner had been replaced by a pair of leggings and a fleece, the makeup gone from her face as well. But as far as I was concerned, she was hotter than anything I'd ever seen.

As much as I wanted her naked, I didn't care if we spent the rest of the night just kissing. She was in my bed, and as long as she was still in it when I woke up, that was all I needed.

I kicked off my boots, pulling my lips away from her mouth long enough to talk. "Get under the covers, Hayden. It's been a really long day and it's going to end before either of us wants it to."

She smiled, watching me as I lifted off her and started to strip. It wasn't my intention to give her a show, but if that's what she wanted, I had no problem with it.

"You want to talk about tonight? You find the guy you were looking for?" Her eyes locked on my chest, making their downward sweep to the boxer briefs I'd yet to take off.

I laughed, wondering if she was trying to be polite or was genuinely interested. Because as much as she'd asked the question, her attention was on anything *other* than how I'd spent my night. "Nothing to talk about. I'd rather hear about you. Tell me what you did. And you might want to lose the clothes too. I wasn't kidding about getting into bed." I dropped my boxer briefs, standing in front of her naked.

Even in the dark I could make out the slow swallow, her hands moving to her fleece and yanking it off. "I don't really want to talk either."

It was my turn for a show, watching as she peeled off the layers and tossed them to the floor.

"Guess we'll have to do something other than talk."

Chapter 17

Hayden

IT WAS EARLY when Mack had left.

I hadn't bothered to check the time, sliding my eyes open long enough to kiss him goodbye and hear him tell me he'd call me later. And whether I wanted to or not, I drifted back to sleep in someone else's bed.

Not only was it something I wasn't accustomed to, but I wasn't even sure I had the ability. To be so at ease with a man who *wasn't* Cooper? Positive I couldn't sleep beside him, wake up, kiss him goodbye, and then go back to sleep in a condo that wasn't mine. But with Mack, the reasons not to, didn't exist.

Yes, we'd had sex. My libido had woken from a long hibernation, the desire to have sex stronger than it had been in years. And if Mack had a problem with it, he sure wasn't showing it. But more than just the orgasms, I really loved being touched, which was a good thing considering Mack constantly had his hands on me.

It had to be midday when I finally woke up. The sheets still smelled of him, my body sore from more activity than it had gotten in years and it was only when I touched my cheeks that I noticed I was smiling for no reason.

Silently.

By myself.

Smiling.

I was happy.

Without questioning my mood or allowing random thoughts to change it, I showered in Mack's amazing bathroom and got into some clean clothes. It wasn't until I was pouring myself a cup of coffee that I realized I hadn't felt like I was intruding or had the urge to leave. Even when I visited my brother and Gayle, I was careful not to overstay my welcome. But it hadn't even occurred to me until I was flipping through Mack's cable channels, snuggled up on his couch, that I should probably go home.

I was just about to leave when my phone rang, my smile spreading wider when I saw the name on my caller ID. "Hey you, good thing your neighbors aren't the suspicious kind. I'm still in your condo, loitering."

He laughed, clearly not annoyed. "I'm glad you're still there. I like the idea of you in my space, so stay as long as you want."

"Well, as much as I would love to do nothing but lay on your couch all day, I have a bunch of laundry I need to do and I'm behind on my transcriptions. I try and use the weekends to catch up since I don't have to work at Target."

"Ouch, sounds brutal. Guess I'm probably not going to see much of you tomorrow then. What time do you get off work?"

"Six," I groaned, the weekend feeling like a fantasy vacation I didn't want to leave. "We could do dinner though. I'll cook."

I hadn't even asked if he wanted to see me, or considered whether because I wanted to see him, it made me seem needy. I didn't think at all—asking for exactly what I wanted. Funny how something so trivial made me feel so powerful, the small assertion—a huge leap.

"Well now you're saying all the right things. Dinner sounds amazing, but you sure you want to spend the time in the kitchen after working an entire day?"

I wasn't the only one saying all the right things. "Mack, you made me *soufflé*. At night. With zero notice. I'm positive I can manage to rustle up something that's suitably delicious."

"Then you'll get no arguments here. I'll pick up some wine on my way over. And beer. I feel like since this is going so well, I don't have to try so hard to impress you." He laughed, having no clue that he *never* had to try to impress me.

Which gave me an idea.

"Hey, so you and Riley work similar hours, right?" The nerves in my stomach jangled, wondering how good of an idea it really was.

"Yep, initially it was pure coincidence we ended up on the same rotation, but I can't say I'm not glad. Now I'm in charge of the teams, it's a little less of a coincidence."

"Good, so why don't you ask him if he and Quinn are free tomorrow night as well."

It was probably a terrible idea.

The worst.

Because it made no sense to extend an invitation when we'd barely started dating. So I was probably making one more mistake in what could very well turn into a series of them.

We were in a bubble, still working things out, with no idea what the future held. Obviously, Mack wasn't going to be some fling, with the feelings I had for him, very real. But life had a way of being unpredictable, and who knew if six months down the road he wouldn't end up being just a really good memory.

But none of that mattered.

I didn't care that we could potentially break up, or if I was inadvertently welcoming in the chaos. Chaos, uncertainty—they weren't the enemy, instead it was the false ideas I'd built up in my head.

"You want me to invite Riley *and* Quinn?" Mack asked, attempting to give me a chance to reconsider. "To dinner?" His voice dipped with slight concern. "Hayden, you sure you want to do that?"

"Well, you did say we'd work out our own tempo. And yes, I know it's probably crazy and they might not even want to come. But Mack, these people are really important to you." *And I'm hoping I will be too,* I finished in my head. "And I think getting to know *them* will help me know *you* better."

"Sweetheart, I appreciate what you are trying to do. Hell, Hayden, just the fact you thought of them means a lot. And I'd love for you to meet Quinn. She's thirty-five shades of crazy, but she's got a good heart. But if you want to keep it just us, you'll get no complaints from me."

"Probably a little late in the game, Chief." I laughed, loving how the name his men called him sounded so natural in my mouth. "You've already introduced me to Riley, Leighton, and Tibbs. And had me tag along on a meeting that I had no business being a part of. I think keeping it between *just us* isn't going to happen."

"Hayden, regardless of how unorthodox the circumstances were, I don't regret that morning. I wasn't ready to leave you, so I didn't. Plain and simple. You want to meet Quinn and have her and Riley over for dinner, I have no problem with it. In fact, you're probably doing me a favor. I'm positive the only reason she hasn't knocked at the door, introduced herself, demanding to know your intentions, is because she is set to deliver any day. If she were any less pregnant, you'd have met her about three minutes after me."

I could hear the smile in his voice, imagining for as much as he pretended Riley and Quinn were a handful, he wouldn't have it any other way. And I loved that about him, that he didn't care about his own discomfort, worried more about the people around him.

"Then she will probably be excited about a night out. And I'm totally fine about being asked my intentions." And I was. It might've been the only thing I was sure about, but at least I had that.

"Yeah? And what are you going to tell her? You worked out if you're comfortable calling me your boyfriend? Or do I get some other title?"

I sighed, wishing I could've been looking into those incredible kind brown eyes instead of just talking to him on the phone. "You're my Mack. And I'm going to tell her that my intentions are for us to be happy. I want to make you feel as good as you make others feel. As good as you make *me* feel. I want us to be together, Mack. And I'm not interested in pretending I don't want you. God, I just haven't got the energy or the time to string it out and play hard to get."

Habits—especially bad ones—had featured highly in the last ten or so years of my life. And I didn't want to perpetuate them anymore. Which was why I was choosing to be brave, even though the uncertainty of it all was terrifying.

"Interesting. Having enough *energy* didn't seem to be a problem last night," he chuckled. "And just hearing all of that is enough to make me happy, Hayden. I'll bring an extra bottle of wine."

"Quinn's pregnant, surely she's not going to drink."

"No, but you might need it."

I shook my head, unable to contain my smile. "One bottle is fine, wiseass. And we still don't know if they are going to say yes. They might have plans."

"Ha! Oh, sweetheart, you have no idea. Trust me, plans or no plans, they'll be there and not because I need to twist their arm." He laughed, before a loud beep interrupted him. "Hayden, I need to go. I'll call you later."

There was no need to ask him what that beep meant. While we hadn't spoken a lot about his work, I had a pretty good idea there weren't many days where emergencies didn't demand his attention. We said our quick goodbyes and ended the call so he could go do his job. And whether we spoke about it or not, what he did was *really* freaking impressive. And yes, it was also very sexy too.

Lifting myself off the couch, I packed my things back into my overnight bag and made sure I locked the door behind me when I left. Usually I was excited to go home, unable to wait to walk in the door and take off my bra. But leaving Mack's and driving back to mine didn't give me the same buzz.

Another thing that didn't fill me with joy was traffic, which surprisingly didn't bother me as much as it used to while I sat in my car heading back up the island. Maybe this was what being in *love* felt like, it had been so long I wasn't sure. But swooning around, being happy about sitting stationary in city traffic was probably a fair indicator. Either that, or those orgasms had indeed been magical. And at that point, I didn't care what was responsible, I was just relieved to be happy.

Gayle had been parked outside, waiting for me when I arrived at my building. It wasn't unusual for her to stop by—living close by in Hudson Heights—but I was guessing her visit was a little more than just social.

"Noticed you removed your dating profile." She got out of her car and walked with me to the front door. "You know they send the *creator* an alert when you do. You decide that casual dating is not for you? Or you met someone you want to see more regularly? And I'm not going to pretend I don't see that overnight bag either."

"Well, hello to you too." I laughed, getting out my keys and letting us both into the building. "And I've been meaning to call you about that."

That wasn't a lie, I had been meaning to call. But initially I hadn't because I didn't know how to define what I was feeling. And then after, well, there was never a good time. "I'm seeing Mack. Have been seeing him." I corrected myself. "Well, I really never stopped."

A knowing smile crossed Gayle's lips as we climbed the stairs to my condo. "You see this look?" She pointed to her face, circling it for good measure in case it hadn't been clear what I was supposed to be looking at. "This is my complete lack of surprise face. You, girlfriend, are a terrible liar, and if he is half as good as you said he was from that first date, then you'd be crazy not to keep seeing him."

I unlocked my front door, letting us both in. "You're right. I just didn't want to feel like I was running from one relationship to another. I wanted to get to know myself again, just be okay with being alone. And I'm not disappointed I found Mack because he's everything I could ever want and more. But part of me feels like it is too soon."

"Hayden. You were separated for a whole year and didn't so much as look at a guy until your divorce was final. And that's not even counting the years that you and Cooper had been disconnected. I think you've got it the other way around, honey. You haven't *been* in a relationship for a very long time. And it was well past due."

That was one way to look at it. "I just want to do it right this time. I really like him."

Gayle pulled me into a hug, and I knew she understood I was underselling that *like*. But it was crazy to think those strong feelings had developed so quickly.

Instant love, love at first sight—whatever you wanted to call it—was for teenagers and twenty-year-olds who didn't know any better. It wasn't easy or effortless, and needed a full page with checks and balances. Plans, time, mutual discovery were all required. That way, when that sheen of the infatuation wore off, there was something *more* there. It was the only way to make sure you didn't waste *years* away in a loveless marriage like I had. Willing to bet that even if I'd lit myself on fire, Cooper would've barely even noticed, let alone cared. But with Mack, it had been *easy* and *effortless*, moving from lust and infatuation so seamlessly alarm bells should be ringing. LOUDLY.

And yet, silence.

"Okay, why don't I put this overnight bag—that you are refusing to ignore—away and we go spend some time with *your* amazing family. I'm positive it's been more than a week since I've seen my darling nephews, and honestly, the idea of sitting at home by myself is kind of depressing."

"Well, far be it for me to turn down an extra pair of hands wrangling children. We'll even get takeout, so no one has to cook. Annnnnnd since there will be no dishes to do, you will have all the time in the world to tell me everything about Mack after we get my little cherubs off to bed." She flashed me a not-so-innocent smile which meant my lack of information had reached its limit.

"Deal, but I'm buying ice cream as well. I need to maintain my place as their favorite aunt, and I'm not above using all means possible."

Gayle laughed, squeezing my hand. "Not that there is any danger of that because they *adore* you. But if you were to take them to a fire station to show them the trucks, you'd probably be elevated to a new level."

"Hmmm." I tapped my finger on my chin in thought. "I know a guy."

"I bet you do."

Chapter 18

Hayden

DINNER WITH GAYLE, Matthew, and their boys had been a lot of fun. Mack had messaged me a couple of times but had been too busy to talk, leaving me a very sweet voice message for when I woke up. I didn't have time to call him back, having slept through my alarm for the first time in forever. I raced through my condo, throwing on clothes and skipping breakfast just so I could make it to work on time. And that pipe dream about catching up on medical transcriptions on the weekend, yeah, that didn't happen either.

Being too happy to be angry at myself, I managed to get into the store, get my personal belongings stowed away and ready before the doors opened. Penny had given me a we're-talkin'-later look, adding a nodding smile as she handed me some new ladies blouses that needed to be hung and put on display. Thank God my job required minimal cerebral involvement. If I'd been a surgeon, someone would have died on the table for sure.

But not only did I make it through my day without killing anyone—not as easy as it sounded when you worked in customer service—but I'd gotten through it relatively unscathed. No one demanded to speak to my manager, sprout the customer-is-always-right speech, or be rude. It was a modern-day miracle, my smile uncontainable as I finished my shift and went to collect my bag.

"I know you were not going to leave here without telling me what happened." Penny's hands rested on her hips as she tapped her foot. "You just were not."

Other sales associates who were finishing at the same time looked at me with wild eyes, likely wondering what I had done and glad they hadn't attracted Penny's attention. Little did they know my infraction hadn't been professional, and I didn't care enough to enlighten them.

"It has to be quick, I'm having guests for dinner." I pulled out my phone, already concerned I wasn't going to have enough time to shop, cook, *and* make myself look presentable before eight. I should have invited them for a midnight feast instead, given myself a fighting chance.

Penny nodded excitedly, pointing to her office as she lowered her voice. "Then be quick and talk fast. Is the Uber driver coming? He's not really an Uber driver is he."

Waiting until she closed the door, I let out a huge breath. "No, he's a fireman. And yes, he and his son and daughter-in-law are coming for dinner. And I haven't cooked for anyone but myself in a long time, and haven't even thought about what I'm going to wear."

"Whoa! He not only has a kid, but one old enough to be *married*? When did he become a dad? When he was like twelve?" Penny's eyes widened, unable to hide her surprise.

I smiled, thinking about how wonderful Mack would have been with a baby. "Well technically, yes, he is old enough, but Riley isn't his biological son. He kind of adopted him—not really, because there's no paperwork—but for all intents and purposes it's his kid. So, yeah, it's complicated."

"Jes-us, I'll say. Still, he looks like that, so I'd put up with all kinds of complications." She elbowed me playfully. "And all jokes aside, find out what moisturizer he uses because his skin is a-mazing. Also, *firemen* are hot. And I'm not trying to be cute by saying "hot" because of fire and all that bullshit, I'm talking h-o-t. Seriously, I was going to offer to set you up with one of my single male friends, but you don't need my help."

"Actually, if you have like five minutes, I would like some help. Short of wearing the same skinny jeans again for like the third time, I don't have anything casual yet nice to wear. I want to make a good first impression, but wearing anything too fancy while I'm trying to cook won't work out well for me either."

The clock was ticking, and heading into the changing room and trying on outfits was a luxury I couldn't afford. It had taken me thirty minutes of umming and ahhhing to decide on the skinny jeans, and they'd *just* been jeans. I needed an objective eye, and I needed it quick.

"Girl, I've got you. Take a seat, I'll be right back." She flicked her long blond hair over her shoulder, disappearing from the office before she'd even finished her sentence.

Dinner was going to be oven-baked chicken pieces with vegetables and a salad. One, because chicken pieces were quicker and easier to cook than a whole fucking chicken, and two, it looked prettier on the plate than hacking chunks of flesh off a bird carcass. I also wasn't sure if Quinn had any issues eating while being pregnant. While I knew she was in her last trimester, Gayle hadn't been able to stomach anything but grilled chicken and vegetables until she delivered. Last thing I wanted when I was trying to impress was send the poor girl running to the bathroom after lowering a plate in front of her.

So, in addition to cooking this—hopefully impressive—masterpiece, I also needed to get the groceries as well. And while there was a Whole Foods on my way home that had precut chicken ready to toss in the oven, I wasn't able to throw my hand out and stop the minutes like Benedict Cumberbatch did in the *Avengers*. Shame too, because as hard as his name was to pronounce, I could have used the skill.

Penny ran back into her office, slamming the door shut behind her while dumping an armful of clothes on the chair opposite her desk. "Okay—and I mean this in the least sexual harassment way—strip."

"I am not wearing fuchsia," I picked up a fitted blazer she'd paired with some tailored black pants before turning to a dress. "And plaid? Really? I'm cooking dinner, not hiking a trail with a lumberjack." I neglected to inform her I managed to survive the entire 90s without a flannel shirt, knowing she was probably too young to even remember the decade.

She rolled her eyes, passing me what looked to be an oversized crew neck sweater. "Fine, then wear the black dress. But belt it so it gives you some shape."

"This isn't a dress. I haven't got the legs for this." I held it against my body, the majority of my khakis visible underneath. "You heard the part where I said I wanted to make a good impression, right? Not have them wondering if I lost my damn mind and forgot my damn pants."

Penny laughed, amused that there'd be a high probability of me flashing my ass to my guests. "Wear thick opaque tights. They're almost like leggings, no one will see, I promise."

Too late to argue, and deciding I was going to take a chance, I did as she said and pulled off my work clothes right there in her office. We were probably breaking about five HR policies, not to mention I was literally in my bra and panties in front of my boss, but I pulled on the sweater/dress, exposing my ghostly white legs.

"See, it's not so short." She handed me the belt. "It looks great."

With no mirror in front of me, I was taking her word for how *great* it looked, but glad it at least felt kind of comfortable. Unfortunately that feeling didn't last long, Penny grabbing me a pair Spanx that sucked me in so tight I felt like an eighteenth-century virgin at her cotillion. And then we added those opaque tights, which thankfully were thick enough that it *was* like wearing pants.

"You look great." Penny took a step back, admiring her handiwork. "Let me cut off the tags and I'll ring them up for you. And don't forget the most important part," she laughed. "Employee discount."

That *was* a positive, grabbing my work clothes and shoving them into a carry bag while following her to the registers. Heads turned as we walked, whispers audible above the music piped through the P.A., wondering why the hell I was dressed up like that. Had to admit, I was kind of wondering myself.

First impressions, I reminded myself. And Penny was a lot closer to Quinn's age than I was, not to mention had gone through the intensive Target merchandising program. So whether I liked it or not, I was going to wear the outfit she'd chosen.

The one positive about the whole episode was at least I didn't need to change. I was already dressed so could get to Whole Foods, grab the groceries and start cooking without needing to stand in front of my closet for an hour. And once I got the food in the oven, I could put some makeup on and do my hair, and get the whole look completed before Mack arrived with Riley and Quinn. I wasn't even sure if they were coming together, almost wishing I'd told him to come earlier and make sure I didn't die from a compressed rib cage courtesy of the Spanx.

It was difficult to move, driving, shopping, and then cooking had been a challenge. But I'd managed to complete all three, getting to the store, and then home, the baking tray of chicken and vegetables sliding into the oven *just* on schedule.

My hair was still a mess and I was still wearing the foundation and mascara from earlier in the day, but unless Mack and company arrived annoyingly early, I had time. Not enough to look at YouTube videos and work out how to make beach waves with aluminum foil and a hairdryer, but ample time to wash my face, reapply makeup and galvanize my hair with the tub of product I'd picked up before leaving work.

I'd just finished looking in the mirror, not overly impressed with the results, when Mack had texted me that he was downstairs, waiting to be buzzed in. While I had managed to make myself look presentable—my hair tamed, my winged eyes almost perfect—I felt like I'd put on a body suit and was walking around in someone else's skin.

Too late to change—and wondering if it wasn't just usual internal self-criticism—I sucked in as deep a breath as the Spanx would allow and hit the release for the external front door. Then I plastered the smile across my face, walked out into the hall and waited for everyone to arrive.

Mack took the last step onto the landing, his eyes looking me up and down like he wasn't sure it was me. "Hey. Riley and Quinn aren't too far behind, they'll be here soon."

There was a weird tension between us. Me, not sure I wanted him to notice how much effort I'd gone to, or whether I pretended like that was how I always looked when I entertained guests. And him, well I had no idea what was going through his mind.

"Should we wait in the hall?" I asked, the fact we were still standing there not helping the situation any. "Or do you want to go inside and have a drink until they get here."

He didn't answer right away, taking a step closer and touching my cheek. "Let's go inside. Let me say hello to you properly before they get here."

My heart flipped, part of the anxiety I felt earlier easing as he followed me back into my condo and closed the door.

The smell of roasted chicken and vegetables wafting through the air mixed with the manly scent of his soap and shampoo. He looked amazing, dressed in a pair of fitted blue jeans and a casual untucked button-down, he pulled off his jacket as his body closed the gap between us. I couldn't breathe—and not just because of the Spanx—my senses rather than my sight tracking his movements as he draped his jacket over the back of my couch as my eyes stayed glued to his. He was unshaven, the stubble smattering across his jaw so sexy I couldn't help but reach up and touch it.

"This is new." It prickled under my fingertips as I followed the line of his face. "I like it."

His eyes moved down my body, sweeping up and down before locking back on mine. "Looks like I'm not the only one trying something new."

He was too hard to read, not sure whether he liked it or not. And I was either going to make out with him to distract myself or just plain ask outright. "My boss—err, Penny, you met her at the club when you picked me up—styled me."

His chin dipped as his brow rose. "Do you like it?"

"I'm not sure yet, but I guess I needed a change." I answered honestly, not feeling exactly like myself but not hating it either. "Do *you* like it? Does it turn you on?" Feeling brave I asked exactly what I wanted to know, not bothering to fish for compliments.

"Hayden, if *you* want to change something—whether it's the way you dress or something else—then do it. But let me make myself clear, as far as *I'm* concerned, you're perfect. And the only thing you need to do to turn me on is show up."

I wasn't sure who moved first, if it was me or him, our mouths somehow meeting in the middle with no further discussion. I loved the feel of it, my lips parting and welcoming his tongue as his hands pulled me roughly against him.

Concerns for my appearance or burning dinner were forgotten as my fingers pushed under his shirt and got cozy with his abs. Lord, Penny was right. When he looked like he did, who cared how complicated things were.

He pushed me against the wall, his hands going on their own exploratory mission as his mouth refused to leave mine. I loved the contradiction; how gentle and considerate he was while still able to kiss me hard and desperate.

A buzzing sound was the first thing that broke the spell, the cursing under his breath, the second, pulling his mouth away while holding me still. "That will be Riley and Quinn."

My head nodded, or at least I thought it did, knowing I should go check dinner or my face or at the very least move from against the wall. It wouldn't be a good look inviting them into my home for the first time disheveled with lipstick smeared across my mouth, but as Mack's hands moved down to my hips, I was seriously considering it.

"Right. We should buzz them up." My breath came out in ragged bursts, suddenly feeling too hot under all my layers. "You want to go down and walk them up? Give me a minute?" To find my brain cells and work out how I was going to get through dinner without crawling into his lap.

A smile edged across his lips. "Sure. We'll pick up where we left off after they leave."

While they were downstairs waiting, I was mentally trying to calculate how long that would be. "I like the sound of that."

Before either of us exercised poor restraint, Mack took a step back and headed to the door. He glanced over his shoulder—his wicked grin freezing me in my spot—before pulling open the door and disappearing out into the hall.

I didn't have much time, gathering my scattered hormones and reining in my pulse as I ran to my room so I could survey the carnage. Thankfully, it wasn't too bad, my lipstick only needing a quick reapplication and my hair to be smoothed out. Making it out into the living room by the time they were entering my condo.

Mack was first, one hand holding the door open and allowing Quinn to go ahead, the stunning blond, more waddling than walking, was followed by her equally impressive husband. They were a good-looking pair, albeit exceptionally tall, Riley at least three inches taller than Mack and Quinn towering over me. Both of them were beaming, wearing matching satisfied smiles while their hands interlocked like they couldn't bear to be away from each other. And if the way they exchanged heated glances was any indication, it was no wonder why she was pregnant.

"Hi! I'm Quinn." Her pretty hazel eyes met mine, unwrapping her hand from her husband's. "And you must be our new mom!"

Mack cursed, mouthing a silent apology as I blinked back in surprise, the energy radiating off her like a bomb blast. "Errr, umm. I'm Hayden. So nice to meet you." I held out my hand, not really sure what to do.

"Psssh, we hug in this family." She shook her head at my offer of a handshake and pulled me into an awkward embrace.

"Quinn," Mack warned, rolling his eyes. "Can we at least get *into* the condo before you start?" He held up the bottle of wine he'd obviously gotten from his car. "I forgot to bring this up earlier." A sheepish grin hinted he'd been just as anxious to see me as I had him.

"And I brought beer." Riley held up the six-pack he had in the hand not around his wife. While she'd let go of him, he'd managed to reposition his palm to her lower back. And if I wasn't so distracted by his cheeky grin, I'd have thought it was adorable.

"Well, that's a good thing." I regretted turning down the second bottle Mack had offered. "Please come in, dinner will be ready soon."

Quinn sniffed the air, pulling away and sidling up against Riley. "Wow, something smells good. You know Mack is a really good cook too. You guys must never want to go out to eat."

The girl had an unshakeable confidence I couldn't help but admire. She walked in without the hesitations I had of meeting her, her large swollen belly barely contained in a relaxed jersey dress and a pair of leggings. She was dressed comfortably—something I envied as well—but stylish, not seeming to care what anyone thought.

I nodded, agreeing I would have no problem with Mack cooking for me every night without pointing out my skills weren't that great. It felt kind of nice to take the compliment without offering a rebuttal, and something I was doing more of since meeting Mack. "Thanks, I hope you like it. My sister-in-law struggled with nausea when she was pregnant with her boys, so I didn't want to make anything too fancy. And I just love your dress."

Quinn beamed, lighting up like a Christmas tree. "Awww, you made something special for me? Hayden, that is so thoughtful, thank you so much." Her hands moved to her belly and gave it a rub. "And this is one of the few things that still fits me. But it's sooooo nice just being comfortable. Honestly, I'd have worn my PJs if I'd known you better."

"God, that sounds great. I'd live in mine if it were socially acceptable." I laughed, only half joking. "Well, I better go into the kitchen and check on dinner. Why don't you all take a seat in the living room and I'll join you shortly."

"You need any help?" Mack offered, hesitating while Quinn and Riley settled on the couch.

"Nope, got it all under control." *Having no idea if I actually did.* "Just relax." *At least I hoped someone would be able to.* "I'll be right back."

Then before I ruined what had been a fairly decent first meeting, I disappeared into the kitchen to make sure I didn't char dinner. And to get a glass for that wine because I sure as hell was going to need it.

Chapter 19

Mack

"**I** THOUGHT I asked you to tone it down." I shook my head as Quinn eased into the loveseat.

She shrugged, not even trying to hide her pleased grin. "Mack, this *is* me toned down. Was it the mom thing? She knows I was joking, and if not, it's important we find out what kind of sense of humor she has right up front."

"Quinn's right. You clearly make piss-poor decisions when it comes to your dating life, so whether you want to admit it or not, you need us." Riley took the seat right beside her, handing me a cold beer. "Although so far, so good. Let's see how she weathers the rest of the night."

"North," I warned, not in the mood for his shenanigans, especially when he had help. "Whatever the two of you plan on doing, don't. It was her idea to invite you, and you are going to sit, be grateful, and not treat her like an experiment. Consider it a personal favor, for me."

"Chief, this *is* for you. You think we're doing it just to amuse ourselves?" He rolled his eyes when I pegged him with a glare. "Okay, *just* to amuse ourselves? You're an important guy to both of us, and it's clear you're not taking your own advice and going slow, so it's up to us to look out for you."

"And how would you know what I'm doing?" He wasn't wrong, but it wasn't like I was dropping a knee and proposing either. And regardless of the timing, it just felt right with Hayden.

"Chief, come on. We've played cards for how many years? You suck at a bluff." His eyes widened to further his point. "Epically bad."

Quinn pointed to my cheek. "You also have lipstick on your face that you obviously tried to wipe off, and we're sitting in her living room waiting for dinner. So if this is a fling, you are doing it completely wrong."

"And do we need to remind you of Melinda?" North unhelpfully added. "She is still trying to screw with your life. I know she's *still* calling you, wanting fuck know's what. And at some point in your life, you thought *she* was a good choice."

I was just about to remind both of them I was a grown-ass man and didn't need their help when Hayden walked in. She had an empty wineglass in one hand, balancing a tumbler filled with ice and some liquid in the other. "It's lemonade. Not homemade, but organic from Whole Foods." She handed it to Quinn. "So, are you done talking about me or should I come back in another ten minutes?"

Fuck.

I wondered how much of it she'd heard, pissed off I hadn't shut it down earlier. "We weren't—"

"We totally were." Quinn cut me off, accepting the glass and taking a sip. "But you can totally talk about me after I leave. In fact, you can start right now while I'm here. I'm fascinated to hear what you think."

Well, I guess a nice night with regular conversation was too much to ask for. "Hayden."

I'd barely gotten her name out when she put her hand on my

arm and joined me on the couch. She shook her head, reaching for the wine and opening up the bottle. "I think you're stunning. There aren't many women who would look as radiant as you do so close to delivering and I love that you speak your mind. It's a good quality to have, and no one should ever make you feel like you need to stop. And if I could go back in time, it's exactly what I'd tell myself when I was your age."

My mouth shut, whatever I was going to say lost as she poured herself a glass of the red I'd brought and lifted it to her lips. "I also know Mack is a special guy, and if I were you, I'd want to make sure whoever he dates is worthy of him."

North leaned forward. "Look, it's not personal. He has always looked out for me, I'm just returning the favor."

"Hey," I waved my hand, feeling the need to remind everyone I was still in the room. "I don't need looking out for." *Especially not where Hayden was concerned.* "And I'm not sure what you overheard—"

"Most of it." She grimaced in apology. "The walls aren't very thick, and the condo isn't big. But if it makes you feel better, I love that they're so concerned." She shifted her focus to North and Quinn. "Honestly, I'm not offended. And Melinda . . ." She stopped, measuring what she was about to say. "Well, obviously she must be crazy."

"I like her," Riley leaned toward me, stage-whispering. "And calling Melinda crazy is an insult to crazy people." He winked at Hayden.

Jesus Christ.

"Surely we have better things to talk about?" I was positive discussing my ex-wife with my current girlfriend, North, and Quinn wasn't a good idea. But that horse had already bolted. "But if there's something you want to ask me, go ahead and ask."

Last thing I wanted was for Hayden to think I was keeping shit from her. Didn't matter it was neither the time nor the place for the discussion, and I'd rather get a root canal. I wasn't interested in being an asshole who she thought was playing her.

She bit her lip, hesitating. "She's still trying to screw with you?"

Thanks a lot, North.

"Melinda has issues with boundaries. But they are her issues, not mine. And maybe earlier in the piece, I felt sorry for her, so I wasn't as firm with her as I should've been. And now that I am, it pissed her off. Again, *her* issue, not mine."

What I didn't mention was Melinda's request I impregnate her. Partly because it was too fucking insane to even repeat. Insane. And partly because there'd be a better chance of North fathering Melinda's child, and he'd hack off his own dick before he'd cheat on Quinn, least of all with someone he hated.

It wouldn't happen.

Ever.

Which was the same way I felt about it.

Yeah, it was early days and we were still feeling it out, but I've never so much as glanced at another woman once I'd made a commitment, and I sure as shit wasn't going to start.

Of course, Hayden didn't have the benefit of that rock-solid understanding so letting her know my ex-wife was looking for a sperm donor wasn't going to do me any favors. Especially since none of it mattered. I hadn't spoken—and wouldn't be—to Melinda since the day after my birthday, so all of it was a moot point. Not that it changed the fact I was a hypocrite, deliberately withholding that piece of information after I made a big song and dance about not playing her, but it was for the best.

At least that was the bullshit I told myself so I didn't feel like a complete dick.

"Anything else?" I looked around, waiting for commentary from the peanut gallery. "Let's not be shy. I'd say the expectations of this being a run-of-the-mill dinner have well and truly gone, so no point holding anything back."

"So, I set up the dating profile for Mack." Quinn raised her hand. "But I never expected him to actually use it, and I almost died when Riley said he had. I still can't believe he is dating someone." She laughed, clearly pleased at the result. "I think I've even impressed myself."

Riley wrapped his arm around his wife. "She can't help herself."

"She can, she chooses not to," I pointed out, not sure why the hell she set the damn thing up if she didn't think I was going to use it. Of course it worked out for the best even if we were having the strangest dinner conversation I'd ever had.

Hayden blew out a long breath, putting down her glass of wine. "Well if we're being honest, I *really* want to change out of these clothes. I feel like I'm dying."

She pulled at the collar of her dress, fanning her face. "I don't have an ex-husband who calls me. Pretty sure he did it as little as possible even when we were married. And I didn't have to be coerced into setting up the dating profile, I may have even begged my sister-in-law to help me so I could find a match. But this," she pinched the fabric of her dress, "isn't me. I don't want to look like someone I'm not. And now I just feel like I'm wearing someone else's clothes."

"Girlfriend, life is too short to wear stuff you don't like," Quinn laughed. "And while that sweater dress is really cute, you should really wear what you want."

It had been obvious when I arrived that Hayden had gone to some effort. The dress, the hair, the makeup—all of it not really her style. Not that I'd have given a shit, if that's what she wanted. But I could tell she was hot and uncomfortable and that didn't sit right with me. That she'd done it for my benefit? Well that just made it a hundred-times worse.

"Okay, so here is what's going to happen." I slapped my hands on my thighs, wanting to get the night back on track.

"Hayden, I want you to go into your room and change. Put on your pajamas if that's what you want, no one will care."

Quinn coughed into her hand, not even attempting to be tactful. "Well I will because I didn't get to wear mine, but sure, okay."

"*No one* will care." I ignored Quinn, knowing she wasn't serious. "And while you change, I'll check on dinner. North and Quinn . . . I don't know, you guys can set the table or something."

Telling someone what to do in their house wasn't cool. The possibility Hayden was going to tell me to go fuck myself was high. But she didn't. Instead, reaching across kissing me before kicking up her chin and rising to her feet.

"I'll be right back and I promise it won't be pajamas." She nodded at Quinn. "And Mack, thanks so much for checking on dinner. It should almost be time to eat anyway."

With a promise I was on my way to the kitchen, she disappeared into the bedroom, leaving Quinn and North to hopefully stay out of trouble. I wasn't sure their initial plan had been sidelined, but I was hoping we could at least eat before any drama developed. And Hayden's chicken smelled really good.

Like she'd predicted, it was ready so I got it out of the oven, then went to check on her in the bedroom. It wasn't so much that I thought she needed my help —more like *knew* she didn't—but I wanted to have a word without the audience.

"Hey, can I come in?" I rapped my knuckles on the closed door. "It's just me."

She pulled it open, her arm sliding into a top as she finished getting dressed. "I'm almost done. But you can come in as long as you promise not to distract me."

"Not making any such promises." I kissed her gently before closing the door. "And for the record, I like this much better."

Most of the makeup had been washed from her face, her hair loosened so it hung around her shoulders. She'd also lost the dress and put on a pair of black leggings like Quinn, the bright red V-neck top another big improvement. That I could see her cleavage was an added bonus.

"I wanted to make a good impression. I know how much they both mean to you." She fixed the hem of her top, letting her arms drop to her side.

I tilted her chin, forcing myself not to kiss her because I knew I wouldn't be able to stop. "They do mean a lot to me. As do you."

Her eyes got wide, my words a surprise to her even though they weren't to me. "So, let's go out there and enjoy dinner without worrying about anything else. Because they're going to love you."

There was more I'd wanted to say but saved it for another time. I wanted her alone, to be able to say what was in my head and heart without a clock running down. And when I got that chance, I wouldn't be sharing her either.

Ignoring my efforts to keep my mouth to myself, she reached up anyway and kissed me. It was dangerous, my hands automatically locking on her hips as I wanted more. It would have to wait. The rest of the kiss and everything that went with it put on the backburner for later. And then I promised there wasn't going to be any holding back.

"We better go. I don't want them to think we're in here having sex." She tugged at my shirt, leading me to her bedroom door.

I nodded, my hand hitting the handle as I cracked it open. "Especially since I didn't get the pleasure of it."

North had put himself to good use and dished out dinner onto plates. I wasn't sure if he'd set the table or Hayden had done it before I got there, but everything was laid out ready for us to start eating.

"So, Quinn, do you know if you're having a girl or a boy?" Hayden passed around the salad before settling into her seat.

Quinn smiled, the scratch of cutlery hitting china as she shrugged. "We want it to be a surprise."

Bull. Shit.

She might not have done one of those fancy reveals—no pink cake or blue smoke—but I had no doubt she knew. And if she knew, the man sitting beside her knew too, which meant the surprise was meant for us.

"Guess we'll find out soon enough." I lifted my beer, smirking as I took a sip. "And I'm not the only one who isn't good at a bluff."

Quinn coughed, Riley's grin all but confirming it as Hayden laughed. I didn't care we weren't in on their secret, satisfied that they knew *I knew* they were full of shit.

And after the rocky start, dinner ended up being pretty fucking awesome. Quinn and Hayden talked about their jobs, Hayden confessing she had minored in photography before she quit college. Of course that was back when you needed film and a dark room, the revelation prompting a million questions from Quinn.

The only one she *didn't* ask, was the one that had been on my mind.

No, not the reason she'd quit college, her excuse of being bored and wanting to earn money given when Quinn had poked. But what she would be doing if she'd given herself a chance. There had to be something, and I could almost guarantee it *wasn't* her job at Target or transcribing medical records. But it never came up, Hayden going on to explain how she supported her shithead husband while he made his dreams come true.

Never had I felt so much dislike for a person I'd never met. Completely bewildered how he could have been so clueless to the amazing wife he'd had, utterly unconcerned for anyone other than himself. Sure, if he hadn't been such a selfish prick with no balls, who didn't know how to treat a woman, I'd have never gotten my chance with Hayden. But that he'd had a hand in her unhappiness, really jerked my chain.

Figuring she was volunteering as much as she was comfortable doing, I saved my curiosity for later, instead letting the conversation switch to Quinn and Riley. They each took turns, giving their version of how they met. *Uh-hum, Quinn's inclination to get involved in other people's relationships had her sending lace panties to Riley instead of the person they were intended for.* Not as shady as it sounded, but every bit as complicated, the two of them ended up together like it was meant to be. It was a treat to watch them tell it, both of them animated as they took her on the twisty road until they said I do. Standing up beside North as we watched Quinn walk down the aisle with her mom, one of the proudest days of my life.

"Well, if everyone is done with dinner," Hayden stood and started to clear plates. "We can move to dessert."

Quinn groaned, rubbing her belly. "Not sure I can fit another thing in. Dinner was sooooo good."

"It's nothing fancy. I just picked up some ice cream, but I have chocolate syrup and whipped cream. I have two nephews. They get treated to ice cream sundaes whenever they visit," Hayden admitted, her smile hinting she was probably their favorite aunt.

I grinned, the opportunity too good to ignore. "Sugaring them up before you send them home, huh? Here I thought you were sweet, but underneath it all you're diabolical."

"Payback on my baby brother is a bitch," she laughed.

Deciding to give dessert a pass, Quinn and Riley thought it was better if they headed home. Quinn had put in a decent effort, but Baby North was sucking the life out of her, her eyelids drooping while trying to maintain a conversation. I could tell Riley was getting anxious too. They lived over the bridge in Brooklyn, so had a drive ahead of them, and he was already on high alert with Quinn's due date looming.

"It was so nice meeting you." Hayden gave Quinn a hug, the difference between the one they'd shared at the start of the night, worlds apart. "And next time I go to visit my parents, I'll check out their basement. I'm positive I still have my old Nikon down there."

Quinn hugged her back. "I'd love to see it. I have my dad's vintage Pentax I still use from time to time."

"Easy there using the word *vintage*, Quinn. That camera isn't that old," I warned, having seen it firsthand and knowing it had been the flash new thing in '89.

"Relax, Chief." North clapped me on the back. "Vintage is popular now. You should probably go through your closet and see what you can sell on eBay, bet you're sitting on a goldmine."

I flipped him off, showing him exactly where he could put his suggestion. "Go home, North, or I'll show you how *non-vintage* I am."

We said our goodbyes, both Quinn and Riley giving me a not-so-discreet thumbs up before leaving. It wasn't needed, obvious how much they adored Hayden when they thanked her for the invitation. Meant a lot to me too, especially knowing how long a day she'd had.

"Dishes," she groaned, almost falling into my arms as we closed the front door. "If I don't do them now, I'm going to hate myself tomorrow."

My lips found hers, staying away for as long as they were going to and kissing her hard. "Here's an idea. You go get into bed, and I'll clean up."

"Mack, the kitchen's a mess. I'm a decent enough cook but I suck at keeping my workspace tidy. It will take at least an hour," she protested, obviously forgetting I'd already eyeballed her kitchen and seen the mountain of baking dishes and plates when I'd gone into check dinner.

"Either you're assuming I can't deal with a mess or that I've never done it before. And before you answer which it is, I'll remind you that neither of those is flattering for me. So go to bed, let me take care of it, and then I'll show you what other manly things I'm capable of." It wasn't so much a warning as a promise, determined to get her estimate of an hour shaved down to thirty minutes. Then I had other plans, ones I was very much looking forward to.

Her tongue flicked across her lips, a sexy moan spilling out that made me instantly hard. "That is probably one of the hottest things I've ever heard. A man offering to clean my kitchen and then come to my bed. How I haven't orgasmed already is a mystery."

"Just go get naked, wiseass." I playfully smacked her ass, not entirely sure if she was serious or joking. I'd never made a woman orgasm with words alone, but I was up for the challenge.

Her hands gripped the front of my shirt, fingers slipping underneath and tracing my abs. "Promise me you'll wake me if I fall asleep."

I shook my head, willing to curl up beside her and let her sleep. "Hayden."

"Promise or I won't go."

She didn't move, locked in a staring competition I didn't want to win. Hell, my dick had already agreed, volunteering to be the one who woke her if she happened to doze off.

"Fine, I'll wake you." I spun her around in my arms, facing her toward the bedroom. "Naked. Bed. You." The instructions as clear as I could make them.

She nodded, turning around and pulling me down for one final kiss. "Careful Mack, you're going to make it really hard for me to ever leave you. And I know how creepy that sounds, and I'm still saying it."

"Sweetheart, you're assuming that hasn't been my plan all along. And I know how creepy *that* sounds, and I'm still saying it."

As far as I was concerned it was a done deal, and I wasn't going anywhere.

Chapter 20

Hayden

SOMETHING HAPPENED WHEN meeting Quinn and Riley. Like a switch that had been long dormant had suddenly been flicked.

I'd heard them talking when I was in the kitchen, their private conversation about me initially making me want to pretend I hadn't heard. It's what I would've done months ago, smiled as I returned and played along. But for the first time in a really long time, I didn't want to, wanting to return to that girl in that club who didn't back down from what she wanted. And the one thing I knew was I *really* wanted Mack.

And not for a meaningless one/two/three-night stand which I clearly sucked at.

Nope, I wanted more.

Needed more.

And knew that it had to be with him.

So I ditched the Spanx, the dress, the façade I'd been trying to create and went with the *me* I'd shown Mack. It was liberating, and not just because I was no longer encased in shapeware. And guess what? They liked me anyway.

And when Mack came to bed—after the ultimate foreplay that was cleaning my kitchen—we made love like I didn't think was possible. It wasn't just sex, a silent understanding passing between us when he looked in my eyes that it was more.

And for someone who didn't want to be in a relationship, I'd found myself in one.

We saw each other as often as we could. It was challenging—with my two jobs and his rotating shifts—but we made it work. And for two whole weeks, I'd been walking on air.

"You sure about this. My nephews can be a bit . . ." *How could I phrase 'hyperactive lunatics' without making it sound like I didn't love them?* "High strung."

Gayle had demanded to meet Mack especially after hearing I'd met Riley and Quinn. Not that it was a competition, but she very clearly illustrated that his family and friends had met me. And other than exchanging some inebriated pleasantries with Penny, Mack hadn't gotten the full "Hayden experience."

"You've met some of the guys I work with. As well as Riley and Quinn. You think a six and eight-year-old are going to scare me away?" he chuckled, having no idea that Dean and Luka weren't average six and eight-year-olds. "Just ring the buzzer already. I love kids and it's freezing."

While there was no snow on the ground, the artic chill was unforgiving as we stood outside on the stoop. And even though Gayle and Matthew only lived a couple of blocks away from my condo, their street was littered with do-gooder neighbors who would call the cops if we loitered too long outside their beautiful house with a yard.

"Okay, okay. But don't say I didn't warn you." Figuring we were already deep in the hole, I pressed the buzzer, preparing myself for the onslaught.

Like demons had been summoned, the thundering footsteps and shrieking came soon after, Mack standing rock solid as the door flew open.

"Aunty Hayden!" Luka ran full speed toward us, tossing himself into my arms with no regard for his personal safety. "Did you bring treats? I want candy."

"Luka," I gasped, just managing to catch him before a trip to the emergency room was required. He'd already had two broken arms in the last two years and I didn't want to be responsible for a third. "You need to slow down. And no candy until *after*."

Dean, the older of the two, had yet to make his appearance which could only mean bad things. He wasn't shy, so it was unusual for him not to be beside his brother, his position finally revealed when both Mack and I were assaulted by a barrage of Nerf bullets. "Got you both!" he screamed from his perch beside the couch.

"You can still leave," I whispered, a wriggling six-year-old still in my arms and Nerf bullets tangled in my hair. "Turn around, Mack, and run."

It was too late for me, but he could still make it and head back to the safety of his nice place in Midtown.

"I'm not leaving, Hayden. And nothing they do or you say is going to change my mind." He shook his head, his feet staying right where they were beside me.

Obviously he was some kind of saint.

"Luka, Dean! I thought I told you not to answer the door." Gayle's voice was firm but kind, wiping her hands on a tea towel as she walked toward us. "I'm sorry guys, please, please come in."

Originally the plan was for dinner. Mack and I would come visit Gayle, Matthew and the boys and sit down for a meal where they would be free to grill him, or whatever else was required for the family meet-and-greet. But Dean and Luka were going to make that difficult. Mainly because dinner wasn't so much of a meal as it was a three-ring circus. Food went flying, arms and legs flailed, and conversation was reduced to shouting over the mayhem. So I thought it would be better to take a field trip instead, Mack generously escorting all of us to the fire station on his day off.

"I'm Mack, it's a pleasure to meet you." Mack held out his hand to Luka, who was spider monkey crawling up my torso. Luka slapped him a high five instead of a handshake. "And it's good to meet you too." His hand extended to Gayle.

Gayle grinned, giving me an appreciative nod and completely throwing me under the bus. "Likewise, glad I've *finally* got the chance. I've heard so much about you."

With hellos being exchanged, Gayle ushered us into the house, demanding Dean cease fire. Dean emerged to greet us, each hand occupied with foam-based weaponry as he nodded. "My dad says you're Aunty Hayden's new boyfriend and you better not be a douche. Just letting you know—if you are—I've got plenty more where these came from." He waved his plastic blasters like a South American drug lord.

"Jesus," I sighed under my breath, my cheeks flushing red.

Mack didn't laugh, which is what I expected from a grown man being cautioned by a child. Instead he sank to his haunches, getting eyelevel with Dean and held out his hand. "I could tell you I'm not a douche, but you have no reason to believe me yet. So how about we shake hands and get to know each other better, so I can prove it to you instead."

Dean's lip jutted out, considering the offer before ditching one of his blasters and slapping Mack's hand in a shake. "Yeah, okay."

With a peace deal brokered, and hopefully the capacity of further embarrassment shelved, Gayle hustled the boys upstairs to put their toys away while we walked into the living room where my brother Matthew was waiting.

"Hayden," he nodded to both of us before stepping forward. "Mack."

"Matthew." Mack held out his hand and shakes were exchanged.

It was tense, Matt attempting to play the part of a concerned brother with a conservative detached glare. But at five-eleven, he was coming up "short" against Mack's six-three in the intimidation department. That wasn't even taking into account the weight difference, my brother's job selling real estate not leaving a lot of time for the gym. And while he'd thrown a punch or two in his younger days, he was more versed in Mortal Kombat on the PlayStation than going a few rounds in an alley.

"Okay, you can stop, Matthew," I warned, not needing the pissing contest.

While I appreciated the effort, it reeked of too little, too late. He'd never so much as raised a brow when Cooper was treating me as his live-in maid, forgetting to turn up to family occasions. Even going so far as asking me to reconsider when I finally moved out and left my husband.

He—like my parents—couldn't understand why I'd walk out on a steady man with a decent job, chalking it up to me being bored. It took a lot of time before he finally understood how unhappy I'd been, the corpse of my marriage rotting away along with my self-esteem.

Matt tipped his chin, ready to argue. "I'm just—"

"I know what you're just doing," I cut him off, wondering if I was cursed when it came to first impressions. "But I'm an adult and can take care of myself. And I'm really happy." I looped my arm through Mack's, sidling up to his body. "So you don't have to worry."

Mack had been silent during the whole exchange, not buying into Matt's initial hostility and remaining neutral. I was positive no one was that Zen, his ability to observe instead of act an impressive feat I couldn't help but admire.

"I'm not going to hurt her," Mack added when it was clear I was done. "But like I told your son, I have no issue with you coming to that judgment on your own. Likewise, I feel it's only fair that I let you know I'm not going to let anything come between me and your sister. So if she wants me gone, that's going to have to come from *her*, and not *you*."

Chills traveled up and down my spine, Mack making it clear that, while he hadn't participated in the initial chest-thumping, he was far from lying down. That was exactly Mack's way, able to temper the extremes of the spectrum with just the right measure.

"Coming through!" hollered Luka, his coat in his hand as he barreled into the living room. "We going to see the trucks yet? I want to turn on a hose! Oh, can we go see a fire? I want to turn on the lights and siren."

Dean rolled his eyes, his impatience with his younger brother growing daily. "You can't see a fire, dummy. They don't let kids do that. You need to wear a special suit."

Mack grinned, giving the boys his full attention. "That's right. They're called turnouts and we wear other protective gear as well. And if there's a call you'll be able to see the guys get suited up, but then we have to let them go do their jobs, okay?"

Luka pouted, clearly disappointed he wasn't going to be riding shotgun to an alarm. "But I wanted to turn on the lights and siren."

"Oh buddy, we can do that right in the bays. No fire necessary." Mack laughed.

Dean tried to not show his excitement, probably thinking he was too old to be impressed. "Won't you get into trouble?"

Mack leaned down, trying to get as close to their level without folding himself in half. "Hard to get in trouble when you're the boss."

"Cool!"

"All right!"

Cheers from the boys erupted as they took turns high fiving Mack. Even Matt seemed impressed, giving his wife a hug while he witnessed his hellions being tamed.

It was so endearing to watch, my ovaries clenching at the thought of him raising a child from birth.

A baby.

Our baby.

God, I couldn't even think about it. It was waaaaaaaay too soon in our relationship to even talk about kids, and with my biological clock more like a ticking time bomb, I wasn't sure there'd even be a chance. So putting aside something that was probably never going to happen, I grabbed Luka and flipped him upside down. "Just remember I'm still your favorite even after he shows you all the cool stuff."

We arrived at Mack's station in Midtown shortly before noon. While we'd attempted to stay at Gayle and Matt's house a little longer, the boys were growing impatient. So the conversation was going to have to wait, Matt and his family following us in their SUV while I rode with Mack in his truck.

"Oh for fuck's sake," Mack cursed, pulling into the parking lot of his station, four men I didn't recognize waiting on us.

"Chief!" One of the men grinned, his hand going to my door and opening it. "Was beginning to think you weren't coming. Hey Hayden, where's the fam?"

I laughed, stepping outside the truck. "Hi, they're on their way, got caught up at a light."

Mack walked around to where I'd stepped out. Pointing to each of the four and blowing out a frustrated breath. "Hayden, this is Casey, Anderson, Phillips, and James. It must be a slow day."

"Come on, Chief, you know there's no such thing." The one he called James winked. "But we heard you were bringing visitors for a tour and wanted to make sure we rolled out the red carpet. Cap warned us to be on our best behavior."

Anderson stepped forward. "And Tibbs was here earlier, told us you were dating a hottie. Had to come out and see for ourselves."

Mack shook his head, dropping a quick kiss on my forehead. "He was right. And now you've seen her. Why was Tibbs here, anything I need to know about?"

One of the others—I couldn't remember if it was Casey or Anderson—was about to fill him in when Matt's SUV pulled up. Dean and Luka's eyes opened wide when they saw the four, dressed in their station blues.

"Save it," Mack instructed, walking over to the SUV and helping the kids out.

Luka and Dean could barely contain their excitement, ignoring my brother and sister-in-law's calls to slow down as they raced toward us. Not wasting any time, they got busy making friends, Luka asking where the trucks were, while Dean wanted to see the protective gear.

"Okay, let's go inside and start the tour." Mack's authoritative voice called everyone to attention. "Boys, you stick with me. Important people need to be up front."

Like he'd promised them flashy new iPhones, they snapped to his side like diligent recruits. It was impressive to see, following behind them with Matt and Gayle as he took us into the station.

"This is the breakroom, or the dayroom, and we have all our meals in here." We spilled out into a large dining room, the tables and chairs empty. "And if your parents say it's okay, we might see if we can rustle up some ice cream sundaes later."

Both boys cheered, their hero worship increasing, and we'd barely started. "Let's go check out the rest of the station."

Mack went from room to room, explaining its purpose. He stopped, answering any questions along the way, and introducing us to anyone who happened to be around. It was fascinating, seeing where he worked. The weight room was more impressive than some of the gyms I'd seen, Gayle and I needing a moment or two to stop and appreciate it. Of course that had nothing to do with the couple of guys in there working out with their shirts off, Matt rolling his eyes when his wife suddenly stopped talking.

"Don't get any ideas." Mack grinned, whispering in my ear. "And if you want someone to take their shirt off, all you have to do is ask."

I bit my lip, secretly thrilled he was a little jealous as I discreetly ran my hand down his chest. "Funny you say that, because I know exactly *how* I want to eat my ice cream sundae."

Mack laughed, linking his fingers with mine as we moved into the bays.

The doors were shut, three massive shiny trucks parked side by side aweing everyone into silence. It was strange that an inanimate object demanded such reverence, but to say they were impressive would be an understatement.

"This one is called a Ladder," Mack went on to explain, moving us all closer to the largest one. "And it does more than just put out fires. It can get us in places normal trucks can't, get on top of the flames so we can run lines into buildings, facilitate ventilation, and of course, search and rescue. And that ladder on the back can go a hundred feet in the air."

Luka tilted his head back, taking it all in. "That's so high. Don't you get scared?"

Mack laughed, resting a hand on his shoulder. "That's what training is for. You don't have time to be scared when you're on a call. You are doing your job, concentrating really hard and making sure that everyone gets to go home at the end of the day."

It was a really good way of putting it, and I was positive there were times that some people didn't make it home. Mack answered more questions about the difference between engines and ladders, and finally sat the boys in the cabin of the biggest one. He hit a switch that opened the bay doors, helping me into the truck with the kids before climbing in himself.

"Everyone ready?" he asked, grinning almost as wide as Luka and Dean. "It's about to get loud." He nodded to Gayle and Matthew who decided they'd catch the action from the ground.

The wail of the siren pierced the air, both the boys laughing as they covered their ears. Next came the lights, the flashing beams bouncing off the brick walls inside the bays. It was amazing, my pulse racing even though all we were doing was sitting stationary. And I could only imagine the surge of adrenaline you'd face if it were real.

Mack had just killed the siren and the lights when a call came in. The boys getting their wish, Mack helping us out of the truck so that Dean and Luka could go see the men get into their turnouts.

"Chief," the captain we'd been introduced to earlier nodded as he passed us on the way to the truck. "You might want to check your phone. North just called and is trying to get a hold of you. Think it might be show time."

Mack looked at me, pulling his silenced phone from his pocket and noticing the three missed calls. "Okay boys, we're going to have to take a raincheck on those ice cream sundaes. I've just got a call out of my own."

Chapter 21

Mack

WHILE I WAS a man of my word, sometimes a promise just needed to be broken. And as much as I wanted to deliver on the ice cream I'd promised Luka and Dean, Riley had called on his way to the hospital, Quinn having gone into labor.

"Thanks for the tour, and talking to the boys." Hayden's brother held out his hand before getting in his car. "Would really like to have the two of you over for dinner." He looked at the boys sitting in the backseat fighting over an iPad. "Maybe we can get a sitter, and go out somewhere and have a proper chance to talk."

I nodded, returning his shake. "I'd like that. We'll have to get it on the calendar, and sorry about the ice cream. Hope the boys aren't too disappointed."

Matthew shook his head and laughed. "We'll pick some up on the way home. And good luck at the hospital."

Hayden molded to my side, waving goodbye to her family as we stood in the parking lot. I was really glad she'd been with me when I'd gotten the call. Hearing North tell me he was about to become a dad, making me more emotional than I'd thought.

"I should go home." She turned to me as the SUV disappeared. "I can get a cab so you can go to the hospital."

"Do you want to go home?" I tipped her chin toward me, hoping the answer was no. "Because I'd prefer you got into my truck, and we both go meet baby North."

It was a lot to ask, sitting around a hospital waiting room for who knew how long, waiting for a kid whose parents she'd only recently met. But there was no way I wasn't going to be there for Riley, and I really wanted her to be there with me.

Her eyes were conflicted, but she hadn't said no. "You think they'll want me there? It's not the kind of event you bring a date to."

"Hayden, I think we can both agree you're not just a woman I'm dating. You're in here." I tapped my chest, the side that housed my heart. "And I don't want to say the words until you're ready to hear them, but it doesn't make them any less real."

There were a lot of things I knew.

And most of them involved the building we were standing behind. I could lead a team, bring everyone home safe, and run a battalion better than the man who'd taught me. I'd helped shape kids into men and women, watched them perform feats of unparalleled bravery alongside me. And I knew when I saw a kid destined for a prison cell, that he had the capacity to turn into one of the finest human beings I'd ever seen if someone would give him a chance. But of all those things, there was one I was even more sure of. And that was that I loved the woman in front of me.

"Come with me, Hayden. I want you with me."

Now.

Always.

Her fingers knotted at my shirt, and her answer wasn't a sure bet. But she had to feel what was between us, had to know it wasn't fake. "Okay, but if they ask me to go, I'm not going to be offended."

"Sweetheart, no one is going to ask you to leave." I pulled her in close, taking her mouth like I'd been dying to do. "Now let's get to the hospital. First babies usually take a while but with North and Quinn, there are too many variables."

Tearing myself away, I opened the truck door and let her climb inside. I moved around to the driver's seat, getting in and starting the ignition while Hayden's hands white-knuckled in her lap.

I got she was nervous, and not just because she thought she might not be welcome. But neither of us could have known we'd find each other on that website, and soul mate promises can ring sort of hollow when you've heard them before. Fuck knows, I understood that, seen it firsthand with my own dumpster fire of a marriage, and with Hayden, forever was going to have to mean more than just a ring.

We drove in relative silence to New York Presbyterian, Hayden keeping my phone in her lap and checking for any updates. Quinn was only five centimeters dilated so I knew we had time, easing off weaving through the traffic and getting to the parking garage without a speeding ticket or rear ending some asshole's car.

"Here," she handed me back my phone, "he said she's just measured at six, and to let him know when we got there."

Shooting off a quick message to North, we walked to the entrance of the hospital and headed to the maternity ward. I had a hunch her best friend and her mom would already be there so wasn't surprised to find Karli sitting in the waiting room, nervously flipping a magazine. "Mack," she gasped, giving me a hug. "Can you believe it's almost time? Oh my God, it feels like yesterday we were sitting in that coffee shop, and you were pulling those panties out of your pocket."

"Yeah, it does," I laughed, the day forever burned into my mind. "Karli, I'd like you to meet Hayden. Hayden, this is Quinn's best friend, Karli."

Karli didn't bother with a greeting, pulling Hayden into a huge hug. "Hi Hayden, so glad you could be here with us. I'm Karli."

"Hi, and I'm happy to be here," Hayden laughed, tapping Karli awkwardly on the back.

With the promise we'd text if there was any word, Karli left the waiting room to go get coffee. Quinn's mom was still driving in from Jersey, so for the time being, it was just us.

It was only once we were alone and I put my arms around Hayden that I realized how tense she was. "Hospitals make you nervous?" I asked, wondering if there wasn't a story she hadn't told me. "I'll admit they're not my favorite place either, but maternity wards aren't so bad."

Her body stiffened, either the attention I was giving her or the conversation making her edgy. "Hayden, if there's something wrong, I want you to tell me."

"It's not the time," her head shook, wringing her hands as she pulled away from me. "I'm fine, honestly. Maybe I should go get a coffee with Karli."

I grabbed her arm, knowing there was nothing *honest* about that *fine*. "Now is exactly the time. If there's something upsetting you, then I want to know. Was it what I said back at the station? Because Hayden, I'm not trying to rush you—"

"I want a baby." It came out of her mouth before I had a chance to finish. "I want to have a baby and I don't know if I'll ever get the chance. When I was married, well . . . it just wouldn't have been a good choice. But now, I worry I've missed my window. And things are going great with us, and I love being with you, but I'm forty-two, Mack. And the last thing I want to do is ruin what we have with something that might not even be possible."

It wasn't the hospital.

Or what I'd said.

Or concern about being unwelcome.

No, Hayden looked like she was about to jump out of her skin because she wanted a baby. And there we were, front row and center, showcasing what she thought she couldn't have.

"Is there any reason you wouldn't be able to have a baby?" I asked, not sure if there was extra info she hadn't shared.

"Other than not trying? Not that I know of. I mean, all my parts work, but nature is a funny thing. And I swear, this is not how I wanted to have this conversation. Please know I'm not trying to guilt you into something, or worse, trap you." Her eyes were desperate, the wringing of her hands stopping as she gripped my arms. "I know this is too soon. I know, and we can put this discussion on hold for later. I promise you that I will pull myself together and not make this about me."

Her admission took me by surprise, the idea of having a kid—well, I assumed that ship had sailed. Then came the whole mess of Melinda and her bullshit—it had probably messed with my head more than I cared to admit.

And sure, I wanted to tell her that I would give anything for her to be the mother of my child. And if it wouldn't get us tossed out and probably arrested, I'd strip her down and put a baby in her right now. Didn't care how long it took, or what we had to do to make it happen. And fuck me, I wouldn't walk away from her if my life depended on it, so "trapping" me was a non-issue. But the hesitation in me spoke loud and clear, and I wasn't going to lie and agree when I wasn't sure. Besides, I had a concession that I *knew* was going to be a game changer for her.

I needed for us to be married.

Yep.

Call me old fashioned, or delusional, or that I had my head up my ass. It made no difference to me anyone else's thoughts on the matter. But I wanted my son or daughter to have my last name, and I needed that commitment.

And as much as I'd like nothing more than to head down to City Hall, make it all legal, and then get busy knocking her up. But she was going to have to know about all of it first. Melinda, the attempts, the false hope—all of it. I was positive the enthusiasm for that knowledge wouldn't be shared.

"Hayden." I tried to think of something that didn't make me sound like a pussy, not knowing how long I had before Karli came back. "I, umm—" My mouth was dry, the words I wanted to say getting stuck in my throat as I opened my lips and nothing came out.

I loved her and nothing she said—included wanting a baby—was going to change that or scare me away. But instead I stared at her, unable to say any of it because I knew it would sound like I was dodging the issue or trying to change the subject. "Can we talk about this later?"

It wasn't even close to what I wanted to say, seeing the disappointment on her face as I tried to convince her I wasn't slamming the door shut. "I'm not saying no, I'm just—"

"Anyone want coffee?" Karli was back, two extra cups balancing in a takeaway tray. "I know you like Americano, Mack, but I wasn't sure about Hayden. It's black, but I got sugar, sweetener, cream, and almond milk, just to be safe. And it's caffeinated, which might be an issue if you prefer decaf. Unless you don't drink coffee at all, in which case sorry."

"Black is fine," Hayden smiled, pretending like she hadn't looked devastated three minutes ago. "Thank you so much."

I nodded to Karli, taking my cup and playing along with the bullshit. "Thanks Karli, I'll get the next round."

I'd barely taken a sip when our phones lit up. Quinn had progressed quicker than expected and North was letting us know it was go time. Next time we'd hear from him, he'd be making an announcement, and I had a hunch he'd be doing that face to face.

Hayden didn't keep her distance, taking her seat right beside me as we waited. She let me hold her hand, making small talk with Karli while we waited for Quinn's mom. If she was mad, she didn't show it, burying the hurt I knew she had to be feeling and laughing like nothing had happened.

Lori—Quinn's mom—arrived just in time, managing to say hello to all of us right before Riley walked into the waiting room. His eyes were glassy, swallowing hard as he cleared his throat. "It's a girl. Ava. She has a massive set of lungs, and looks exactly like her mother."

"A baby girl!" Lori cried, sniffling into a tissue. "Oh, can I go see her? Is Quinn okay?"

"Quinn is exhausted but fine. She was a warrior, didn't complain once. And I swear if there was a way I could love my wife more, that would have done it." He didn't need to say any more, Lori hugging him before Karli took her turn.

Knowing Quinn might appreciate some alone time with her mom and Karli, Riley told them to go on ahead and meet his daughter, and he'd be in soon. I could see it was killing him to leave Quinn's side, the scars of his early childhood probably rearing their ugly head.

"You did good, kid." I shook his hand, Riley pulling me in for a hug.

"Thanks, Mack. Kind of terrified, to be honest. She's so small and so perfect. I'm going to make sure I don't screw this up, or die fucking trying."

Those were words he never had to say. "Don't ever doubt yourself. Go be with your ladies, we'll come in and say hello once Lori and Karli have had their turn."

Nothing more I wanted than to go meet the newest member of our family, and yeah, even though there was no blood link, Ava was part of *my* family. But I was happy to sit back and let the others go first, maybe give me a chance to make sure Hayden was okay.

"Mack . . ." Riley hesitated, before heading back out the door. "Thanks."

He didn't need to say anything else because I knew exactly what that thank you was for. Had to swallow hard a few times myself, needing a minute to get my shit back together.

Hayden had watched it unfold, but had kept silent. Given the new information I had, I was fairly sure I knew what she was thinking. "Hey, you doing okay?" I wrapped my arms around her knowing it was a stupid question. How the fuck could she be okay with it? It was pretty obvious that she wasn't.

"Mack," her hands moved up to my face, stroking my jaw. "You don't have to protect me. I know it's your instinct and it is sooooo attractive. But I'm okay."

Wasn't sure I believed her, but didn't have much of an option to do much else.

After Lori and Karli had returned, both of them red-eyed and gushing about how cute Ava was, North invited us back to see Quinn. I slung my arm around Hayden, hoping she didn't think I was the biggest jerk of all time.

"Oh my God, she's so perfect." Hayden's eyes misted, Quinn peeling back the blankets so we could get a better look. "Riley's right, she looks like you."

"Well, she has her father's height," Quinn smiled. "Measured at twenty-two inches, and you don't have to be so smug." She glanced over at North who looked like he couldn't be prouder.

"Couldn't be helped, beautiful. You knew what you were getting into." He turned to me. "You want to hold her?"

I nodded, getting closer to Quinn, Ava sleeping in her arms. "Of course, but only if it's not going to mess with her too much."

Quinn grinned, extending her hands a little. "She'll be fine. Here you go."

It wasn't the first time I'd held a baby. Besides having two nephews, I'd also delivered a few myself. But it had been a while, the tiny bundle weighing almost nothing. "She's beautiful. And I think it's only fair I be upfront and tell you both this kid is gonna want for nothing. You guys say no, she's gonna get it from me."

"Funny, I remember you being more of a hard ass. Still are." North laughed, his assessment accurate.

"She's cuter than you, North. And grandparents get privileges."

As much as I wanted to enjoy the moment, I didn't want to be an insensitive prick either. Hayden might say she was cool with everything, but rubbing her face in it wasn't my style. She'd been catching up with Quinn, asking her important questions like how much she weighed and if the delivery had been difficult, and to the outsider, it looked like business as usual. She was too good a woman to have them believe otherwise, willing to put her own happiness aside for someone else's.

Deciding it would be better to go, I gave the newest North a hug and handed her back to her mom. There'd be time for more of that later, and Quinn had to be ready to throw us all out and get some sleep.

"We should go. Let you guys be a family and get some rest." I tipped my chin to North, hoping to convey how proud I was. "You need anything, you call me. Day or night."

"Thanks, Chief. Guess I won't be turning up to work for a few days." Riley rubbed the back of his neck, his leave not scheduled for another week.

That North had even given it a second thought was laughable. "Take as much time as you need, kid. And lucky for you, you have friends in high places. We'll amend your paperwork and I'll approve it. As much as your ego would like to think we'd fall in a heap, the station will work just fine without you."

Riley slapped me on the back, and I could tell he was wiped. It was definitely time to go. "I'll call you, and don't get too comfortable without me."

"Never, North. Now go be with your girls."

Hayden's eyes met mine and I nodded it was time to go. I wasn't sure if she wanted to hold Ava but she'd remained hands off, saying a final goodbye to both the baby and Quinn while I waited. And even though she'd been all smiles, I could see the lingering hurt underneath. Worst part was, I knew as much as I didn't want to, I'd had a hand in it.

It was only once we were outside of the hospital that either of us talked. Both of us opening our mouths at the same time, her "please forget about what I said," drowned out by my, "we need to talk."

"No, no we don't. Please, Mack. Things are good between us and I'm happy. You have no idea how long it's been since I've been able to say that."

We'd stopped walking, her hands wrapped around me as I did the same. "This is important to you, we should talk about it." And I wanted to. Wanted to tell her that green lighting the idea was high on my list of priorities, I just needed a little more time.

"Okay, then let's compromise. We'll talk about it later." She kicked up her chin, meeting my eyes. "Can you do that for me?"

Do that for her?

Hell, she had no idea what I'd do if she asked and that was the point. *She didn't know.* And I needed for there to be no doubts. Not from me. Never from me.

"Yeah, of course. Let's go enjoy the rest of our day off. Maybe I'll even cook for you." I kissed her lips, slinging my arm around her waist.

"Oh, I like the sound of that. I love it when you cook."

The smile was genuine, and while I knew we'd just put a Band-Aid over it, nothing was being solved at that moment. I could work with time and her being happy, content to spend the rest of the day in our own world. And the weekends were prized when I didn't have to work. During the week, our time was limited, so I wasn't going to waste a second of it fighting a battle that could wait.

"Good." I cinched her closer to me. "Then let's get you back to my house because I'm going to make you a feast."

Chapter 22

Hayden

"TOUCH ME."

It was my usual request whenever we were in bed, the contact never seeming to be enough as Mack's hands moved from my waist to my breasts. He was on top of me, his weight held off by core muscles that defied explanation.

"I want you to ride me." A guttural growl spilled out of his lips as he rolled onto his back and pulled me along with him. "Ride me, Hayden."

It had been a long time since I'd had that kind of confidence, to be visible while I took my pleasure. But it was easy to feel like a goddess when you were being treated like one.

Without hesitation my knees settled either side of him, my hands sliding up Mack's chest treated to all the peaks and valleys his muscular torso provided.

"Give me your cock."

God, I loved saying it out loud. Unafraid of sounding needy or vulgar, all my insecurities were ditched as I took what I wanted.

His fingers reached down between us, grabbing his shaft and giving himself a stroke while I watched. But only once, his fist gliding down the base, holding himself steady as I lifted my hips.

I didn't wait, glad he was already wearing the condom, sinking down onto him fast, making him curse out the rawest "fuck" I'd ever heard. His hands moved to my hips, encouraging me to rock while I held still, enjoying the fullness inside of me. "Just because I'm on the bottom, doesn't mean I can't fuck you, Hayden," he warned, his dark brown eyes simmering with heat.

The intensity was always there, whether we went fast or slow, in my bed or in his, that desperate need I felt for him was always reciprocated. And I loved it. Loved how powerful it made me feel, the confidence I'd once had returning as I teased him a little.

"I thought you wanted me to *ride* you." My hips moved slow, circling up and then down as my hands cupped my breasts. His thighs underneath me twitched, his eyes sliding down my body as I continued my agonizingly slow glide.

His hips bucked, filling me completely as I cursed out a moan. "Then do it," he thrust again. "Like you mean it."

In case his words weren't enough, his fingers moved to my clit and circled, driving me insane. My eyes slammed shut, a hand reaching out for purchase on the wall above the bedframe as I tilted my hips.

I didn't stop, rocking against him while *he* teased *me* as the tempo increased. It was unrestrained, both of us dueling for control as each one of my thrusts was answered with one of his. I loved it, the frenzied heat creeping up my back and exploding across my skin.

His back shot up off the mattress, meeting my lips while I writhed on top, his tongue plunging into my mouth as I grabbed onto his shoulders. "You're so fucking beautiful," he groaned against my lips. "And sexy. Got me so turned on I'm going to blow right through this condom."

It was a threat that wasn't idle, his cock so hard I wasn't sure how he hadn't come already, and my body taking every last inch he was giving me.

Without warning, my body tilted. His strong arms circled my torso as he lifted me, lying me down on the bed while still fucking me. Not only was it an incredible display of strength, but the action got him in deeper, making my eyes roll back into my head in euphoric bliss.

"Come for me, Hayden," he pushed in all the way to the root. "You're so close, I can feel it."

He wasn't wrong, my body teetering on the edge while he impaled me faster and deeper with each thrust, his fingers circling my clit. It was sensation overload, my body ignited with so much that felt good that the minute he dropped his lips to my nipple and sucked, I detonated.

My body spasmed, waves of pleasure flooding me as I panted for breath. He hadn't stopped though, the shudders shaking my body as I felt myself crest again.

"Wait, I think I'm going to—"

I didn't get to finish the sentence, tears spilling from my eyes as every nerve in my body twitched out of control. I'd never orgasmed again so quickly, the spasms shaking us both as he kissed me, growling my name.

His cock pulsed, coming hard and fast inside of me as he rode it out. Curses mixing with my name, as we both panted out of control. I was glad it had been like that, worried our earlier discussion had made him cautious—or worse, hesitant—with me.

"Mmmmmm," he chuckled, his lips moving from my lips to my neck. "That was nice."

I laughed, wondering out of all the adjectives he could have picked, how he'd settled on that one. "I'd say earth-shattering would be more accurate. How the hell did you even do that?"

"Not hard when I can read your body. It tells me everything I need to know." He shuffled onto his side, slowly pulling out before collapsing beside me.

"Well, not sure who to address the thank-you card to, but I am overwhelmed with gratitude." I rolled onto my side, snuggling against him. "I wish you didn't have to go to work tomorrow."

Selfishly, I wanted to have the whole weekend with him. For us to wake up late, spend the entire day inside, where all we did was eat and have sex. It was hedonistic and over the top, but I was greedy, not wanting to share him.

"You could come visit for dinner." His hand slid down my ass and gave it a squeeze. "I'll even cook if it helps convince you."

The offer was tempting, especially since I had no plans. Obviously, I could have spent the time more productively, like getting ahead on my transcripts or doing laundry, but I couldn't motivate myself to care. I wanted to see him, no *needed* to see him.

"You want to follow me into the bathroom? Join me for a shower?" Mack asked, not pushing for an answer on my plans for the next evening. He never did. Refusing to pressure me either way even though my indecision probably drove him crazy.

I grinned, my aching muscles longing for the spray of the hot water. "I'd like that. Will you wash my hair again?"

"Anything you want, sweetheart." He kissed me again, lifting himself off the bed and extending a hand.

Strong arms wrapped around me as we walked to his bathroom, only letting go when we got inside and he closed the door. He discarded the condom, grabbing two huge fluffy towels and laying them on the bench beside his shower and turned on the faucet. I loved the large stall—a treat from my shower/tub combo—both of us fitting inside easily once he was satisfied with the temperature.

Warm water and steam filled the space, our bodies intertwining underneath the spray. And when I looked at him, his large hands brushing away the wet hair from my face, it was easy to feel like it would last forever. He was so good, so kind, so sexy, so—everything, the most decent man I'd ever met, and I didn't think I could ever give him up.

"What are you thinking about?" His hands tilted my chin forcing me to look him in the eyes. "That smile is really good for my ego, but I'd love to know what's on your mind."

"I'm *really* happy, Mack. Things in my life aren't exactly where I'd want them to be, but being here with you is the rightest thing I've ever done. I'm in love with you. I know I should wait longer to tell you, but my feelings aren't going to change. I love you, Mack."

My body sagged against him, feeling relieved at finally telling him. I'd been nervous about the timing, hoping he wasn't going to think it was to convince him to get me pregnant. Or worse, worried he wouldn't feel the same way, and what that would mean for us. But the minute I'd said it, none of those things mattered. He didn't need to say it back, the freedom of being able to love him without worrying about him hurting me, enough. He just wouldn't do that. Even if he didn't love me like I loved him, he'd never hurt me.

I'd thought I'd been in love before, made a commitment to be with someone forever. And what I felt for Cooper—even in the beginning—didn't come close to what I felt for Mack.

"Hayden," his hands tangled in my wet hair. "God, I love you too. You have no idea how good it is to hear that. That you're happy—happy with me, happy with us—because, sweetheart, I feel the exact same way. And I'm so in love with you I can't think straight."

I laughed against his chest, amused that there was anything that could make steady, dependable Mack discombobulated. "Well, that makes two of us. I'm glad I'm not the only one who is wandering around in a daze."

His hands tilted my chin, and I knew he felt it. "It's different with you, Hayden. I swear, it defies logic and makes no sense. But this thing between us," he stopped, shaking his head like he couldn't find the words. "I wish I could take tomorrow off, do something special. But I'm not easily replaced and with Riley out—"

"I get it," I hugged him tighter. "But if that offer of dinner is still good, I'd love to come visit you. Maybe, you can give me another tour. A private one this time."

A wicked grin spread across his mouth. "You trying to get me in trouble, Hayden? I've got an example to set, and won't take kindly to being tempted when I can't act on it."

"Well, we'll just have to see then, won't we," I threatened, already scheming to find something ridiculously sexy to taunt him with.

His hand gently tapped my ass, not hard enough to sting but enough for the noise to echo. "Yeah, guess we will."

Dropping a kiss on my shoulder, he turned and got the shampoo, washing my hair with such care it was hard not to wonder how many times he'd done it before. But before I could let those evil and unhelpful thoughts take root, I pushed them aside, enjoying what was mine. *Mine.* It didn't matter what he'd done before and who with, I would let a past that had nothing to do with me steal the joy I had now.

From my hair he moved to my body, washing every part of me with such reverent care I felt guilty. I returned the favor, doing my best to make him feel as special and loved as he'd made me. The hot water heater was put to the test though, the stream thundering down on us running cold just as we were rinsing off.

"Here," he got out first, holding out a towel and wrapping it around my body while he stood naked and dripping in the cool air. "I don't want you to get cold."

It was those little things that made me love him more, only reaching for his own towel once he was satisfied I was warm.

"We should probably go to sleep. I know you have to get up early." My greedy eyes watched as he toweled himself off, rubbing his muscular body without the care he'd shown mine.

"You sure you don't want to grab a snack? You didn't eat much at dinner," he tossed the towel in the hamper, smirking when he noticed I'd been staring. "And I mean food, Hayden."

I laughed, my face probably spelling out exactly what had been on my mind. "I ate plenty, you cooked enough for an army. And unless you stop doing that, I'm going to need to go on a diet."

"Nope, I'm not stopping shit. And you don't need a diet, I love your curves." His hands wandered down my torso landing on my hips, showing me his appreciation. "So if you're not hungry for my cooking, let's see what else I can do to satisfy you."

"But you need to get up early," I half protested, wanting whatever he had planned to give me.

His lips came down hard on mine, kissing me and stopping the argument. "So I guess I'll be tired tomorrow."

Chapter 23

Hayden

MACK HAD WOKEN me briefly before he left, kissing me and telling me to call him later. I loved being in his condo, enjoying his comfy king-sized bed before taking a long hot shower in his amazing bathroom.

After I dressed—and shared the news of baby Ava with Gayle and Matt—I left Mack's condo and walked around Midtown. I'd left my car back in Inwood, Mack offering to drive me home Monday morning before my shift started at Target. So since I had some time to kill before meeting him later for dinner, and not wanting to blow up his phone with a million calls or messages, I window shopped. Wandering slowly down the streets of Manhattan, looking for that perfect sexy dress I knew would blow his mind when I turned up at the stationhouse later.

Most of what I saw was out of my price range or geared toward a size zero, but I managed to find a beautiful black, off-the-shoulder dress in H&M which fit and didn't require a second mortgage. I grinned in the mirror, imagining what he'd think when he saw me, excited about turning him on. I paid for my purchases, enjoying lunch by myself before heading back to his condo to get ready. I'd packed an overnight bag, anticipating spending another night even though it would be solo, doing my makeup while old-school hits streamed on my phone. My regrowth was starting to show, my hands playing with my hair as I contemplated it. I was sick of the color, the flat drugstore box blond doing nothing for my complexion. Maybe if I asked Penny for some overtime, I could justify going to a salon. It had seemed so frivolous and unnecessary before, but I shouldn't feel guilty about something that made me feel good about myself.

Unable to fix anything at that moment, I did what I could to make it work, without feeling as critical as I usually did. It was good to feel confident, to not automatically see my flaws and to know that regardless of what happened with Mack, I was changed for the better.

I was better.

And when it was finally six—the time we'd prearranged for me to visit—I could barely contain my excitement as I walked the short distance from Mack's condo to the fire station.

"Hey, you must be Hayden." A tall woman who looked like she should be a model greeted me at the door. "I'm Presley."

She was stunning, dark brown hair tumbling around her shoulders in perfect blown-out curls. And her makeup was flawless, the smoky shadow on her lids accentuating her gorgeous light brown eyes. Not to mention she had legs for days, the hem of her bodycon dress skimming her mid-thigh while showing off her ridiculous figure. I'd have been jealous if I weren't so happy, the twenty-something in front of me no threat at all.

"Tibbs's sister?" I asked, remembering when her name had been mentioned at the coffee shop a few weeks ago. "Wow, you're gorgeous."

"Thanks, and yeah, the jerk is my brother, but don't hold it against me. Mack told me you were coming and wanted you to wait." She hooked her hand on her hip, assessing me silently. Not that I could blame her, it's sort of what I'd been doing.

"Oh, did he need to go?" I asked, wondering where he'd gone and why he hadn't given me the message himself. "He doesn't usually go out with the crew."

She nodded, a small smile edging across her lips. "Chief is riding with them tonight because Riley's home being a daddy and they got called out. Probably just as well you didn't get here early, would have been harder for him to get into the truck after he'd seen you."

"Well thanks." My cheeks heated, glad my effort hadn't gone to waste. "I thought it might have been too much, but I just got this and wanted to wear it." My hands moved down my body as I stood up straight.

"Oh no, it's not too much. And his eyes are going to launch out of his head, trust me." Presley laughed. "If I didn't have to go to work, I'd stick around just to see it."

"You need to go?" I asked, hoping I'd have someone to wait with. I wasn't sure if there were other fireman in the station but didn't really know anyone.

"Yeah, I like to be at the club early. Meet with my front of house and security before it gets busy. Once the doors open, I like to be on the floor." She pulled out her phone and checked the time. "And I'd have already been there if my pain in the ass brother hadn't texted me to meet him here. Not sure why he couldn't just have left me a message. Weekends are insane for me."

"Is it as exciting as it sounds? Running a nightclub." I felt guilty for keeping her, especially since she'd just finished telling me how she needed to leave. But curiosity got the better of me and she seemed so nice.

She laughed, her smile making her even prettier. "It has its moments. You want to come hangout with me until they get back? It's not far, and at least there I can buy you a drink."

The offer was more than I'd hoped. Accepting the invitation so fast Presley probably thought I never went out. I even surprised myself, willing to put aside the venue—a club—in an effort to get to know her better. "Yes, I'd love that." I left off the *if you're sure*, I'd usually include.

"Then let's get out of here. I'll text Tibbs and let him know you're with me. Mack can call you when he gets back." She tossed her phone back into her handbag and motioned to the door. "I should probably let you know I have ulterior motives," she grinned. "Chief hasn't dated anyone seriously since he split up with his wife. Well, not anyone we've seen. And considering the amount of time he spends with my brother—who no shit couldn't keep a secret if his life depended on it—we would've totally known if he had. There's been no one. Well, not until you. So, naturally I want to know everything."

I couldn't help but smile, liking her even more. "Hey, if you're buying me drinks, I'll tell you anything you want to know. I'm pretty much a lightweight these days."

Presley shimmered, pulling open the door and leading the way. "Oh, we're gonna have some fun tonight."

She wasn't kidding when she said the club was close, the short walk to *Diablo*—the name of Presley's club—taking us almost no time at all despite Presley wearing sky-high heels. "The owner is an investor from Hong Kong. As long as I keep up profits, he doesn't care what I do with it." She flipped her hair over her shoulder. "It's a rare thing, usually they want to interfere or assume I need my hand held because I'm a woman. Doesn't matter I have a business degree and worked in clubs all through college. In this world, unless you have a penis, they want you either serving their drinks or dancing on a pole, and they can kiss my ass if I'm doing either of those things."

In what little time I'd spent with Presley, I could tell she was amazing. She was beautiful, yes, but she was also smart with a take-no-prisoners attitude that demanded respect. I could see it in the faces of her staff, each of them greeting her with status reports as she walked in, no one questioning who I was or what I was doing there as I followed her to the bar. "So what about you? What do you do?"

Ugh, the question I assumed would come up at some point. It was a little hard to dress up my job and make it sound impressive, which is why I just went with the truth. "I'm a sales associate at Target. And do some medical transcription at home. It pays the bills." My habit of justifying my work still making its way out of my mouth even though I'd been more confident lately.

"Well, I sure as hell wouldn't turn down that discount." She shrugged, lowering two highball glasses on the bar. "I can't go into the place without spending like a hundred bucks. Last week I went in for a throw rug and ended up with a cart full of stuff I didn't need. Oh, and I totally forgot the throw rug so had to go back."

"Oh, trust me, it's worse when you work there. I see everything when it comes in. How I make any money at all is a mystery," I laughed, watching her thank the bartender but letting him know she was fine to make our drinks.

It was nice to see, the staff being treated with respect instead of snapped at with demands. I'm sure they appreciated it too, the bartender smiling broadly at Presley before returning to slicing lemons.

"They have a lot of respect for you. Lots of bosses would have sat down, asked for drinks, not caring about what they had to get done." I nodded to the bartender who'd moved onto limes. "I bet they love working here."

Presley looked over at her bartender, his knife working steadily as he ignored us. "It's not hard to treat people with respect. And just because I have a degree doesn't make me any more important than any of them. You can replace a club manager fairly easily, but good staff are hard to find. The place would fall in a heap. And I'm not above making my own drinks.

I said I wouldn't make them for misogynistic assholes, but for us is a different story." She grinned as she poured in vodka, topping up with soda from a bar gun and then dropping in some of the freshly cut lime.

"So tell me, Hayden. You like working at Target? And I say that with no judgment. But I did warn you I was going to pry, and I get the feeling it wasn't the dream job you had in mind." She moved the drink closer to me, the interrogation having already started.

I sighed, wishing I had a better answer. "I dropped out of college my second year, and kind of got stuck. I've waitressed, worked in bars, but retail hours are more reliable, and no one tries to grab my ass."

The drink was perfect, not too heavy on the vodka, the lime adding a splash of citrus. "Wow, this is really good."

"Thanks, but it's hard to mess up a lime, vodka and soda. I leave all the fancy stuff to the professionals. And you still haven't answered my question. All you did was justify why you're there."

She was right about that. I hadn't answered whether I was happy, or what I'd rather be doing. Instead, giving her the explanation of why I wasn't doing something better. "It's okay. Am I happy? No, not really, but I'd be less happy if I was unemployed and living on the streets. Given a choice—and if I had a chance to go back and finish my degree—I'd probably go into compliance. Risk assessment. That kind of thing. It might sound boring—and my younger self would be horrified—but it's what I'm good at. Organizing comes naturally to me, my manager usually gets me to do the displays or rearrange the shelves when things aren't working. I can look at something and see a problem, even if there's no code violation. It's weird, but mentally I assess the environmental factors, the foot traffic, the store layout, and it all comes together. And I'm good at remembering things, and learning on the fly, which is why I do so well with my transcriptions. I haven't been to medical school, but I could give you a step-by-step account of what is required for a triple bypass, who needs to be notified, and the procedure to file with the insurance."

"It's not too late," Presley lifted her glass and took a sip. "You could take night classes. Online colleges."

I laughed, the idea of me studying after all those years almost ridiculous. "Or I could stay at Target and keep my amazing discount."

"True, but if you ever change your mind, decide you want to do something else? Give me a call. No one says you have to stay on the road you're on, just remember that."

My smile tightened, feeling slightly more exposed than I would have liked. It wasn't that I was offended, more that the whole idea seemed overwhelming. I'd known what it had taken when Cooper had gone back, and I'd been ten years younger then. Anyway, it didn't matter, I'd never be able to afford the tuition, and probably wouldn't qualify for student loans.

"So if you're allowed to pry, then I am too," I said, lifting my glass. "What do you know about Mack's ex-wife?"

Deep down I knew I shouldn't be asking, or at the very least talk to Mack about it. But I was curious, wanting to know what she was like from someone who didn't have a vested interest. And yeah, I wanted to know what kind of woman would toss away a man like Mack. Because no matter which way I looked at it, it didn't make sense.

Presley screwed up her face in disgust. "Melinda? Enough to know she's bad news. In any case, you're here and she isn't, so I wouldn't worry about her."

It was good advice, which I probably shouldn't have needed. Mack would've mentioned if she was still calling and I didn't want to seem like the insecure needy girlfriend who didn't trust him. I did. I totally trusted him. But something told me I shouldn't trust her.

Moving the conversation along to something more pleasant, Presley asked about Ava. Riley had sent everyone a photo with details, but Mack and I were lucky enough to see her firsthand. "God, she's gorgeous," I gushed, unable to describe her any other way. "Not that there was any doubt given her parents, but she was so incredibly sweet."

I'd been desperate to hold her but didn't want to intrude, figuring demanding a cuddle when I barely knew her parents was highly inappropriate. And I knew Mack was probably worried, catching the concerned glances even though he was trying to hide them. He probably assumed being so close to a baby would set off some deep-seated depression, like the smell of a baby could stir up post-traumatic stress. And maybe it did hurt, the longing in my heart a little harder seeing it up close, but I'd never begrudge anyone for having something I didn't.

"You going to be okay around here for a bit by yourself?" Presley asked, hesitating at the bar. "I have some meetings I need to take, but it shouldn't take too long. I can come and chat in between my tasks until Mack gets back."

I nodded, having no expectations of her sitting around entertaining me. After all, I knew she had to work. "Of course, I'm fine. And thanks so much for the drink. If I'm not going to be in the way, I'd love to just hang around. I'd rather wait in here than sit at the stationhouse."

My eyes floated to the stunning purple walls, the contrasting matte silver columns and bar lacked the tackiness of most clubs, playing off the blacker-than-black floor. It was beautiful, classy, and decadent all at the same time. And maybe I'd been desensitized or somehow brainwashed, because spending time in *Diablo* didn't seem like it would be a hardship.

"You're welcome to stay as long as you like, and I don't blame you. That place is made for function but isn't as sexy as *Diablo*. I totally picked the color scheme, the designer almost having a heart attack." She threw her head back and laughed.

Then taking her drink and instructing her bartender to look after me if I needed anything, she disappeared to the back of the club where I assumed her office was.

Despite being alone at the bar, I didn't feel lonely or weird, enjoying my drink as the bartender fixed me another without even asking.

"Probably should slow down on these," I lifted the vodka, soda and lime to my lips and took another sip. "I'm not sure how long I'm going to be waiting around, and I'm a lightweight. I'm Hayden, by the way."

"Hank," he grinned. "And it took you almost an hour to get through the last one, so I think you're safe from being drunk."

"An hour?" I asked, not realizing it had been that long. "It hadn't seemed like that long."

"Yep, the boss just finished her staff meeting with the front of house and we're opening soon. You seemed like you were in your own world, so I didn't want to disturb you."

A stupid grin spread across my face, most of the hour spent thinking about Mack. which was probably why I hadn't realized it had been so long. "Sorry, I wasn't trying to be rude."

"No need for apologies. Whatever you were thinking about must have been good." Hank winked. "Enjoy your drink."

I checked my phone, looking to see if I had any missed calls or unread texts. But there was nothing, no activity at all on my cell with the reception down to an intermittent one bar. Like an idiot, I waved it in the air, as if tilting it in a different direction would give me better service.

"You need to head to the back end of the club." Hank nodded to the phone in my hand. "These walls are lead-lined, makes it hard to get a signal. Or if you need to make a call, you can slip out the side exit. It's where the staff sneak out for cigarettes, so you'll be able to get back in."

I lowered my phone, shoving it back in my bag. "Thanks for the tip. I might go outside real quick and check my phone,

I'm expecting a call. If Presley comes back, can you let her know where I am?" I wasn't sure if Tibbs was going to let her know or if Mack was going to call me. In any case, I didn't want to miss the message and have Mack wondering why I didn't show up.

Hank nodded, pointing out the direction to the side door. "Yep, and if you see a redhead with a neck tattoo out there, tell her I need her back."

"No problem." I waved goodbye, making my way through the mostly empty club to where the side door was located. It was hidden by a small enclave, a false wall making it look like a dead end, but directly behind it was a door with a push bar.

It was unlocked, giving way under my weight as I walked outside into the cold night air. It was dark, my breath coming out in frosty bursts as a redhead turned toward me. "Um, you're wanted back at the bar." I pointed to the door I'd just come from, watching her stub out her cigarette and leave without question.

Alone, I pulled out my phone and checked the reception, the display on the top showing service had been fully restored. Unfortunately there were still no missed calls or unread texts, Mack obviously still busy. Tossing my phone back in my bag and trying to tell myself my disappointment was stupid, I turned to go back into the club when I heard a rustling coming from the hedge.

I wasn't an idiot, knowing that all bad horror movies started with some dumbass going to look for trouble in the dark instead of getting themselves out of there and calling someone more qualified i.e. the police.

My heart was thumping as I moved closer to the door, trying not to panic, the thundering sound of footsteps coming toward me.

Shit.

My arm was grabbed, my body spun around so I could see who had me, shocked when I saw their eyes, their words surprising me even more.

"It's *you*, I knew it."

Chapter 24

Mack

SHOP FIRE.

Two engines and two ladders.

The captain pointed to the side alley, "Chief and Leighton, around the back. There's access to the basement through there and the owner is unaccounted for."

Ain't going to lie, providing cover for North and going out on a call was an adrenaline rush. I missed being part of the crew, deferring the authority to someone else. And currently it was Cap running the show, even if technically I outranked him.

Leighton nodded, sticking to my side as we jogged down the alley. "Just like old times, huh, Chief? Bet you hope North makes a habit of knocking up his wife and taking unplanned leave."

"Maybe I need to make it a habit just to make sure you all stay in line." I pulled on my SCBA. "I'll take point, see if you can keep up."

Like I'd done a million times before—my mind switched gears, my body moving automatically—experience and training doing their jobs. Testing it first for heat, I busted the storm doors open, smoke pouring up the stairs that led to the sidewalk.

The fire was at the front of the building but spreading fast, the fumes and smoke pumping through the old HVAC system and making shit even harder. If the owner was down there, he'd be unconscious for sure. And that was best-case scenario, the idea he was trapped in the front where line teams were trying to access, not something I wanted to think about.

It was dark, our lights needed as we descended into the basement. Thankfully whoever owned the building hadn't pulled a reno, so it was still open plan. The beam of our lights able to get through the space without running into *Chip and Joanna* style walls. A shadowy figure was distinguishable a few feet away, no clue if it was a person, mannequin, or an illusion from the smoke. But whatever it was, wasn't moving. Leighton and I double-timed to the backend corner, the figure slumped on a chair, not responding to either of our calls.

"Do a quick sweep of the area, make sure he's alone." I signaled to Leighton, grabbing the guy off the chair and checking for a response. "Stay in my line of sight, Leighton. The ceiling could go at any second." He nodded, calling out into the smoke and doing a visual. Even though only one person was unaccounted for, I needed to be sure.

The guy was still breathing, but his pulse was weak as fuck. And with stairs our only access, I hauled him onto my shoulders, preparing to navigate our way out.

"Clear," Leighton screamed through his mask, nodding to the direction we'd come from.

"Let's bail."

The guy was heavy set, had to have weighed at least two-hundred pounds. But slung on my back, with my hands locked in, I moved with purpose, pushing up the stairs into the open air.

Leighton was right behind me, helping me lower him to the stretcher of the waiting medics. The guy hadn't so much as twitched the whole time, but as long as his ticker was still going, I knew they still had a chance.

Same couldn't be said for the shop, fire engulfing the entire structure. There was no hope of saving it, our priorities shifting to protecting the neighboring buildings and "surrounding and drowning" the blaze until it collapsed on itself. It was two hours before it was down to its foundations, the lines still running just to be sure.

"You miss it?" Cap tapped me on the shoulder as I pulled off my helmet, wiping my face. "You looked pretty good out there."

I laughed, having known Cap a lot of years. "Didn't realize you were checking me out. If I'd known, I'd have done my hair."

"Yeah, save that for Hayden, Chief. I have a hard enough time noticing when my wife does her hair." He laughed, walking over to give last-minute instructions to the crew.

Just the mention of her name put a smile on my face, hoping she'd stuck around. I wouldn't have blamed her if she didn't, our plans for dinner at least three hours ago, and I hadn't gotten a chance to call. Not there was a lot I could do, calls were unpredictable, and to say I was thrilled to be back on the engines was an understatement.

Taking the desk job had been the right thing to do. If it hadn't been for Melinda and a chance to start a family, I'd have probably waited and stayed on the engines a little longer. I fucking loved being in the field. But it was the one area I didn't have any regrets. Just like the woman I was itching to see, hoping that I hadn't pissed her off too much by being so late.

Presley had showed up just as we were leaving, Tibbs having said he wanted to share some intel he'd gotten on the cocksucker she used to date. Not that he'd shared it with me, but I was grateful she'd offered to wait around until Hayden arrived so she didn't think I'd completely bailed.

Pity I wasn't feeling all that grateful when we got back to the stationhouse and found it empty. No Hayden or Presley, and no note either.

"Chief, you got a second?" Tibbs was at my door as I pulled my cell from my desk drawer. "By the way, Presley left a message that she took Hayden to the club to wait. I'd like to think she was being considerate but we both know it was probably an interrogation mission. Sorry, but you know I've got no control over my sister."

"Jesus Christ." I scrubbed my face with my hand, Presley was almost as bad as Quinn when it came to other people's business. Fuck only knew what they'd talked about. Still, I was glad she had someone to wait with, hoping Presley hadn't gotten her so liquored up she could no longer walk straight.

"Let me get things squared away with my woman, and then we'll have that chat." I nodded to Tibbs making it clear that call would be happening in private.

"Got it. I'll call Presley while I'm waiting. Give me a yell when you're ready but take your time." He grinned, closing the door behind him as he left.

Not a lot I could do about that smirk, or what he was thinking, and I didn't give a shit. It was clear to anyone who knew me that Hayden wasn't some passing phase and if they wanted to ride my ass about it, I welcomed it.

And what do you know, she'd left a message.

Trying not to have the same smug ass look on my face that Tibbs had when he left, I swiped the screen to open the unread text. I wanted to see her, hoping she would consider coming back to the station and I could make good on that promise of dinner.

"WHAT THE FUCK!"

The adrenaline I'd felt back in the engine was nothing compared to that moment. My chest felt tight, my pulse drumming so fast I wasn't sure I wasn't having a heart attack as I slammed my fist down so hard on my desk the wood actually groaned.

"You okay, Chief?" The door swung open, Tibbs and Leighton both looking in. "We heard you yell."

"What the hell did your fucking sister say?" I fought the urge not to pick up the kid and put him through a wall. "You get Presley on the phone right now!"

I could feel my blood pressure rising, my muscles twitching with the need to do something as I couldn't stand still. I paced, reading the message over and over, like giving it another look would change the words.

Nope.

No such luck.

"What's going on?" Tibbs looked confused, his phone still in his hand instead of up against his ear like I fucking asked. I swear, if it was someone's idea of a sick joke, heads were going to roll.

"Hayden sent me a message." I looked down at my phone again, rereading it for what felt like the hundredth time. "It's just. . . . she's. . . ." The words not making sense even as I said them. "Said she was done."

I couldn't even continue, too many emotions going through my body to trust myself to make a coherent sentence. What the fuck had happened in a few hours? We'd been happy, telling each other that we loved each other, and then she what? Decided she changed her mind? Nope, she wouldn't have come to that conclusion on her own. So whatever was responsible was more than just a change in fucking heart.

"What?" Leighton looked surprised so at least I knew he wasn't in on it. "You sure you didn't read it wrong?"

"Did I read it wrong?" I laughed, the fucking joke on me because there was no other interpretation. "You tell me." I tossed my phone to Leighton, the message on the screen still burned into my mind even though I was no longer looking at it.

Mack,
It's over between us. We clearly want different
things and if we continue, someone is bound to

get hurt. Please, don't try and call me, I won't answer. Trust me, this is for the best. Goodbye. Hayden

Tibbs read over his shoulder, shaking his head. "Chief, this has to be a mistake. She doesn't seem like—"

"Get your sister on the phone now." The words barely audible through my clenched jaw. "She was probably the last person who spoke to her, and I want to fucking know what the hell was said."

Wising up and not wasting time with stupid questions, Tibbs got busy on his phone and dialed. Not that I even knew what I was going to do with the information, or how I was gonna fix it, but accepting shit was over between me and Hayden wasn't happening. If she wanted it over, she was going to have to tell me to my face. No way in hell I was giving her the easy way out.

What was probably seconds felt like hours as we waited for Presley to answer, Tibbs giving his sister the rundown of the situation. I didn't even give a fuck that my business was out there when previously I didn't share shit. The need for me to find out what happened, superseding my desire to maintain my privacy. Fuck, if it got me a resolution and I was able to work things out with Hayden, I'd take out an ad in *The New York Times*.

"Presley said she left the club a little bit ago, so she assumed she was with you. Bartender saw her go outside to check her phone and didn't come back." Tibbs held his phone from his ear, relaying what his sister had told him. "Chief, apparently she'd asked about Melinda."

"Fuck!"

Like a bad dream, every worst-case scenario raced through my mind. The mystery of *someone bound to get hurt* probably connected to the worst mistake of my life. No, not the time I stood in a church and married a woman who clearly didn't have a heart or a fucking soul. But not telling Hayden about Melinda's stupid plan about me fathering her child.

What had been intended as protecting her, had probably blown up in my face, Melinda's habit of hanging around *Diablo* and Hayden's sudden goodbye, more than just a coincidence.

I shook my head, unable to think straight. "Ask Presley if Melinda is there, I have a hunch I already know the answer."

Tibbs brought the phone back to his mouth, the question asked and answered as he nodded his head. "She's sitting at the bar."

And there was my complete lack of surprise.

It wasn't a secret I'd started dating, my new relationship probably reaching Melinda's ears. And it didn't take a rocket scientist to work out that in an effort to piss me off and get my attention, she'd probably confronted Hayden. Because that's what Hayden needed to hear, that I—even though there wasn't a chance—was considering fathering someone else's baby when I hadn't agreed to hers. And if ever there was a point I could go back in time, it would have been at that moment.

"Good, tell Presley to keep her there if she tries to leave. I'm on my way." I grabbed the phone and started to dial. Hayden's request for me not to contact her was only going to last until I'd spoken to my ex-wife, and after that, she was going to be shit out of luck on me staying silent. "Hey, Keys, it's Mack. I know it's short notice, but I've got a personal situation I need to take care of. Any chance you could cover me for a few hours?"

Tibbs and Leighton looked on, no doubt wondering if they should leave or hang around. Honestly, I didn't give much of a fuck what they did, my focus making sure I didn't screw over my crew when I walked out the door. And make no mistake, I wasn't waiting until tomorrow to work it out, the need for me to set shit straight so high I wouldn't be any good anyway.

Keys knew that me asking was enough for it to be an emergency, not bothering to question my motives. He probably assumed it had something to do with North and the baby, and I didn't have time or the inclination to set him straight. Instead, he was already in the car on his way over, me ending the call and letting Cap know the situation before I left.

"You need anything?" Cap asked, the serious look in his eyes reflecting the one I was wearing. "I can call Marques down in the precinct, get him to do a wellness check at her address."

Yeah, that would go down well. One, for using public resources for sorting out my love life, and two, having Hayden even more pissed off at the invasion of her privacy. Nope, this shit needed to be handled personally. By me.

"Nope, I've got it. But I'll call you if anything changes. Keys is on his way. I'd wait for him to get here but—"

"Go," Cap nodded, knowing the clock was ticking and I had no plans to wait. "We're good here."

Just as well.

Without a final goodbye, I grabbed my keys and drove to *Diablo*. It would have been quicker to walk—the traffic on the streets making the journey take longer than it should—but I was going to need my wheels when I went after Hayden, and didn't want to double back.

I parked behind the club with no shits given the area was reserved for staff. Getting out of my truck and heading to the side door, going into *Diablo* through the staff entrance rather than circling round to the front.

"Mack." Presley saw me the minute I had made it into the main part of the club. "Just calm down. I know she's a bitch, but you can't lose your cool in here or I'll have to kick you out."

It was bewildering to me she even needed to issue the warning, the idea I'd ever hurt a woman so fucking foreign it wouldn't even be a possibility. But I guess the look in my eyes was new too, so there wasn't a lot of precedent on what I was going to do.

"I've never so much as raised my voice to that woman, let alone a hand. But I swear to God, Presley, if she has fucked this up for me, you're going to need a lot more than your beefed-up security to toss me out."

Ignoring the warning both from Presley and the one in my head, I stalked over to the woman who once shared my last name. Predictably she was busy flirting with some douchebag at the bar. "Melinda."

The sound of her name made her turn, her eyes opening so wide they almost dropped out of her head as she took me in. And I wasn't sure if it was because I was standing there, or because I was ready to start World War III.

"Mack, oh my God. I can't believe you're here. I just *knew* you'd turn up eventually." She ignored the douchebag, jumping off of her stool and launching herself at me. Her hands around my neck felt like acid, her touch so repulsive I had to fight the urge to throw up.

Ripping her arms from my body, I took a step back. I didn't know how or what her involvement was, but I was determined to find out. "What the fuck did you do?"

She had the nerve to look surprised, her brows scrunching in confusion like she wasn't the devil incarnate.

"What do you mean? Is this about me offering one of your guys a blowjob? I mean, they're cute and all, Mack, but I only offered because I knew they'd turn me down and then go running to you." She laughed, finding the whole thing amusing, as I moved her to the side, my hands around her arm gripping tighter than I probably should.

"I don't give a fuck who you blow. This is about Hayden."

She pulled her arm from my grasp, narrowing her eyes as the smile slipped from her mouth. "Who the hell is Hayden? Is that why you won't give me a baby? I swear, you're such a pussy, Mack. If you don't want to fuck me, just jack off into a jar and I'll take care of it."

There was a time when I thought I loved her.

I must have had a brain injury or psychosis, but there definitely was a time when I looked at her and thought she was it for me. What I didn't know was it had never been love, me mistaking her need for me, the hunger for my attention as anything other than the narcissism it was. And since meeting Hayden, and falling in love with her, there was no denying I'd had no clue before.

"Melinda, I'm going to ask you one last time." I leveled her with a stare. "Do you have anything to do with Hayden leaving?"

She didn't get to answer, Presley yanking on my arm so hard I was positive it was one of her goons. "Mack, it wasn't her. I went and checked the surveillance footage. You need to come with me."

Chapter 25

Hayden

LEWIS WRIGHT WAS the younger brother of my ex-husband. They didn't get along, Cooper not having spoken to Lewis for at least two years before our divorce. I knew money had been involved, a cash transfer for five grand from our joint account to Lewis had never been paid back. But like the dutiful wife I'd become, I didn't ask questions, assuming if Lewis was asking for the cash, there must have been a good reason. And while we'd never been super close, I sympathized with him and his plight of being misunderstood.

"What the hell, Hayden? I can't believe you got yourself messed up with these people. They aren't like you or me." His eyes looking left and right as he tossed me into a waiting car before getting into the driver's seat. "That was the staff entrance, so don't even try and tell me you aren't involved."

When he'd grabbed my arm outside the club, I'd assumed he was some lowlife looking to rob or attack me. I never expected to *know* the lowlife. But hadn't it been a not-so-lovely surprise when it was discovered that not only was he my ex-brother-in-law, but Presley's ex-boyfriend—the same guy Mack and the others had been looking for. I'd thought about struggling, making enough noise to attract attention but something inside stopped me. Knowing he would do something worse.

"I'm dating Mack," I answered, wondering if he was going to kill me or had other plans. "It's new."

His head whipped around, eyes widening as he started the car. "You're dating Mack? Did you lose your fucking mind? What the hell is wrong with you? He's an even bigger asshole than Cooper. And have you seen his ex-wife? No offense, but she's sexy as hell. He's probably just using you to make her jealous, assholes like him do it all the time. Trust me, he is playing with you for sure. And if for some reason he doesn't end up back with his hot piece of ass ex, he'll find a new toy. They're all the same, Hayden. And they don't give a fuck. You should be thanking me for setting you straight; I'm doing you a favor."

Hearing Mack's ex-wife was beautiful felt like a slap in the face. I'd always suspected, but could've lived without the confirmation, ignoring his past and everything that came with it. And I hated that Lewis knew him—knew them both—trying to taint what I knew wasn't true. Mack didn't want Melinda, and beautiful or not, he wasn't trying to win her back. But there was no hiding the hostility, the mention of Mack's name making the anger rise in Lewis.

"What are you going to do with me?" I asked, watching as he entered traffic, his Audi easing in behind a huge SUV. "What is it that you want?"

He sneered, rubbing his face erratically like he was on something. "Well, considering you totally fucked up my plans of getting into the storeroom and robbing the place, I figure you owe me. We're going to go to your place. I need time to think."

"You were going to rob *Diablo*?" I asked, not understanding how he'd planned to do that. There was security, cameras, not to mention he'd already been flagged for breaking into her apartment. What was he going to do? Pull a pair of pantyhose over his head and try and take it with a single 9mm?

His jaw clenched, swearing under his breath in annoyance. "Well I definitely can't let you go now, can I? And yes, I might not have gotten a run at the safe but her storeroom is a fucking sitting duck. You know how much money is just sitting in her inventory? All those fancy bottles of liquor, waiting for cocksuckers to just drop their black AmExes? Please. I know a guy who can move that shit in a night and have ten Gs sitting in my hand by morning. Now, where the fuck do you live? Don't make me ask again."

"Go to 40 West 225th Street in the Bronx." I shook my head, my grip tightening on the door handle.

He grabbed my arm, while keeping his other hand on the wheel. "That better be where you live and not some game, Hayden." He hissed low, his warning unnecessary. "Fucking Mack is stupid, but screwing me over will be terminal."

It was dumb luck he'd seen me, questioning my motives for loitering around the staff exit. Assuming it was some freaky coincidence that we were at the same place at the same time. It wasn't until I saw the gun in his waistband that I started to panic, knowing our meeting—both of us being there—wasn't so much of a chance.

"I'm not," I whispered back, not wanting to agitate him further. The distance between us wasn't enough. If Lewis fired, there was a very good chance that shot would be fatal, so I needed to play it smart. "I can see the gun, Lewis and I'm not stupid. As for dating Mack, he was a nobody. Someone to distract me because I was lonely after the divorce."

He didn't trust me, keeping the tight grip around my arm as he looked ahead out the windshield. "So where the fuck are we going?"

"We're going to where I work, okay. I'm not taking you to my house."

Not sure if his plan to rob Presley's inventory would have worked, but that had changed when he saw me. I had no doubt he probably would have tried to hurt Presley, or someone else, so that I'd managed to get him away from there—and from her—made me feel good even though I was scared. I tried not to shake, refusing to let him see how rattled I was, focusing on the man I used to know when he hadn't threatened my life.

"What the fuck? I said I wasn't playing games, Hayden. You think taking me to a Taco Bell is going to save you? I said I need time to think."

Fear bubbled at my throat, wondering if I should've put up a fight and risked it at the club. I had no idea what I was doing, literally making it up as I went along. "I don't work at Taco Bell, and haven't for a very long time. Target has a big parking lot, no one will even notice this orange car. It's less obvious than going to my place."

"Fine," he released my arm, returning both hands to the steering wheel. "But I'm only giving you one warning."

There was no way I'd bring him to my condo. Not only did I not want to be alone with him, but having him know where I lived was something to be avoided at all costs. My senses screamed with the need to get away, but I forced myself to be brave. I had a chance to change the narrative, and I was going to take it no matter how slim it was.

Trust.

I needed to earn his trust.

"I need to text Mack, he was expecting me." I fumbled in my purse for my phone, his body immediately tensing. "You can read what I write, Lewis. No funny business, I swear. But if I don't say anything, he's going to come try and find me." *Or worse—I finished in my head—track my phone and put himself in danger.*

He nodded, his eyes dropping to my screen as I typed out a message I knew would hurt Mack as much as it would hurt me.

It was the only thing I could think of that would stop him from coming after us. He'd hate me, no doubt be confused, and think I'd played the game that I promised I wouldn't. But he'd never pushed, giving me space whenever I needed it, and I was relying on that.

My body didn't relax until after I'd hit send, Lewis raising a brow over my breakup via text. He seemed pleased, a smile crossing his lips as he relaxed. "You should have told him you were fucking someone else," he laughed. "Not like he isn't used to it, his wife sure was. I wish I could see his face when he reads it. Fuck him. Fuck all of them."

I knew what I was doing was stupid. That I needed to call the police somehow and let them deal with it. You know, the people actually trained for these kinds of situations. And if anyone else were doing what I was, I'd have told them they needed to be committed.

Barely knowing Presley, I wasn't bound to action like if it had been Gayle or even Penny. But if Mack were in my place, he absolutely would have done something. Without even thinking about it, he'd have put his own safety on the line. If it meant possibly saving someone else, he'd have done it without a second of hesitation. And I had the chance to do that, for once in my life do something that was bigger than myself. Not just for Mack, or Presley, and not to prove the point. But because it was the right thing to do, and I was done being scared.

"What did she do?" I asked, hoping to gain more information. "It's unlike you to be angry for no reason. She must have done something to provoke you." The words felt thick in my throat, my faux compassion making me want to vomit.

He nodded, believing the lie at least in part as he kept his voice low. "That fucking spoiled bitch used me just like that piece-of-shit fireman was using you. That's what they do. Treat us—the people beneath them—like garbage."

She used him?

It didn't make sense. What could he give her that she couldn't have gotten herself?

"People like us?" The question unintentional, wondering how he saw me as anything like him.

His voice hardened, throwing me a hateful glance before returning his eyes back to the road. "They fuck *us*, Hayden. Pretend to give a shit but they don't. We're just amusement. That's what you were to Mack, a way to get his dick wet until his hot wife came to her senses and took him back. And Presley was just slumming it with me. She fed me bullshit about wanting me to be successful, when really she was looking to keep me down. All she had to do was pick up a phone and get me into the clubs like we fucking agreed. Instead, she kept blowing me off, telling me the timing wasn't right. The fucking timing was perfect, my DJ sets were tight and I was pulling good numbers on the socials. But she didn't give a fuck. Didn't drop my name once or so much as lift her perfectly manicured finger to help. Nothing. And then she had the fucking nerve to tell me to contribute to her fucking rent, like she wasn't pulling six figures sucking dick at that club. Yeah, manager, whatever. Like I believe that shit."

I nodded, pretending to agree and finding it hard to swallow. "Is that why you were going to rob *Diablo*? And why you broke into her apartment? To teach her a lesson?"

"I couldn't give a fuck about that whore. She wasn't going to help me so I'd find someone who will. But I know she's got money stashed in that place, and I deserved to be paid for the time I invested. Why do you think I went when she wasn't home? But the princess just had to get other people involved, playing the fucking victim. When in reality, the real person who got fucked is me. Man, she's a vindictive slut. I should've fucking shot her when I had the chance."

"Money? You need money?" I forced myself to look at him, knowing we were getting closer to our destination. The store was still open, Penny working late. And as much as I didn't want to put anyone else in danger, I had an idea that might just work. "I can get you money, Lewis."

His eyes narrowed, his knee bouncing with impatience. "Yeah, how much have you got?"

"I don't have a lot, Lewis. Between the divorce and the mortgage for my new place, I might be able to scrape a thousand? Fifteen hundred maybe? But I know a place we can get more." I pointed to the windshield, the red sign coming into view. "But you're going to have to trust me, and I need to know what it's for."

He pulled into the parking lot, choosing a spot away from the entrance that wasn't flooded by the huge overhead lights. We were just another parked car in a sea of parked cars, disguised by a battalion of SUVs, trucks, and sedans owned by non-suspecting people getting their late-night shopping fix. I'd been stalling up until that point, but if I was going to go all the way through with it, then I needed to know why.

"Tell me, Lewis. Is it drugs?"

People wandered in and out of the lot, ignoring us entirely. To them we were just another couple, possibly having a disagreement because I'd dragged him out to the store on a Sunday night.

He grinned, seeming to find the question amusing. "Like you and Cooper didn't smoke weed when you first met. Please. Who do you think bought me my first joint? I've dabbled, but my drug of choice is the ponies. And the people I owe money to aren't the forgiving kind."

I was just about to ask how much when my phone buzzed in my hand, his eyes connected with mine as the screen lit up with an incoming message. It was Mack, both of us going for my cell at the same time.

"Don't fuck me, Hayden." He gave me a pointed look. "Read it. Out loud."

Nodding, I opened the message, clearing my throat as I read Mack's brief response. "*Hayden, you want it over, then it's over. Have a good life. Mack.*"

My heart pounded, the bile from my stomach churning like I was going to throw up as I tried not to react. He was done. Walking away without a fight, even though he'd said he loved me. Not that I could blame him, he'd probably assumed that's what I had done.

"I told you he wasn't going to stick around. Better you find out now." Lewis seemed pleased, pointing to the phone. "See, complete asshole. And if for nothing else, you should be paying me because I totally called it. Way I see it, you owe me for saving you from wasting your time."

I was desperate not to cry, begging the tears not to fall as I kicked up my chin and refocused on making it out alive. I was on my own. "You're right," I sucked in a breath. "It would never have lasted."

Part of me believed the last part, wondering if we hadn't fallen in love too fast. I should have taken it slower, and kept my goddamn mouth shut about wanting a baby. Hell, he'd probably been looking for a way out. My message giving him the free pass he'd been praying for.

"Now fucking tell me how you're going to get me my money, Hayden. I've told you why, now it's your turn to talk."

"I told you I work here." I pointed to the store. "And there's money in the safe. A whole day's takings, and I can get it for you. All you have to do is let me walk in and get it, and I'll hand it over."

He laughed, grabbing my arm again and bringing me in closer. "You think I'm stupid, Hayden? Think I'm just going to let you walk into the store? And what's to stop you from going inside and calling the cops? We might have been family once, but that don't count for shit now."

"I am not going to turn you in. It's not my money, what do I care if you take it? They're covered by insurance, it's not even really a loss. Not to mention, I would not only lose my job if they found out but also face criminal charges. You don't have to trust me, Lewis, my participation makes me an accessory."

Most of it was true.

The money wasn't mine. And if I did what I said I'd do, a conviction and criminal record would probably be in my future. But despite the store having insurance, I did care. I just hoped he didn't see through that part of the lie.

His head tilted, considering it. "That's right. You are an accessory, you volunteered for this."

I nodded, hoping to appease him. "I did, no one forced me. You know I'm a terrible liar, Lewis. They'll know if they interrogate me that I did this by choice, I can't pretend you forced me. We're in this together."

"Still don't trust you. So here's what's going to happen. We're going to go in there together. You're going to give me the money and then I'm going to be fucking gone. You can go back to your shitty life, working your shitty job, fucking dickheads who don't care about you. And if you ever tell anyone about this, it won't be Presley's apartment I'll be breaking into." His voice was ice cold, the kid I'd once known completely gone as he made threats I one-hundred percent believed.

He was desperate, the debt he owed probably way past due to people who didn't believe in a payment plan. And if hurting me got him in the clear, he'd do it without a second thought.

"If we go in together, it will look suspicious. Not to mention the security footage," I tried to reason. "It will be easier if I do this myself."

"Work it out, Hayden. Prove you're not as dumb as my brother told me you were." He shook his head.

It didn't surprise me to hear Cooper had thought I was dumb. It was probably the reason he'd never wanted me to finish school, loving he could lord his MBA over me. Before it would have crushed me, tearing apart what little self-esteem I'd had. But I'd grown stronger, and even without a fancy piece of paper, I knew I was smart. And I wasn't going to let someone's words hurt me. Especially when that someone was so insignificant.

"Fine, but we need to go through the staff entrance. And you have to do exactly as I say, Lewis. I don't care if you trust me or not, but if you want this money, we're doing it my way."

Chapter 26

Hayden

IF THERE EVER was a moment to get in touch with my inner badass, that was the moment for it. I didn't have time to worry about Mack's message or my broken heart, or whether or not Lewis was going to get impatient and do something stupid. All I had was the chance I could make it right, the confidence I'd gained in the last few weeks making me believe I could.

We'd climbed out of his car, Lewis keeping a tight grip on me as we walked toward the store. I'd barely been able to breathe, his fingers digging into my arm so hard I could feel the skin bruising.

"Fine, lead." He tipped his head to his side, letting me go and putting his hand on the butt of the gun. Not sure if it was to remind me he still had it—unnecessary—or because he was planning on using it.

Either way, it was too late, walking around to the rear of the store where there was a staff entrance. It had a pin-code door, allowing us access into an internal hallway when the main doors were locked. At night when the store was closed, a key was needed as well as the code, but as the store was still open, I hoped it still worked.

My fingers pressed the number sequence, praying it didn't trigger some internal alarm. Or maybe that was what I should be hoping for, my hand twisting the handle after the last number had been entered.

Success.

I couldn't believe it worked.

"If anyone sees us, pretend you're my date." The thought of him touching me, repulsive. "I forgot my purse in my locker, and we're just here to collect it."

He rolled his eyes, chuckling. "No one would believe I was with you, but sure, whatever. Just hurry up."

Ignoring his insult, I continued down the hall. The staff lockers were in one direction, the cash room in the other.

"Hayden, what are you doing here on your day off?" Penny appeared in the hall, smiling brightly despite me technically trespassing.

"Hey, Penny, I forgot my purse." I tried to smile, hoping Lewis didn't panic. "We're just going to get it."

Her brow rose, positive she wasn't buying it. "And who is this?" She turned to Lewis. "Another Uber driver?"

I laughed nervously, not sure how it was going to go. "Noooooooo, this is my boyfriend." I slung my arm around Lewis, trying to look at him with adoration when my skin was crawling. "We were on a date when I noticed. Thought I'd quickly stop in and get it."

If it had been anyone else, I might have gotten away with it. I rarely spoke about my personal life to any of my coworkers, most of them oblivious to who I was dating, and not caring either way. But Penny was different, having met Mack and knowing what my feelings were for him. She'd never believe if we'd broken up, that I wouldn't have mentioned it, or that I would have moved on so fast.

I braced, expecting everything to unravel in the hall, with the demand to know exactly what I was doing.

Instead she smiled at Lewis, extending her hand. "Oh, your boyfriend, huh? Well, that's just great. I'm Penny, Hayden's boss. I'm pleased to meet you."

Lewis looked at her hand but didn't accept it, keeping his palm close to his gun as he nodded instead. "Lewis. And not to be rude, but we're in a hurry. Reservations."

With no idea what was going on, I was forced to play along and nod. Either Penny had been drinking in an effort to make her weekend night shift pass quicker, or there was some other force at work. And as long as no one got hurt, I didn't care what was responsible.

"Really? Where are you guys going?" Penny asked, ignoring his insistence we were in a hurry.

"Medici's in Brooklyn," Lewis answered, "Get your purse, Hayden. We need to go."

Medici's?

Of all the places in the whole city, he'd picked the one place I'd never go. It was crowded and noisy, filled with pretentious suits trying to prove how much money they had to their dates. It also had a strict dress code, which we weren't even close to meeting.

"Wow, nice place. No wonder you need that purse." Penny's large eyes widened, not missing a beat. "Well, I won't keep you then. Enjoy your night."

Without any more questions—which was uncharacteristic in itself—she waved goodbye and headed to her office. I wasn't sure what was going on but short of aliens inhabiting her body, I didn't have time to work it out.

Lewis laughed as she disappeared. "She's just as dumb as you. Guess that's why you both work here."

"Yeah, guess so." My smile tightened. "The cash room is in there," I pointed to another door with a pin code. "Maybe you should just wait out here?"

I knew he wouldn't agree, too worried that I'd *screw* him or worse, take the money for myself. Any logical person would be worried since we'd already been ID'd by my boss, our connection to any theft almost guaranteed. But he—like his brother—had never been a big-picture kind of guy, getting distracted by details and his own desperation.

"I'm not waiting anywhere. Put in the goddamn code, Hayden. I'm going in first."

He didn't even notice the door was slightly ajar, my hand holding it steady while I pressed on the numbers. Instead he asked me how many thousands I expected to be in the safe, pushing me aside once the last of the code had been entered, and stalking in ahead just like he said.

"What the fuck?"

I pulled the door closed on his surprised face, the loud click of the lock engaging. It wasn't the cash room, instead a closet that housed our cleaning supplies, which he'd have seen right away if the light had been on. But again, he hadn't even bothered with the details, barreling inside looking for his payday. What he also didn't know was it had a faulty lock, logged for maintenance since Friday with explicit instructions that no staff use it until it was fixed. Probably because the chances of getting locked in were high, as was the current case.

"Hayden," Penny reappeared, running toward me, holding a taser. "The police are on their way."

"You called them?" I almost cried with relief, still not having had the time to grab my phone and dial 9-1-1.

"Your *boyfriend*? *Medici's*? Girl, you were hot and heavy for your fireman last time I checked, was no way you'd dump him for that loser. I didn't know exactly what was going on, but I figured it had to be some kind of trouble. I called the minute I got to my office. I have this as well." She pressed the trigger, the electrical current zapping between the poles. "You know, for my late-night closes."

Lewis banged on the door, his voice yelling through the wood. "Open the goddamn door, you bitch. When I get out of here, I'm going to make you regret the day you were ever born."

There was a gunshot, the sound of wood splintering making Penny and I scatter. Up until that moment, I hadn't been sure it was loaded, the second bullet coming soon after.

"Jesus, he has a gun?" Penny looked panicked, handing me the taser while grabbing her cell and dialing. "This is Penny, we have an active-shooter situation. Evacuate the store and lock all doors leading to back of house."

The door jangled, Lewis testing the lock. He either had poor aim or the lock was more stubborn than anyone thought, the door holding despite being shot at twice. "You need to go, Penny." I shoved her down the hallway. "Go make sure everyone stays safe."

"You're coming with me. Fuck it, Hayden. He's obviously crazy and he has a gun. It's not worth it. Let the police deal with it." She tugged on my arm, pulling me with her.

It was a split-second decision, which was all I had time for, shaking my head and holding up the taser she'd handed to me. "No, if he gets away, they'll never find him. Go." I pressed the trigger, ready to use it. "I'll be fine."

"Hayden—" Her voice drowned out by another gunshot, her legs moving back automatically.

"Go, Penny. Go." I shook my head, keeping my feet rooted to the floor. I wouldn't leave, refusing to accept an outcome where Lewis didn't end up in cuffs and everyone was safe. All I had to do was zap him when he walked out, the current able to incapacitate him enough until the cops arrived. It was what Mack would have done, and even though I wasn't even sure if we were together anymore, it wouldn't change the outcome. I was doing it for me. To gain back what I'd almost never had, knowing I was enough all by myself.

The door flew open on the fourth gunshot, Penny running in the opposite direction even though she hadn't wanted to. I was scared but unmoved as I met his crazy wild eyes, the barrel of the pistol pointed directly at me.

I pushed my arms out, the zapping of the stun gun aimed at his chest, hoping to make contact. He was caught off guard, managing to angle out of the way but making the gun go off. Lucky for me, it had been pointed at the ground, saving me from a wound I probably wouldn't have survived.

"You're a crazy bitch. And I told you not to fuck me." He lunged, frustratingly trying to grab my arm while I waved the taser in front of my body. His hand was still tightly holding the gun, but thankfully no longer aimed at me, making me feel like I still had a chance.

He wasn't going to kill me.

If he wanted to do that, he'd have done that already.

A surge of adrenaline took hold, forcing myself forward, but was stopped as he swung the gun around and cocked the trigger. "So fucking stupid."

Oh, shit. I'd been wrong.

My heart raced, my lungs struggling to expand as I came face to face with possibly the last thing I'd ever see.

I regretted not telling Mack sooner that I loved him.

Thinking it had been too soon.

He should have known.

Should have been told the minute I felt it. I should have been braver. It wouldn't have mattered if he didn't say it back. I would've been okay.

God, I'd been happy.

Happier with him in the last few weeks than I'd been throughout my entire marriage.

I wish I could've told him.

It felt important that he know.

But other than that, I had no regrets.

None.

Not about getting into the car with Lewis, not trying to stop him, not about dying today if that was the way my story ended.

Blood roared through my ears as the last shot fired, my body collapsing on the floor. I had no idea where I'd been hit, other than I wasn't dead. I laid still, my body paralyzed more from fear than pain as I heard thundering footsteps heading in our direction. I'd done enough. The police had arrived, they'd take him away, and whatever else happened didn't matter. I'd done what I said I was going to do, and kept everyone safe.

My body sagged in relief, my eyes filling with tears as voices echoed around me. I couldn't hear properly, another gunshot piercing the commotion as my vision faded in and out. It wasn't until I saw Lewis fall to the ground that I knew it hadn't been aimed at me.

I needed to sleep, the fatigue overwhelming as I heard my name shouted again and again, turning me over onto my back.

Hands.

Hands ran over my face as I tried to focus, wiping away tears I didn't realize had fallen as the voice begged me to stay awake. I wasn't sure I could to be honest, wanting to just close my eyes for a minute or two and catch my breath.

"Hayden." The voice was more insistent, shaking me a little. "Don't you dare close your eyes. You stay with me, okay? Stay with me."

It was Mack.

His hands, his voice, his demands—somehow in the room with me. And I didn't know if I was hallucinating, if he was really there, or I'd already died. I didn't care, using the last of my strength to reach up and touch his hands and whisper that I loved him, that I didn't mean what I said, and that I knew he'd never hurt me.

He said something I couldn't make out, coldness flooding my body, and my eyes closing, even though I didn't want them to.

I was glad I'd gotten one last chance.

Even if it was only to say goodbye.

Chapter 27

Mack

"MACK, SHE IS in shock. You need to let us work." Maree pushed me away, covering Hayden's body with thermal foil blankets while sliding on an oxygen mask. Taylor, the other EMT had pressure on her chest, the blood from the wound pouring out of her way too fast.

It was dumb luck Lewis was such a terrible shot, the range at which he'd fired would've been deadly if he'd aimed more center and lower. Still, I wasn't feeling gratitude as I watched Hayden's eyes slide shut, her pupils flat and dilated, ready to kill Lewis with my bare hands if he hadn't already been shot.

Tibbs had done some digging and found out Lewis was in deep to the tune of fifty Gs. It's what he'd wanted to tell Presley before we'd gotten called out, the mystery of why he'd broken into her apartment, solved. We couldn't be sure, but assumed he'd been looking for money, hoping some cash would appease the loan sharks. Pity that wasn't how it worked, which is why he was getting increasingly desperate and showed up at the club. What he'd intended to do, we had no idea.

What Tibbs hadn't found out—the police filling us in as they hauled him away—was Lewis Goodman, AKA DJ Lewis G, was actually Lewis *Wright*, brother to Cooper Wright, Hayden's ex-husband. He'd changed his name after a falling out with the family and had been estranged from what they could tell, but the Lewis who had been dating Presley had been the same Lewis, Hayden had once called brother-in-law.

"Her pulse is stabilizing. We need to move her," Maree shouted, Taylor helping roll her onto a stretcher while I stood by and watched. I didn't even realize arms had been holding me back, Tibbs on one side and Leighton on the other.

"I'm going." I moved forward the four-hundred pounds holding me back not strong enough to stop me. "Move your arms or I'll rip them from their sockets."

"You're no good to her if you're getting in the way." North pushed me in the chest, nodding to the other two as the medic unit took Hayden out. "I'll take you to the hospital, but you're riding with me."

Seeing that piece of shit grab Hayden and drag her away on the security footage, had spiked my anger to a level I'd never experienced. And there wasn't a doubt in my mind that when I found him, I was going to kill him. Didn't care what the consequences were or why he'd put hands on her in the first place. All I knew was we had to find them, like yesterday.

That film made it clear her message had been bogus. Why, she'd sent it hadn't been apparent, but her telling me we were done via a text was bullshit, and I should have questioned it from the start. Hardest thing I'd ever had to do was send that response, hoping if I played along it might keep her safe. Not that I meant a word of it, Presley calling the police and getting a trace put on her phone, dispatch calling us as soon as Penny's 9-1-1 had come in. I'd never driven so fast in my life, Tibbs and Leighton hearing it over the emergency scanner and meeting me in the parking lot while SWAT went in.

The puzzle pieces started to come together even if the whole picture hadn't been revealed, but her intent had been clear. She'd been trying to protect us, putting herself on the line to make sure Presley and everyone else stayed safe. And I couldn't have loved her anymore if I'd tried. Penny made her statement how Hayden wouldn't leave, my brave—and fucking crazy—warrior staying there until the end.

"What are you doing here?" I met Riley's gaze; his focus unmoving. "Why aren't you home with Quinn and Ava?"

"Because I was needed here. Now stand down, Mack. You might be able to take on one of us, but not even you can take on all three." It was without the usual old-man ridicule, illustrating that he wasn't joking. And while I wasn't sure he was right, we didn't need anyone else ending up in a stretcher.

"Fine, you drive. But you drive like you have a purpose, North." I fingered him in the chest, unable to even think straight. "And someone find out where the hell they're taking her. We also need to call her family."

"I can do that. Her brother is her emergency contact. I'll call." I hadn't even noticed Penny had still been standing there, her eyes connecting with mine. "Go, just get one of your guys to let me know which hospital."

I nodded, Leighton already on the phone as North pulled out his keys. "We're out of here. Text me the info."

North and I jogged out to the truck, his Explorer parked beside my Chevy. "Tibbs call you?"

"Leighton, and I'm glad he did." He started the truck as I buckled up, slamming it into drive and accelerating.

"She's at New York-Presbyterian Allen on Broadway, not even five minutes away." I said a silent prayer of thanks. "You can drop me off and go back home."

"I think it's hilarious that you think you have any say right now, Chief. I'm on leave, so you're currently not my boss. And I'm too old for you to pull your dad card. Because we both know if that were Quinn, you wouldn't be leaving me." He signaled, making a left onto Broadway and looking for a parking spot.

"It's not the same—" I didn't finish, unable to say the words. Because even I knew it was bullshit. The connection Hayden and I had was no less than what he had with Quinn, and fuck if he wasn't right in that I wouldn't have left his side.

"Yeah, that's what I thought. So how about you let me be there for you for a change, and trust I'm man enough to handle it. Now, stop arguing and let's find out where she is."

Shutting my mouth and doing exactly what he said, I waited until the car had come to a complete stop before getting out. I wasn't crazy about the dynamic, liking to be the one in charge, but I had to admit my judgment was more than a little cloudy. And if I was honest, I was really glad I wasn't alone. We fell into step as we went through the ER doors, not stopping until we hit the nurses' station.

"Hey, Mack," Lou, a transfer from my neighborhood cracked a smile. "We got one of yours in here tonight?"

"Hayden Green. Gunshot. Arrived in the last ten minutes or so. I need to know her status." I'd attempted to pay her the same courtesy she'd shown me, but fell short. I needed to know where Hayden was, my brain flipping to automatic with my manners being left behind.

If Lou's feelings were hurt, she didn't show it, tapping on her keyboard without so much as a raised brow. "She's being moved to surgery. We're waiting on her next of kin and you didn't hear any of that from me."

Whether she knew me or not, she didn't have to tell me shit. It wasn't one of my charges in that bed, and I wasn't even in uniform. But first responders had a special relationship with the ER staff, having seen more of each other than probably either of us liked. So sometimes lines were blurred, and HIPAA could kiss my ass.

"Thanks."

I saved the explanation I knew she didn't have time to hear and shoved my ass into a chair in the waiting room. Riley sat beside me saying nothing, my mind trying to make intelligent assessments despite my heart not giving a fuck about logic.

It was a non-fatal wound.

Chances of recovery were better than average.

She'd been conscious, vitals steady.

Unless the bullet ricocheted and nicked an artery.

Or she went into V fib on the way.

"Fuck," I tried to get out of my own head, not possessing my usual calm as I scrubbed my face. "She's going to be okay. She is going to be okay."

North's heavy hand rested on my shoulder. "She is. And while we wait until the doc comes and confirms what we already know, why don't you tell me about this breakup, Melinda, the club, and how any of them are connected. I know I've had a lot going on with Quinn and Ava, but that's not a conversation I'd have forgotten."

Of all the conversations I wanted to have, that probably came in dead last. But it was probably going to come out anyway, so it was better he'd heard it from me.

I blew out a long breath, my muscles so tense they were starting to burn. "Melinda had designs on me being her baby daddy. Not sure where she got the idea, or why she was so fucking insistent, but it's the reason she keeps calling me. When I heard Presley had taken Hayden to *Diablo*, I assumed Melinda had tried to stack the deck. It wouldn't be the first time she's tried to sabotage something that made me happy to further her own agenda."

"Ha, I'd say that was pretty much your whole marriage wasn't it?" Riley laughed, not needing another reason to dislike her. "I swear, you need a ring of salt and a fucking priest anytime you deal with her. I assume you hadn't told Hayden about any of it?"

"You would assume right. And considering Hayden had said she wanted a baby, it didn't seem like a good time to bring it up." I still should have said something, if for no other reason to explain my initial hesitation.

Riley's face pulled into a grimace. "Oh shit."

"Yep." My fingers squeezed the bridge of my nose. *Oh shit* was putting it mildly.

He shrugged, shooting me a sympathetic smile. "Yeah, probably not the best time to bring it up. But you want them, right? Kids. I mean, I know they're not going to be as perfect as your first, but I'm sure you'll love us all the same."

"Here I thought fatherhood would make you more mature." I rolled my eyes while shaking my head.

"Honesty trumps maturity, Mack. I'm just keeping it real. And stop avoiding."

"Yes. I'd assumed that ship had sailed, but given the chance with Hayden, yes, I want that. Fuck, right now I'd give her a truck load of kids, keep her pregnant for the next five years just to hear she's okay." My chest expanded, the knot between my rib cage making it hard to breathe. "I want all of it. The trip to City Hall, the rings, the anniversary dinners, fighting over television stations, and growing old together. And, yeah, I want kids, Riley. I want *her* babies because she'd be one hell of a mother. But more than any of that, I need her back. I need her in my fucking arms where I know she's safe."

If I got that chance, I'd never let her go, willing to take whatever hardship life had in store. Ironic that of all the good I'd accomplished, the commendations, the medals, and all that other stuff, I hadn't been able to do the one thing that mattered.

"It's not your fault," Riley pulled me from the shit in my head, making me wonder if I hadn't said it out loud. "I know you try harder than any person I know, Mack, but you can't stop bad things from happening."

"I should have been able to stop this one." I wasn't sure how, but it felt like it was on me. If I'd just dug deeper on the

Lewis thing, told her about Melinda, just fuck—I don't know. "I just should've."

North punched me lightly in the shoulder, getting my attention. "Did you ever think maybe she doesn't need saving, Mack? Maybe that's why you feel the way you do about her, because she doesn't need you to ride in on your white horse. Sounds to me like she more than handled herself. And while I'd be just as out of my head if it were Quinn, I'd have been fucking proud. She looked that bastard in the eye, Mack. She didn't run. And when she wakes up, she's not going to run from you either."

"Christ, Riley," I shook my head, swallowing hard a few times so I didn't lose it. "When the fuck did you get to be so fucking smart?"

The kid had come a long way, seeing things in me that I probably didn't much notice. And he wasn't wrong. I had a tendency of wanting to make shit right, to fix things, to make everyone else okay. But Hayden hadn't needed that, not *really*. She was stronger than any woman I'd ever met, and the only thing she'd needed from me was to love her.

That's it.

And I did.

Completely.

Gayle and her brother ran in, looking frantically at the front desk. I knew that look, saw it too many times to count, and needed to man up and let them know as much as I could.

"Hey," I stepped toward them, both of them turning at the sound of my voice. "She's in surgery."

Gayle threw herself at me, hugging me before I'd even noticed what was happening. "I can't believe she was shot. She *has* to be okay."

North and I filled them in as best we could, Lou adding what she was able. And then the four of us sat down and waited, because apparently that was all we could do.

"She's going to be fine." I turned to Gayle, and for the first time actually believing it. "Better than fine because she has all of us."

Chapter 28

Hayden

IT DIDN'T HURT when I was shot.

At least not that I remembered.

There was an impact, my body being unable to stand but I didn't feel pain.

But waking up was a *different* story.

"Hurts." I tried to pull off the oxygen mask, realizing I was at a hospital. Hopefully that would make getting drugs easier, the need for some pain relief of the utmost importance.

"Hi, Hayden, we're going to give you some morphine now you've woken up. It should help make you feel more comfortable."

There was a kind face above me, coming into focus as I blinked. I assumed she was a nurse. Or a doctor. Hell, she could have been the janitor and I wouldn't have cared as long as she gave me morphine. Her hands worked quickly, injecting something into the IV in my hand.

I had no idea how long I'd been out, waking from what felt like a weeklong sleep with memories of before really hazy.

Mack.

Mack had been there before I'd gone to sleep.

"Mack," I croaked, my throat feeling raw and scratchy. "Where's Mack?"

What I probably should have asked was where was I shot and am I going to be okay? I assumed since I didn't die at least half of the question was redundant. And the searing pain radiating from my upper chest to under my arm answered the first part. So since I'd solved most of the riddle, I needed to know where Mack was, so I could tell him that I loved him.

I'd tried to tell him before, thinking it was going to be my only chance. But I wasn't sure if he'd heard the words, my mouth having a difficult time trying to work when my body wanted to shut down. He needed to know. Know I hadn't meant what I'd said before and that I didn't care if it still meant we weren't together, I wanted him to have the truth.

"You're still in recovery. We'll be wheeling you down in a minute, and then you can see him. He's waiting with the rest of your family. You've got quite a crowd." Her smile widened even if her words didn't make sense. I assumed Gayle and Matt would be there, maybe they'd brought the kids? Other than that, I had no idea who would be waiting. Unless Riley was with Mack for moral support as well.

"Thank you," I sighed, feeling my body relax as the morphine started to kick in. Everything still hurt, but it wasn't as unbearable as before, my eyes closing as I felt myself wheeled from the room. The gentle rock of the bed combined with the drugs made me want to sleep, but the nurse had mentioned me being able to see Mack and I didn't want to miss it.

The movement stopped, hands lifting me from one bed to another and then the oxygen mask being removed. A tube was inserted up my nose, the hiss of cool air not feeling as invasive as I'd imagined as they positioned me more comfortably. I hadn't even noticed my arm was in a sling, bandages wrapped around my chest and shoulder making my hospital gown hang off awkwardly.

"There, that should be better," she appraised her handiwork, the two other nurses/orderlies/janitors who'd joined us on our journey leaving the room. "You can have visitors, but only one or two at a time. Is there someone you want to see first?"

"Mack, I want to see Mack." My throat still felt raw, my body exhausted but it didn't matter. I forced my eyes open, watching as she left and not blinking as I looked at the door.

And then he was there. One minute the gap between the frame empty, and then filled with his huge, hot body.

His eyes locked on me.

"Hayden."

I wasn't sure if he'd said more than my name, my attempt to lift my arm and reach for him hindered by the bandages. He didn't care, not needing the invitation as he came closer, dropping his mouth to mine. "I love you. I love you so goddamn much and I was terrified I'd never be able to say it again."

I tried to kiss him back, my lips not cooperating as they smashed against his with no coordination. "I love you too. I'm sorry for the message."

"Listen to me," his hands tilted my chin. "You have nothing to be sorry for. Ever. I know why you sent it. The same reason why I sent one back. Neither of them meant anything, because I know what's in your heart. And, Hayden, you have to know what's in mine."

I nodded, feeling overwhelmed. "I had to stop him, Mack. He would have kept going. Hurt Presley. Hurt you." I became frustrated, unable to finish my sentences. "Had to be over."

His eyes closed, every muscle in his jaw tensing. "You're the bravest person I've ever met, Hayden. What you did for Presley? For me? No one has ever put themselves on the line like that. But please let it be the first *and* the last time, okay? Not sure my heart can take it a second time."

My lips tried to smile, wondering how hard it was for him not to demand I didn't. I'd seen the way he'd been with Riley, with Tibbs and Leighton and the other guys but never with me. He didn't demand a thing, letting me come to decisions on my own even though it was in his nature to take over. "Well, Cooper doesn't have any other crazy brothers. Think we're safe. Unless . . . Melinda."

It was supposed to be a joke. Well, mostly. Although, if I needed to take on his ex-wife I'd do it without hesitation, the woman not getting a second chance on something she'd clearly never deserved.

Although Mack didn't find it funny, his face hardening at the mention of her name. And when he looked at me, his eyes were serious, my heartbeat racing even though he hadn't said a word.

"Yeah, Melinda isn't going to be a problem. But there's something I need to tell you. And I know now is not the fucking time, but I made the mistake of waiting before and I'm not doing it again."

"What is it?" I asked, even though part of me was terrified of finding out. I knew he didn't love her. Not buying into the bullshit Lewis had told me about them eventually getting back together. Beautiful or not, if he'd wanted to be with her, he would. But whatever it was, didn't look good.

He took a breath, taking a seat in the chair beside my bed and holding my hand. "She asked me to father her baby. I turned her down, and I'd rather have no children than have one with her. Hayden." His hand tightened on mine. "She lied to me when we were married, made me think we were trying for years when she never stopped taking the pill. Every month, I'd get disappointed, wondering if it was me. Exposure to chemicals can sometimes do that. And, well, who knew? But I found the pills eventually, confronted her and then actually apologized because maybe I'd pushed too hard. No one should be forced to be a parent if they didn't want to, and I'd never forgive myself if that's what I'd done. So I just kind of got my head around it wouldn't happen for me, you know? And then her fucking request, well, it messed with my head a little. So when you mentioned kids. . . I know you're not like her. And I should've told you why I didn't say yes. Should've told you that I'd want nothing more than to get you pregnant. But part of me . . . was scared."

My chest hurt, and not from the gunshot. The ache in my heart breaking for such an amazing man whose opportunity for more children had been weaponized against him. It had been a chip, a bargaining tool—and I couldn't stand it.

"Okay, so I guess I'll have to go after her too." I squeezed his hand. "Riley was right, she is an evil bitch."

He laughed, kissing my fingertips. "Yeah, she is. And I should've seen that a long time ago. But if that offer is still good, I have *big* plans." He winked.

I nodded, not even pretending like I didn't want it. "I don't even know if it's possible, Mack, but I want you to know that I'm never going to lie to you. And if it ends up that it's just us, it's more than enough. Besides, we still have Riley. And Quinn and Ava. Not to mention Gayle, Matt, and the boys. It's not like we're going to be lonely on the holidays."

"Yeah, I feel the same. Still, it's going to be fun trying." Mack chuckled. "And while you're in the mood to agree, I have one other question to ask you. It's the one time I'm going to insist, Hayden. And I'm not taking no for an answer."

He didn't need to say it, the proposal written all over his face. And as much as it had been a surprise, it was exactly the right time.

"Yes. Yes, Mack, yes."

"I haven't even asked yet." He laughed, standing from the chair and getting down on one knee. "You've already said yes, so we're taking your first answer. But I need to say the words. Hayden, I love you. I love you even though I wasn't looking, believing I'd never do this again. But now that I've got you, I can't ever go back, the alternative no longer an option. I need you to be my wife, Hayden. For us to be together for whatever the future throws at us. I need for you to be my person, and to let me be yours, and I'll promise I will never take you for granted."

Tears filled my eyes as I nodded, saying yes for a second time. "Yes, I'll marry you. I can't wait for you to be my husband."

Never thought I'd say those words again, especially since I'd decided to put myself first. But with Mack I didn't have to choose, able to love myself and still love him. It didn't matter that I hadn't been divorced that long, or that the idea of getting married was something I hadn't even considered. I wasn't worried about the future, knowing no matter what happened, I'd be okay.

And that was what it was all about, being with someone when you were enough all by yourself.

He kissed me, trying to be gentle but failing as his lips crushed mine. I was glad he didn't hold back, needing to feel him so that I knew it was real. "I'm going to get you a ring, and whatever else you want." He mumbled against my mouth. "And probably a bulletproof vest, just to be sure."

My body hurt as I laughed, wishing I could wrap my arms around him. "Well, let's start with the ring and we'll take it from there."

I wanted to get out of the bed, to go home with him and start our new life, the beeping beside us reminding me I couldn't. "Hey," I pulled my mouth from his, curious about something. "The nurse said there was a crowd waiting to see me? Did Gayle and Matt bring the boys?"

"No, sweetheart. The boys are with your parents. Gayle and Matt are in the waiting room with Riley and Quinn. As is Tibbs, Leighton, and Presley. And Penny, she told me to tell you you're getting a new name badge at work that says Wonder Woman."

My throat tightened. I couldn't remember a time there'd been so many people wanting to see me. "They're all here for *me*?" I asked, not really believing it.

Mack brushed the hair away from my face, the smile spreading across his lips. "Of course, sweetheart. They love you too."

I'd gone from having no friends, to having so many I couldn't fit in a room. And my heart felt like it was going to burst. "Can you please tell them to come in, I want to see them."

"Yeah, the nurse said only one or two of us at a time. It's against the rules." He chuckled, kissing my forehead.

"Fuck the rules, Mack," I coughed out. "I think we established we weren't really playing by any."

He laughed, shaking his head. "Yeah. Okay. I'll go get them."

My eyes followed him as he left, knowing he'd be back soon, and enjoying the stillness of the empty room.

I was happy.

Truly.

Madly.

Deeply.

Happy.

Chapter 29

Mack

"**Y**OU KNOW WE can wait, Hayden." I zipped up the back of her dress, thinking someone needed to be the voice of reason. "You only just got out of the bandages. We probably should have held off another week or two."

The 9mm had pierced Hayden's side between two ribs. It was a million-to-one shot, the gap so narrow it was a miracle it hadn't hit bone. But miracle or not, blood loss had made surgery necessary, the doctors able to repair the damage and make sure her lungs were okay. I'd never been more relieved than when the doc came out and told us she was in recovery. Willing to wait however long it took before I could see her.

In the end, I hadn't needed to wait that long.

I'd proposed, she'd said yes, and then we got into all kinds of trouble with the hospital staff when everyone descended on her room.

And the second I was able to take her home, I did.

To my place in Midtown.

Which was where we'd been for the last few weeks.

"Why wait? Unless you've changed your mind? You having second thoughts?" She grinned, spinning around to let me look at her. She was beautiful, the smile on her face brighter than any sunrise I'd ever seen.

"You know I'm not having second thoughts and I'd *never* change my mind. I just want to be sure this is what you want. We can do the wedding thing, Hayden. Have it as big as you want it."

It wasn't the first go around for either of us, but it didn't mean I wouldn't do the whole big saga all over again. Hell, we'd make it even bigger, invite the whole city if that was what she wanted.

She straightened my tie, the suit feeling a little tighter in the shoulders than I remembered it. I'd been working out a little more lately, liking the way her eyes lit up when I took off my shirt. "This is what I want. Now stop stalling and marry me already."

I kissed her, not able to deny her anything even if I'd wanted to and loving the way her body fit against mine. "Fine, but we are having a proper honeymoon, and I'm planning it. Nothing but beach, cocktails, and a whole bunch of lying around."

Her hands hooked around my neck, tipping her face to kiss me. "And sex. Lots, and lots of sex."

"That was implied." I pinched her ass, the fitted black dress showing all her amazing curves. "So much sex you won't be able to walk, hence the whole bunch of lying around."

"Then we better hurry up and make it official. Because you look pretty damn sexy in this suit, and getting started on the honeymoon sounds like a *really* good idea."

Wasn't sure I'd ever get used to that smile, cherishing every single one she gave me. And to think it had almost been taken away, the piece of shit responsible locked away awaiting trial.

Unfortunately, the cocksucker hadn't died. Which was a shame because no one deserved a dirt nap more than he did. But even with an airtight case and a prosecution unwilling to plea out, I wasn't worried about the son of the bitch getting out.

Because if he did, I'd kill him myself.

So it was just as well he was in the can, meant I still had my civil liberties to enjoy. And marrying the woman in my arms, was of paramount importance.

"Okay, future Mrs. McPherson, let's go make it official."

We'd driven to the courthouse in my truck, meeting everyone else there. We might not be doing the big fancy wedding, but that didn't mean we weren't going to be surrounded by friends and family. Even my parents flew in, leaving the Florida sun and joining my brother, sister-in-law, and their family, to see me say those vows one last time.

Riley grinned, cradling his baby daughter in his arms while Quinn beamed alongside of him. Both of them had been cocky as fuck, claiming responsibility for our relationship. But I didn't care, willing to be gracious to whoever had made it happen.

"You look so handsome, Chief." Quinn nodded at me before turning her attention to my bride. "And, Hayden, you're simply stunning."

She was right.

There wasn't a woman in the world who was more beautiful than Hayden, her arm slipping under mine as we led the inappropriately large crowd into the building. We'd called ahead, not wanting to put anyone out, the good people at the Office of the City Clerk clearing a room for us. I'm sure being a Chief with the FDNY hadn't hurt, many of the guys who served the city showing up to shake my hand.

And while she didn't walk down an aisle and was without the white dress, there'd never been a more perfect bride than the one who turned to me and said, "I do."

The ceremony went quick, the words and rings exchanged while we looked in each other's eyes. And when I was told I could kiss the bride, I didn't need to be told twice.

Everyone cheered, my arms wrapping around Hayden as I pulled her close and ignored the wolf whistles around us. I'd deal with them later, wanting to remember the perfect memory forever.

"Easy there, Chief." Leighton laughed behind us. "There are kids present."

I rolled my eyes, fighting the urge to flip him off, because as annoying as it was to admit, he wasn't wrong.

Hayden stood beside me as we accepted everyone's congratulations, getting more hugs and handshakes than I'd had in an entire year. And once everyone had settled a bit, we'd invited them back to Gino's. Which was not only the place we were having the reception, but had been the venue of our first date.

I'd assumed Hayden would have wanted somewhere fancier. A ballroom, or restaurant that didn't have plastic tumblers and checkered tablecloths. But she'd wanted it to be relaxed, giving the kids space to run around, and for our guests to just enjoy. Gino couldn't have been happier when I'd told him, giving us the upstairs function room and giving us such a good deal on the food and drink, I'd almost felt guilty. Of course, he'd probably make the money back and then some next time the station ordered, the tip I was planning on leaving more than making up the difference.

We'd just finished our entrees, when Melinda appeared. Because clearly the woman wanted to attempt to ruin what was otherwise a perfect day.

"John?" She looked at me and Hayden and the shiny gold bands on our fingers. "Oh my God, it's true."

I was just about to raise holy hell, not willing to give her any more time than I'd already had.

"Melinda—"

Hayden put her hand on my arm, stopping me from finishing. She smiled, standing gracefully and looking Melinda in the eyes as she met my ex-wife for the first time.

"I'm not sure what happened to you, or why you feel the need to be the way you are. But I'm sorry. And whatever the reasons, you lost an amazing man who would have loved you unconditionally. But I bet you know that, which is why it's been hard to let go. You know, if I'd had seen you when Mack and I had started dating, I'd probably been intimidated. You're beautiful. Pity it's not reflected in your heart."

Melinda planted her hands on her hips, her face flushing so many shades of red I wasn't sure her cheeks hadn't combusted. "You feel sorry for me? Why don't you go fuck yourself, you fat whore."

"Get out of here." I stood up, my willingness to sit down while she insulted my wife, nonexistent. "You ever contact either one of us again—" I had to stop, distracted by Hayden laughing.

Her arms were around her waist, almost doubled over as she giggled hysterically. A double-take needed just to be sure I was seeing it right. "Hayden?"

"Fat whore? That's the best you can do? You think I care what you think, or whether or not you believe I need to lose a few pounds? He's with *me*, Melinda. He chose *me*. And I'm never going to let him go. So insult me if it makes you feel better, but it's not going to do a damn thing to change how wonderful my life is."

Riley coughed, rising to his feet. "You have no power here, Melinda. Now run along before someone drops a house on you." He waved his hand dramatically, unable to hide his smirk.

Melinda turned, every set of eyes on her and not one of them filled with pity. Hayden was right, it didn't matter what she said. Nothing was going to change what we had. Doing what I should've done a long time ago, I turned my back and ignored her. She didn't matter, and she sure as hell was not getting my attention anymore.

"I thought you hated the *Wizard of Oz*," I tossed a napkin at North. "You're not hiding a closet fetish for musicals, are you?"

His grin widened, shaking his head. "It was on last night when Ava woke up, and I swear the resemblance was uncanny. Still wondering if I should toss a glass of water at her to see if she'd melt. But I don't want to make a mess on Gino's floor."

Melinda gasped, sticking around despite no one paying her any mind. She'd have to get used to that, storming off when it was clear she wasn't getting what she wanted. Who knew if it was that easy? Or if she was working on her second wind. Either way, it didn't matter, the amazing woman I'd just married making me the luckiest man alive.

"You ready to get to work on the honeymoon?" I grabbed Hayden around the waist and pulled her against me. The dress had me hard most of the day, and given we were in company, I figured it was better to show than to tell.

She laughed against my neck, letting out a small groan. "Mack, we haven't even cut the cake. We can't just leave in the middle of our own wedding."

"Sure we can. We're adults, we can do whatever the hell we want. And fuck the cake, I'll bake you one. You know I've got the skills." I kept my voice low, not advertising what skills I was referring to. Not that it mattered, kitchen or bedroom—I could dominate in either.

Hayden's eyes darkened, her smile telling me exactly what was on her mind. "You know, we have a *really* hard time finishing our dinner in this place."

I held out my hand, having already made the decision we were leaving. "Yeah, well, I was always more of an eating-at-home kind of guy."

And now that Hayden was my home, I had even more incentive.

Epilogue

Hayden

"HAYDEN!" PENNY APPEARED around the corner, her arms filled with stock that needed to be displayed. "You want to help me out? Old time's sake?"

I'd quit my job after I'd been released from the hospital, knowing it was going to be a HR nightmare. While it would have been easy to argue I'd given Lewis access to the store and put people at risk while under duress, I didn't want to put Penny or anyone else in a difficult position. Part of me felt guilty, wishing I'd thought of another way. And the other part of me didn't want the reminder, having to walk past that closet and remember that day. Needless to say, they accepted my resignation, and we parted ways on good terms. I still spent way too much money in the store, so it was just as well that after Mack and I got married I'd gotten a new, higher-paying job.

Marriage the second time around had been completely different, and not just because Mack was amazing with more integrity in his little finger than Cooper had in his whole entire body. He loved me unconditionally, gave me the space to be myself, cheering me on as I flourished. And I did that for him, though I had to admit that part of me was glad he rarely went out on calls. The idea of something happening to him was terrifying beyond belief. I wasn't sure how those other women did it, especially knowing Mack wouldn't think twice about putting his life on the line to save someone else.

I held out my arms, smiling at my good friend. Because that's what she'd become, adding to the collection of people who had the same title. "Sure, but I have to tell you, having this display is a tripping hazard. The material of the shirts is slippery, making them hard to stay folded. You're better off hanging them, less chance of theft too."

"Look at you, talking all fancy." She grinned. "But you're right, they probably should be hung. If for no other reason than some poor son of a bitch is going to have to keep folding them. Hey, Brenda," she called to another khaki, polo-wearing compatriot mindlessly zapping merchandise with a price gun. "Can you grab me some hangers from the storeroom. We're gonna hang these shirts."

Brenda looked at her for a full five minutes, her attention shifting to Penny and then the shirts. "Hangers?"

"Yes, you know, the plastic things we hang things on. They're in the storeroom. Go get some." Penny rolled her eyes before turning back to me. "Come back to me. I know I can't pay you what Presley is, but consider it your charitable contribution."

She was right, Target couldn't match what I made at *Diablo*, the paycheck I was bringing home almost double what it used to be. Then again, I earned it, handling all Presley's inventory, managing her compliance portfolios, and lowering the club's liabilities with progressive risk assessment. I was still earning my degree through course credits online, but I'd showed enough initiative for her to hire me even without the piece of paper. It gave her time to expand the *Diablo* brand, a second site in the meatpacking district, already in the works.

I tilted my head, giving it some consideration. "I'd love to but, I'm already having a hard time juggling *Diablo* and school. Throw in impending motherhood and I'm not sure I'd cope."

Penny blinked, her big eyes getting wider as she sorted through my words. "Holy Shhhhhhhhhh," she clasped her hand over her mouth, realizing we were on the shop floor. "Jesus, you two work fast. You've been married for what? Three months? Lord, that Uber driver is really earning that five-star rating."

I laughed, her early nickname for Mack still getting a mention every now and again. "Guess we got lucky. But keep it to yourself, it's early days."

"Who am I gonna tell?" She looked around, shoppers filling their carts and ignoring us. "But for the record, it's awesome and I'm happy for you. Let me know if you want me to help you pick maternity outfits. You know I can deck you out."

"Yeah, let's *not* do that. Those Spanx you made me squeeze into still give me PTSD." I absently rubbed my tummy even though there was no bump. I knew our little baby was in there, and I was going to enjoy every second of it.

"Fine, fine. But I'll fight Gayle for a chance to throw the baby shower." She folded her arms across her chest, looking determined.

"Why don't you do it together? I'll even give you both full autonomy. Just promise me there will be lots of food. I swear, most people have their head down the toilet the first trimester, and I can't stop eating. And you know Mack isn't helping. I've already gained three pounds, and I can't even blame the baby."

Mack had suspected I was pregnant even before I had. Not sure if it was wishful thinking or he knew he was packing super sperm, hounding me to take a pregnancy test before I'd even missed my period. He just knew, he'd said, putting the early detection test on the counter and telling me to put him out of his misery. I agreed, figuring it was easier to just get the disappointment out of the way, fully expecting the result to be negative. I'd only come off the pill after the wedding, knowing that a long stint with the hormones could sometimes mess with your cycle. That wasn't even taking my age into account. Needless to say, I almost passed out when it read positive, Mack smug for an entire week that he'd totally known.

"Pssssh, you look great." Penny dismissed my concerns, offloading the shirts to Brenda who'd returned with hangers. "And there will be *lots* of food."

I hugged her, the pregnancy emotions already in full force as I tried to stop my eyes from watering. "You were a good friend to me. I know I'm older, and I was your employee, and you didn't have to."

Penny laughed, hugging me back. "Honey, no one is dying. And I didn't care how old you were, or if you were my employee. You were worthy of my friendship. And still are."

And that had been the crux of it. Knowing I'd been worthy.

Of friendship.

Of love.

Of being who I wanted to be.

"I should go." I pulled myself from her embrace. "I know hugging on the shop floor is frowned upon, and I wanted to go meet Mack for dinner at the station."

She groaned, throwing her hands up dramatically. "Fine, leave me here to rot. Go, go be with your hot husband, in your perfect life."

"I intend to," I waved, smiling to myself as I walked out the door.

The smile didn't slip as I got into my car and drove to Midtown, parking in the back of the stationhouse and walking inside. I was greeted by hellos and heys as I walked through to Mack's office, giving everyone a friendly hello as I didn't stop.

"Hey, sexy." I rapped on his open doorway, his head snapping up at the first sound of my voice. "Thought I might surprise you for dinner."

He came at me like a freight train, pushing out of his chair and grabbing me around the waist, kissing me so I couldn't talk.

I laughed, running my hands along his muscular back. "You know I'm already pregnant. You could probably cool it, if you want to."

"That's just it. I don't want to." His hands moved suggestively over my hips. "And knowing our baby is inside of you just makes it hotter."

I swatted at his chest playfully, wondering if he'd still feel that way when I was huge. Or after the baby was born, and my body was different, unable to have sex for weeks at a time because of fatigue and who knew what else. "Just remember this when I'm breastfeeding, and I don't look the way I used to."

"You're delusional. Thinking anything could change the way I feel about you." He put the debate to rest, kissing me again and pinning my body against his office wall. Had to admit his insatiable appetite was doing wonders for my ego. And my hormones were totally on board.

"Ewwwwww, Mom and Dad are making out." Riley laughed from behind us. "Pretty sure there's regs against that. And if there isn't, there should be."

"You need something to do, North?" Mack lifted his head, smirking at Riley.

Riley rolled his eyes, reaching for the door. "Nope, but how about I close the door so you don't traumatize anyone else. Thank God you can't get her pregnant twice. And just so we're clear, I'm still the favorite."

"Leave, and I'll think about it," Mack chuckled.

Riley looked horrified, screwing his face up into a scowl. "Fine, I'll share being the favorite. As you were." He waved his hand, pulling the door shut.

"You heard the man," I tilted my chin, my lips parting, ready for his kiss.

Mack's hand trailed along my jaw, sending shivers up my spine. "Yeah, I sure did. Let's see if we can really break some regulations."

THE END

To keep up to date with all T Gephart's news, appearances, and releases, please subscribe to her mailing list (http://eepurl.com/bws5Av).

Also please consider leaving a review on your retailer of choice. They help the author and future readers and we're all eternally grateful.

Acknowledgements

A massive thanks and big love goes to my family—Gep, Jenna, Liam and Woodley. One of these days one of you is going to see these acknowledgments and all my thanks, but until then I'll just have to tell you every day. Not a hardship!

Again, thanks to Kelly Elliott, who was there from the inception of this series and whom I think I spoke to every single day while writing this book. I tried not to spoil any of it for you, act surprised if I did. P.S. Love you, thank you for those daily chats, especially when I was sick. P.P.S. I hope you're still laughing.

Thank you for all the love, support and understanding from my extended family and friends. I'm trying to be better and not turn into a bitter recluse who doesn't wear pants. Thanks for all the walks, movies, dinners, coffees, foodie dates, makeup dates, random outings and basically dragging me out even when I wanted to make excuses for not being an active human. You complete me.

Thanks to Gayle Williams for the check ins, messages, scheduling, chasing up and basically putting up with the hot mess that I was/am trying to write this book. I keep telling you it's gonna get easier, I promise it will one of these days. Love you.

Thanks to Penny Rudge—SNOOP FOR EVA!!! Dude, I'm so glad we found each other. You better be back reading; it's been too long. #FYMForever #TellYourFriends

Thanks to Team Brower—Kimberly, Aimee, and Caroline. Are you sick of my 5,000 emails yet?! LOL Love you guys, dream team.

Thank you to Nichole Strauss from Insight Editing who pushes me to do better. See, not all of my stories are ridiculous. Thanks for all your hard work so my books are the best they can be.

Thank you so much to MK—THE BEST BETA EVER. I love all your little notes, insights and feedback. You honestly see things from a different perspective and I love it. Don't change, girlfriend. You're amazing.

Thanks to Elaine York from Allusion Graphics LLC, Publishing and Book Formatting. I am absolutely in love with my pages. Love working with you and seeing my words looking beautiful after you're done with them.

A bazillion thanks to the amazing HANG LE! My covers, teasers—there just isn't anyone who gets me like you do. Everything you do for me is stunning, and I have cherished every single email, text message and inbox we've ever shared. Friends for life. Ninja hugs!!

Thank you to my eagle-eyed proofreaders, Elaine and Lisa, for finding those typos that I miss despite reading this thing a million times. You're both amazing!! Special thanks to Elaine York for stepping in at the last minute. Lord—you are a super star.

Special thanks to my author friends who will often get random messages from me and ignore the crazy. Sometimes I honestly have to pinch myself and remember acting like a lunatic is not cool. I'll always be your fangirl though, even if we do hang out. And P.S. I still squeal in delight when you send me your ARCs. #FriendsInHighPlaces.

SO MUCH THANKS, love and adoration for all the bloggers, reviewers, bookgramers, group admins and promoters who read, promote, review, and share my work. I will never take any of it for granted and am so thankful for all your LOVE.

Thank you, Liz, MJ, and Jillian at 1001 Dark Nights.

THANK YOU TO THE T GEPHART REVIEW CREW AND ENTOURAGE. I haven't been as active as I would like to be, but am thankful you guys have stuck by me, supporting each book with such excitement. Don't underestimate what it means to me, you all are in my heart.

And lastly, as always, thank YOU. Yep, you the person reading this. You rock my world, thanks for letting me a part of yours.

About the Author

T Gephart is a *USA Today* and International bestselling author from Melbourne, Australia.

With an approach to life that is somewhat unconventional, she prefers to fly by the seat of her pants rather than adhere to some rigid roadmap. Her lack of "plan" has resulted in a rather interesting and eclectic resume, which reads more like the fiction she writes than an actual employment history. She'd tell you all about it, but the statute of limitations hasn't expired yet. But all those crazy twists and turns have led her to a career she loves—writing romantic comedy.

When she isn't filling pages with sassy and sexy characters with attitude, she's living her own reality show in the 'burbs of Melbourne with her American husband, two teenage children, and her fur child—Woodley.

She loves adventure, to laugh, travel, and strives to live her life to the fullest.

Connect with T

tgephart.com
Facebook (https://www.facebook.com/tgephartauthor)
Goodreads
Twitter (https://twitter.com/tinagephart)

Books by this Author
The Lexi Series
Lexi
A Twist of Fate
Twisted Views: Fate's Companion
A Leap of Faith
A Time for Hope

The Power Station Series
High Strung
Crash Ride
Back Stage

The Black Addiction Series
Slide
Sticks
Stand